BATTLE OF ILLARIA

BOOK THREE OF THE ILLARIA SERIES

DYAN CHICK

ILLARIA PUBLISHING LLC

Published by Illaria Publishing LLC

Cover Artwork by Clarissa Yeo
Editing by Laura Kingsley

In memory of all those who went too soon.

1

MAX

Max stood on a hilltop at the edge of Greenville, staring at the smoke rising into the sky. The night was filled with screams as people fled from the sorcerers attacking their homes. He could see the black-cloaked figures throwing flames into the night. Buildings burned and crumbled to the ground. A shrieking made him turn his gaze and he watched a woman fall, body engulfed in fire. This wasn't what he had in mind when he joined forces with the king. He clenched his teeth, forcing himself to stand and watch. He felt the pull of the Darkness, urging him to join in the attack. It was like a warm caress, filling his insides, begging to be released. The Darkness was fueled by destruction and the scene unfolding in front of him was making it hunger for release. The king's plan had worked to open a bridge to the underworld through Etta. Since her return, the pull to the Darkness had grown and was getting harder to resist. Fighting to keep control of his own thoughts, he pushed it away.

"You shouldn't fight it so hard," King Osbert said.

Max glanced at him. "I don't want anything to control me."

"It doesn't control you, it strengthens you."

Max didn't answer. He knew that the times he'd let the Darkness in, he'd done things he wouldn't have done on his own. He also knew the king was still testing him. The wedding couldn't come soon enough. After Max married the king's daughter, Nora, nothing was going to stop him from destroying the king and claiming his throne.

"Go help them." Osbert lifted his chin toward the smoking ruins that used to be the largest city in Illaria. "Teach that sister of yours a lesson. She'll never rule on her own. She joins us, or we kill everyone she ever cared about."

Max's stomach twisted into knots. He hated it when the king threatened the Ravens. Part of him couldn't let go of the past and his life with them. He'd been their leader for fifteen years and while he tried to tell himself he no longer cared for any member of that group, he couldn't find it in him to wish them dead. Hesitating for a moment, Max considered what would happen if he disobeyed the king. After all, he did have a dragon under his command. It would be so easy to surprise the king and let his new friend breathe fire down on the castle. But it wasn't just about getting rid of the king, it was about rising up to claim his throne. His marriage to Nora would make Max the legitimate king once Osbert was dead. It was the best way to ensure a smooth transition and the best way to regain the favor of the Illarian people.

"What are you waiting for?" Osbert narrowed his eyes at Max. "Go."

Max nodded. He didn't want to aid in the destruction of Greenville. The Darkness had a way of taking over once he started using his magic lately and he didn't like the lack of control. But he needed to continue to play the part of loyal servant of the king for a few more weeks. Taking a deep breath, Max walked down the hill into the smoldering city.

Heat rose around him as he walked through the streets, burning buildings on either side of him. The screams had died down, leaving the sound of the crackling flames. Max walked further into the city, where he found the other sorcerers throwing fireballs at the undamaged buildings. The king's sorcerers were no match for the destruction Max could cause. He knew if he channeled the Darkness, he could take out an entire block in one movement of his arms. Looking behind him, he wondered if the king was still watching. All he could see was smoke, but he could feel the pressure of the Darkness growing inside him. The king was pushing him, encouraging him to let the Darkness in.

It was another test. Max took a deep breath in, and dropped his guard. Dark tendrils of anger and hate wound through him, filling his entire body with a rage he'd never felt before. He closed his eyes, letting it wind its way through him. When he opened his eyes, he no longer cared how many people he killed or how many lives he ruined.

Calling to fire, his palms ignited. He swept his arms upward, launching the flames at an untouched street. A tidal wave of fire swept from him, swallowing the street in orange and gold. The screams only lasted a second before they were silenced forever.

2

ETTA

M aster Flanders looked over at me as we walked toward the clearing we used for sorcery lessons. "Things are changing out there. Can you feel it?"

The nightmares I'd been having flashed through my mind and I reached for the familiar comfort of my pendant, squeezing it in my hand. I had woken from sleep last night covered in sweat, screaming. I'd dreamed of monsters pulling me into the darkness of the underworld. It felt so real that I had been afraid to light a lamp and check to see if there were marks on my body. After that, I wasn't able to return to sleep. It was as if something had shifted and nothing was quite the same. I'd hoped I was just being paranoid, but Master Flanders' frown made me realize that wasn't the case. "What happened?"

"The bridge you opened has grown. The Darkness is getting stronger. It will be here sooner than we thought. Even the Oracle is going to have a hard time seeing anyone's future if it gets much wider. Illaria, and all the kingdoms are in grave danger. It's more important than ever we eliminate the king."

Every time Master Flanders mentioned my role in helping the Darkness spread, my palms grew sweaty and my stomach twisted with guilt. It was my fault that it was coming sooner than we thought. I tried to remind myself that the Darkness was going to come either way, coming sooner was just making our plan to destroy the king more difficult. I took a deep breath. "What does that mean for us? For our plans?"

He shook his head. "I had hoped we'd have more time to work on your training before you traveled to Gallia. But I'm afraid we can't put it off any longer."

I dropped the pendant back under my tunic. The plan has always been to destroy the king, but as soon as we involved Gallia, we'd be on a timeline. It would be our first offensive move against King Osbert with me at the helm of the Ravens. We'd contacted the king of Gallia, my uncle, after I'd saved Ashton. He was receptive to meeting, elated, even. Master Flanders recommended I hold off for a month to make sure I could control the Darkness before traveling to another kingdom. Despite the fact he'd kept things from me, I still trusted him. "Should we send word to him? He told us we were welcome any time."

"I think it would be wise for you to go as soon as possible. I'm not sure what caused the change, but we can't take any chances on waiting. If the king has discovered a way to open that bridge faster, it might already be too late."

I'd never heard Master Flanders so grim before. Goosebumps rose on my arms. "We shouldn't have waited. We should have gone right to Gallia."

"I don't think it was wrong to wait. If you lost control in front of them, they'd never believe you could command an army. We needed the time, but we can't wait any longer."

I nodded. "I'll call a council meeting."

We had reached the clearing and I looked around. It was a beautiful fall morning. A cool breeze shifted the grasses and birdsong filled the air. Sorcery lessons didn't seem as important as they had a few minutes ago. "Did you still want to do a lesson?"

"Always. As long as I'm here, I'm going to keep teaching you. We're going to do something different today." Master Flanders sat down on the fallen log that had come to be his usual place during our lessons. We'd spent hours in this clearing every day for the last few weeks, working on building up my resistance to the Darkness and helping me learn to use my magic.

"No fire today?" It was still my weakest element so most lessons started with a review on how to summon and channel at least a little bit of fire.

"It's time for you to learn to prepare yourself against attacks by the Darkness. So far, we've focused on you learning to maintain control. Once we travel outside these wards, things will be different."

It was hard enough trying to keep the Darkness away from within. The idea of having to fend off external attacks made my skin crawl. There wasn't any choice, though. I was the reason why the Darkness was gaining momentum in Illaria. I needed to be the one to fix it. I took my sorcerer stance. "I'm ready."

Master Flanders stood. "I'd like you to summon wind."

Easy enough. I closed my eyes and concentrated on clearing my mind, then moved into my sorcerer stance. Taking a deep breath, I opened my eyes and focused on the air moving around me. Before I was able to finish calling to the wind, a tugging sensation rose inside me, knocking me off balance.

I corrected my stance and looked at Master Flanders, "Was that you?"

He lifted an eyebrow, expression serious. "You need to focus better."

Irritated that I had failed so easily, I squared my shoulders and started again. I didn't even settle into my stance before I toppled over again. I caught myself and glared at Master Flanders. "I wasn't ready."

"The Darkness isn't going to wait for you to be ready when it attacks. It'll come any time it wants. You have to keep your mind clear and focused at all times."

So far, all of our lessons had included methods I could use to prevent the Darkness inside me from surfacing. Occasionally, it would rise up from within me, and I had to learn to send it away. I'd always been on the offensive against myself, never an opposing external force. Determined to get it right, I settled into my stance. "Let's try again."

Master Flanders nodded and I again called to wind. This time, I managed a little gust before the tugging inside me took over, sending me lunging forward to catch my balance. "How am I supposed to do this? As soon as you attack, I lose all focus."

"You have to clear your mind. Have you been working on the meditation we talked about?"

I looked down, not wanting to meet his gaze. "I keep trying, but I can't seem to turn off my thoughts."

Master Flanders walked over to the log and sat down. "You have to learn how to master your own mind. I can only teach you so much and I won't be around forever."

"Stop saying things like that," I said. "You can't go anywhere. I need you."

He smiled, the wrinkles around his mouth and eyes deepened. "I know and I'll do my best to be here for you. But I'm serious, if you can't clear your mind, you'll never keep the Darkness away."

I pressed my palms against my temples. "Every time I try to clear my mind, something takes my focus away. There's Max, the king, trying to get my kingdom back, the Darkness..." The worry never ended.

"This is why we practice. You need to have control over this before you go to Gallia," he said.

"I'll do better." I wanted to be stronger, I wanted to take back my throne. To do that, I needed to gain the support of my uncle in Gallia. I'd only get one chance at a first impression. I couldn't let the Darkness sneak up on me while I was there.

Tucking my hair behind my ears, I turned away from Master Flanders, trying to clear my head. I took a deep breath and got into my sorcerer stance. The tugging sensation began again and I gently pushed back on it. *I can do this.* While still pushing back on the force inside me, I thought about the wind. As I reached for it, my concentration slipped and I toppled over, landing on the ground.

"This is impossible." I stood up and dusted the dirt off of my clothes. "How am I supposed to keep you out and call on my magic at the same time?"

"Practice."

I huffed, knowing he was right. Turning away again, I went through the same thing over and over, failing every time.

After what must have been hours of working, I still had not successfully called to the wind. While not as easy as working with water, it was something I could do without effort most days.

"Please tell me there's a trick I don't know yet and you're making some point by having me fail over and over."

Master Flanders stood and walked over to me. "We're done for today, but you do have homework. You have to complete your meditation time. Every morning and every night. Once you get into the habit of doing that, you'll see more progress. We'll try this exercise again tomorrow."

"That's it?" Usually our lessons were much longer.

Master Flanders lifted his chin toward something behind me. "I have a feeling our time is up for today."

I turned to see Calder running toward us.

I waved to him. "Everything alright?"

He reached us, and took a moment to catch his breath. "Saffron sent me to tell you Sir Henry is here."

Finally. A rush of warmth filled me. My friends here at the Raven camp were wonderful, and I couldn't do anything without them, but none of them knew how to run a kingdom. None of them knew anything about royal courts or politics or how I was supposed to act when I spoke to my uncle in Gallia. Sir Henry did. He had been part of my father's court, and now he would be part of mine. Having him here to help figure out what to do made me feel like some of the weight of the responsibilities I had assumed lessened.

I looked at Master Flanders, he didn't seem as excited as I was. "You two go on, I'm going to get some rest."

I knew Sir Henry didn't like Master Flanders, but I hadn't realized the feeling was mutual. I wondered what had happened between the two of them, but my excitement at seeing my friend won over my curiosity and I followed Calder toward the common area.

As we approached, I spotted Saffron and Celeste among a small crowd that had gathered. Saffron was wearing the first smile I had seen since the night I saved Ashton. Making my way over, my heart leapt into my throat. *Sir Henry.* I broke into a run.

I met him with an embrace. "Thank you for coming."

His round, red face filled with a smile. "Reapers couldn't keep me away."

After a round of introductions, the crowd died down, leaving me standing there with Sir Henry, Saffron, Celeste, and Calder. Sir Henry dropped the smile and his face looked suddenly weary.

"What is it?" I asked.

He glanced at Calder. "Not sure it's safe to speak here."

"It's okay," I said. "This is Calder, he helped me save Ashton. I trust him."

Sir Henry looked around, seemingly checking that we were alone. Satisfied, he turned to me. "It's Greenville."

My forehead creased in concern. We'd been in Greenville a few weeks ago and the city had openly declared their support for me. My stomach knotted, unsure if I wanted to hear any more. "What about it?"

"The king wasn't happy about them sending away all his guards." Sir Henry took a deep breath.

Calder leaned in next to me. "What happened?"

I grabbed hold of Calder's hand. He'd lived in Greenville until he joined us and still had family that lived there.

Sir Henry looked down for a moment before looking back up at me. "He set his sorcerers on the city. They destroyed everything."

3

ETTA

M ax's face filled my mind, blackened with soot, dark eyes flashing with flames. I could practically see him launching fire at the homes of the innocent people in Greenville. Screams filled my ears and I covered them with my hands, squeezing my eyes shut. I wanted the vision to go away. I didn't want to think of Max like that. It couldn't be him. He'd never do that to his own people. He hated the king as much as any of the Ravens. His face was replaced by sweeping dark robes and flames until all I could see in my mind was fire. I opened my eyes, hoping the vision would clear.

My friends stood around me, watching me with concern, but didn't say a word. Hands trembling, I lowered them from my ears as the sounds of screaming faded. This was my fault. The king was punishing the people who stood against him; the people who stood for me. He was sending me a message. My nostrils flared and I squeezed my hands into fists as anger surged through me. The king had to be stopped. "We have to go to Greenville."

"It's too dangerous," Celeste said. "It could be a trap."

"It probably is a trap," Sir Henry agreed.

"Are you sure it's been destroyed? My family's in Greenville." Calder looked at Sir Henry. His face was drained of color. "The whole city? I mean, how is that even possible?"

Sir Henry's expression softened. "I'm sorry, son."

I set my hand on his arm, not sure what to say. "I'm so sorry."

"Can someone take me there?" Calder looked around at the group of sorcerers. "I only need an hour maybe. One of you can teleport me, right? My parents, my little sister, I have to get them out of there. What if the sorcerers come back?"

This was the most I'd ever heard Calder speak of his family. I didn't even know he had a little sister. I turned to look at Celeste. "It would be a quick trip. We've all been there before."

Sir Henry turned to Calder. "What would you do if they were gone, son? Sometimes, it's better not to see these things."

"I've seen too much already. There's no way I'm going to leave them there." Calder turned from Sir Henry to me. "Etta, you know why I have to go."

I nodded. "Yes, I do."

"I can take him," Celeste said. "But I can only teleport two people out. If there are more, I'll need help."

"I'm not any help with that part, yet. I can barely even teleport myself. We're going to need help." I took hold of Calder's hand and started walking. "Come on, let's find the others. We'll get your family out of there."

A hand on my shoulder halted my progress. I turned to see Saffron. Dropping Calder's hand, I stopped moving. "Celeste, can you take Sir Henry to my quarters? Calder, can you find Ashton and Madame Lyndsey? I'll meet you all there."

Saffron and I stood alone and I tried to read the expression on her face. The smile that had come with the arrival of Sir Henry was gone. "You need to stay here this time. It could be a trap aimed at you."

My heart sunk. I wanted to help my friends but I knew it was dangerous. I'd seen how easily I could be convinced to do things I shouldn't when my friend's lives were threatened. What if it was a trap? Saffron didn't know about the Darkness. Nobody did. Master Flanders and I had pledged to keep it a secret. Who would follow a queen who was responsible for opening a bridge between realms? "Will you go with them?"

She narrowed her eyes. "You want me to go? I can't teleport anyone."

"If I can't go, you go for me. If Calder's family..." I couldn't get the rest of the words out. Calder had already suffered the loss of his wife at the hands of the king's guards. Most of the members of the Ravens knew what it was like to lose someone they cared about, but Calder and I seemed to have an understanding. Saffron knew loss, too. Like me, her family had been killed in the Battle of the Dead. "You can help him. He'll need someone to speak reason if things go wrong."

"I can do that." She knew the story of how I met Calder and the vendetta he had against the king. The last thing we needed was for him to go off on a vigilante quest by himself. In the short time he'd been with the Ravens, Calder had already proven his benefit to our group. He and Saffron worked together to train the new recruits. He was good at teaching and good at giving support to those who came to us broken from their own loss.

We didn't speak again as we walked toward my quarters. The destruction of Greenville weighed heavy on my heart. I didn't want to think about the number of people who were making the journey to the underworld today. Then I froze and grabbed hold of Saffron's arm. There could be thousands of dead in Greenville. "The dead. Do you think the king is building his army?"

Saffron's jaw tensed. "We have to hurry."

The two of us ran the rest of the way to my tent.

MASTER FLANDERS, Saffron, Madame Lyndsey, Sir Henry, Ashton, Calder, and Celeste stood around the table that filled most of the tent I used as my quarters. I looked around at the faces of the few people I trusted with my life. These were my friends, my support, they'd grown to feel like family. "First, thank you all for being here."

I gestured to Sir Henry. "We have a new arrival today, my dear friend, Sir Henry. I wish this meeting was simply to celebrate him, however, that is not to be."

The faces of my council told me they already knew why we were here. News traveled quickly in the Raven camp. I wondered if it had already gone beyond my council members. "As you have heard, Greenville was attacked by the king and his sorcerers. This happened because they supported me."

Nobody spoke. In the last few weeks, we'd been preparing strategies and ideas for what I would present when I met with Gallia. Things had seemed promising and optimism was rising in the camp. We had hope again. Today, all of that seemed forgotten as we sat around the table coming to terms with the attack on Greenville.

"This event has two immediate concerns. The first is personal." I nodded to Calder. "One of our own's family lives in Greenville and we have a responsibility to offer them help. The other concern is the dead. While I am heartbroken at any loss of life, the fact is that the king has done this in the past to build up his army. Granted, he usually chose small towns, but this attack could have been for more than to just teach me a lesson. He could be rebuilding his undead army."

"He shouldn't have the power to do that," Sir Henry said. "The numbers would be too great for him. Isn't that why he stuck to smaller villages?"

"If he took the dead, it means he found the stone," Master Flanders said.

My heart raced. There were five power stones created with dark magic the last time the Darkness had descended upon Illaria. King Osbert already had control over two of the stones, the Stone of Morare controlled his Reapers and the Black Onyx could temporarily remove a sorcerer's magic. We had the Dragon stone, which left two remaining. Any of these power stones would be dangerous in a normal sorcerer's hands. In the king's hands, they meant loss of life of epic proportions, one of the remaining stones more so than the other. I knew where Master Flanders was going with this, but I didn't want to admit it to myself. "Which stone?"

"The Skystone."

Sir Henry stood and slammed his fist on the table. He leaned across toward Master Flanders. "I knew your daughter was up to no good, sorcerer."

Master Flanders looked weary. "She has nothing to do with that stone."

"But she could tell him where it was, couldn't she?" Sir Henry said. "I knew it was a bad idea for you to send her there. You should have taken her place. What kind of father sends his daughter away?"

"Enough." Saffron stood, and glared at both men. "It doesn't matter what happened in the past. What matters is that if he has that stone, we need to know. It's not going to stop us from going after him, but we have to be prepared and find a way to match his strength."

Sir Henry sat down. "We're not going to match his strength. Especially if he's got the Oracle on his side."

"The Oracle helped Etta save me," Ashton said. "I don't think she's working with the king."

I bit down on the inside of my lip as all eyes traveled to

me. I hadn't fully shared with Ashton what had happened that night. I never told him about the Oracle's link to the king or that Master Flanders and I suspected the whole thing may have been a set up. How would he feel if he found out he'd been a pawn in the king's game to allow the Darkness a permanent entrance? Or when he found out I was the unwilling cause? Would he even look at me the same way again?

The temperature of the room seemed to have risen and I pulled at the collar of my tunic, moving it off of my neck. I wished I could keep this to myself, I wanted to protect Ashton, but I couldn't protect everyone all the time. Glancing at Master Flanders, I wondered what I should say. He nodded at me. This was the only thing I had kept from Ashton, but now it was time.

"The Oracle did help me save Ashton," I said. "But we do suspect that she's working with the king."

"You can never expect a woman to betray her first love," Sir Henry said.

"What are you talking about?" Ashton asked.

Sir Henry looked over at Master Flanders, seemingly waiting for an objection. None came. "Osbert and Delphina were child-hood sweethearts. She had to take an oath of solitude to become the Oracle. She was supposed to give him up, but I don't think she made that decision on her own." He glanced at Master Flanders. "I don't think she wanted to be an Oracle."

"She was ready, Henry. I assure you, I never forced her. However, it seems I misjudged her affections for Osbert." Master Flanders stood. "That isn't a concern now. Delphina won't be able to see any visions involving the king or Etta. There is too much Darkness coming into Illaria for her to see through its mask."

"Are you saying what I think you're saying?" Madame Lyndsey looked at me. "How is Etta masked by Darkness?"

"When she saved Ashton, she traveled to the underworld and back. It left its mark on her."

My cheeks grew hot and I looked down at the table. Hearing about what I had been through again made it even more clear how much I had hurt our kingdom. I hated that I had helped the king, even if it wasn't on purpose. I was ashamed of my role, but conflicted because it had let me save Ashton. While I would do it again if I had to make the choice over, I didn't want my friends to think poorly of me. I didn't want them to think that I'd let the Darkness change me and I was worried that they wouldn't see me the same way once they found out.

"She's working to control it and it isn't a factor in her ability to rule. In fact, it will be an asset once we conquer the king and can work to vanquish the Darkness. That being said, I need this information to stay in this room. Nobody else can know. They wouldn't understand."

The room was silent for a few moments and I continued to stare at the table.

"So, you're saying that the Oracle can't see what Etta's moves are because she's channeling Darkness?" Celeste said.

"Yes."

"And she's in control of it?" Celeste asked.

"Yes."

"Then I don't see the problem. Keeps the king's Oracle from knowing what we are going to do. It sounds like the best thing we could hope for."

I looked up at Celeste and smiled. What would I do without her eternal optimism? Risking a glance at Ashton, my smile faded. As soon as our eyes met, he looked away. I'd never kept anything from him before and guilt swam through me. I wanted to pull him aside an explain everything. I couldn't stand him being disappointed with me.

"What are we going to do about Greenville?" Saffron brought

the meeting back to our original purpose. I turned away from Ashton.

"We have to send a team in to see what happened and to rescue anyone we can," I said.

"If this is a rescue mission, we need all the help we can get," Madame Lyndsey said.

"Agreed, but volunteer only. Sir Henry thinks this could be a trap so I want you all to consider that before you raise your hands," I said.

"I'm in," Saffron said. "Though, I can't teleport anyone."

"You can't keep me away," Celeste said. I noticed she was holding Calder's hand under the table. I wondered if they'd been sitting like that the whole meeting.

"I can teleport three at a time," Madame Lyndsey said.

"I can take two, maybe three," Ashton said.

"Thank you all," Calder said. "I appreciate what you're doing to help my family but what can we do about the rest of the city?"

"Send Etta," Sir Henry said.

"Etta needs to be here," Master Flanders said.

"She has to go," Sir Henry said. "This is a matter of diplomacy, old man. You need the support of the people. She needs to be seen as the opposite of the king. If she stays in safety while her people die, what is there to make her different from the man who did this to them?"

He had a point. I did want the people to see me as different than the king. And I wanted the opportunity to show them that they mattered to me. The city had been attacked because they stood to support me. I wanted to go.

"She's got a very important meeting next week with Gallia. If we don't get that army, we lose everything," Master Flanders said.

"If she doesn't go, you've already lost everything." Sir Henry glared at Master Flanders.

"That's enough." I hadn't realized that I would need to keep the two of them separated. They seemed to dislike each other more than I could have guessed. "Master Flanders, haven't you taught me well?"

Master Flanders looked away from Sir Henry to me. "You still have much to learn."

"I know," I said. "We teleport in, we talk to some people, we teleport out. We'd be gone for a few hours. You know I can do this."

Master Flanders sat back down in his chair. He looked defeated.

Sir Henry was still standing. "You know this has to be done. All the survivors need to see her. They'll see she's not afraid. She's not hiding. She's here to help her people. The king caused this destruction and the true queen came in to care for the people. It's gold. We can't buy the kind of loyalty that will create." He paused. "You want to see Illaria supporting our queen? Send her in and make a show of it. News will spread. We'll have half the kingdom on our side in a matter of weeks."

"He's right," Saffron said. "We need the support of the people before we send her to Gallia."

"The king's sorcerers could still be there," Master Flanders said.

"Nobody here knows Greenville better than me. We can avoid the main streets," Calder said.

"Master Flanders, come with us. We'll only be a few hours," I said. "If it's too bad, we can come right back here."

Sir Henry turned to me. "Your highness, you know it's your decision."

Over the last few months, I'd had to learn to trust my intuition and listen to those with more experience. Every path I sent us on had consequences. I knew I would never forgive myself if I didn't at least try to help the people of Greenville. "We're going.

Saffron, can you get a cart of supplies ready? We'll send that ahead in with a group of volunteers. The rest of us will teleport there."

Saffron nodded at me, then turned to the rest of the group. "We have a safe house near Greenville. We can teleport there first. It's about two miles outside the city so we won't risk teleporting into an ambush."

I nodded. "That sounds perfect."

Sir Henry slid a full purse of coins across the table. "Take this with you. Help whoever you can."

I covered the bag with my hand. "Thank you." Turning my attention to the whole group, I took a deep breath. If everything went according to plan, we'd be back at the Raven camp by nightfall. "Get whatever supplies you need, we'll meet in the common area in twenty minutes."

People rose and pushed chairs in. Next to me, Ashton stood. I grabbed hold of his arm. "Wait."

He pushed his chair in, then turned to face me. We were the only ones left in the tent.

"I'm sorry I didn't tell you sooner."

He took hold of my hands in his. "Etta, I don't want you risking your life for me anymore."

"I didn't have a choice," I said. "I couldn't let you die."

He pulled me in for a hug and moved his lips next to my ear. "You know I love you, but you have to stop doing things that put you at risk."

Backing away from the embrace, Ashton let out a sigh. "What are we going to do if something happens to you?"

"I can't do this on my own," I said. "If something happens to you, it's over for me, anyway."

"You're wrong," he said. "You are strong and you can do this on your own if you have to. You have lots of people who care about you and want to help you, but you have to let them in. You don't have to do everything by yourself."

"I do let people in," I said. At least I thought I did. I had my council I listened to them and valued every word they said.

"You are going to have to do better than a rag-tag group of people standing around a table in a tent. The people need you, and you need them."

I took a deep breath. He was right, the support of the people was one of the best things we could gain, but so far, it was costing more Illarians their lives at the hands of the king. How was I supposed to ask the people for support when I knew the risk they were taking to follow me?

The tent flap opened and Celeste popped her head in. "You two coming?"

Ashton squeezed my hand. "We better go."

4

MAX

The Oracle crossed the room, silent on bare feet. Her long blonde hair hung loose down her back, joining the flowing movement of the white dress she wore. "I told you, I can't answer his questions anymore. Darkness courses through him. He's impossible to see in my visions."

Max walked into the middle of her tower. "I came on my own."

"You will soon follow in his footsteps if you aren't careful." She circled Max, looking him up and down.

Max glared at her. He'd been intimidated the first few times he'd come to see her, but her tricks didn't work on him anymore. He knew her power was limited. Her magic was helpful, but the sight no longer impressed him. "You know why I'm here."

"I do." She stopped moving, blue eyes locked on Max. "What makes you think I'll take your side over his."

"He knows." Max clasped his hands in front of him. He waited for the words to sink in.

The Oracle was silent for a moment. "He's going after my father?"

Max nodded. "The secret's out. He knows it was your father who protected Etta."

"Osbert knows that if he kills Etta, he's risking his kingdom." The Oracle walked over to a chair and sat down. "I already told him that."

Max followed her. "He's losing patience. And to be honest, he's not making his decisions based on logic anymore."

"The Darkness has claimed him," she said.

Max sat down next to her. "He's not the same person you knew. He's a monster. You know that."

The Oracle glared at Max. "You're going down the same path, you know. I've seen your future. Things aren't going to go the way you want them to. You have no idea what you're going to have to give up to get the things you want. If you rule, it will be over a kingdom of corpses."

Heat rose inside Max. "I've given up everything already. There's nothing more I could lose."

"You have just begun to taste loss. You should go back to the Ravens, Max."

"Did you forget that I have a dragon on my side?" Max leaned closer to her. "I'm not stopping until I have my throne. There may be bloodshed on my path to glory, but I will be king."

She didn't flinch. "You really want my help, Max?"

He didn't want to fight with the Oracle. He knew how powerful she was and what a strong ally she could be. "Tell me what I need to do."

"You're losing yourself, Max. Every time I lose sight of you to the Darkness, your future changes. Once, I saw you as a great king. Those days are gone."

He rose and stood in front of her chair. "You are lying."

"Why would I bother to lie? I'm a prisoner here until another takes my place or the ruler of Illaria lets me go. You know this. What do I have to lose? At this point, death is welcome."

"How do I make it change?" Max asked.

She stood, eyes locked on Max's. "There is only one version of the future where you become king. And you do it with Ashton by your side."

Max winced, then quickly righted himself. He'd always planned on having Ashton as part of the Order of the Dragon but he didn't see how that could happen after what he'd done to him. "There's no other way?"

She shook her head.

Max took a deep breath. "What do you want me to do about your father?"

"Nothing. He made his choice."

5

ETTA

It was a three-day journey to Greenville for the men taking the cart of supplies. We'd loaded in as much as we could spare and the whole camp gathered to watch it leave. The optimistic mood of the camp over the last few weeks was gone and we were left with a jarring reminder of how dangerous our path was. An anger had fallen over the people here, stemmed from the disbelief that the king would cause this much damage.

I faced the crowd as we prepared to teleport to the safe house. "We will return soon and I will bring whatever news I can of Greenville and the rest of Illaria. This changes nothing. We will gain the support of Gallia and we will take down the king."

Jax, one of the Ravens who worked with Saffron regularly training new members stepped forward. "Hurry back. The sooner we get this war started, the sooner we can kill the king and his sorcerers."

His words brought a smile to my face. Not long ago, I worried about the loyalty of the Ravens and wondered if they'd continue to follow me. The hatred of the king wasn't quite enough to unify us after Max left. Now, after my return from the Oracle, and the king's attack on Greenville, there seemed to be a shift in their attitudes. These Ravens were ready to fight with me.

A cheer rose behind him. The Ravens were out for blood. I wondered if the king's attack would have the same effect on the rest of Illaria. Would it drive fear or would it breed hatred? I nodded to Jax then turned away to where the rest of the group waited for me.

I'd learned how to teleport over the last few weeks but this mission was too important for me to risk experimenting with my newfound skill. I clasped Ashton's hand, grateful to have an excuse to be close to him.

He turned to me. "You ready?"

"Let's go." Clouds of gray smoke billowed up around me as our group left the camp.

Feeling solid ground under my feet, I opened my eyes and looked around. I let go of Ashton's hand and waved away the gray smoke that remained from our teleportation. The landscape in front of me seemed more hazy than usual. Where I should see rolling hills in the distance, I could only see clouds. The fog seemed to be creeping toward us, shrouding the fields with mist. It took a second to register that what I was seeing wasn't natural. The scent hit me and I knew in that instant that this smoke could only have come from a fire.

No! I covered my mouth with my hand and icy fear spread through me. Turning around, I found myself face to face with a burning farm house. The air was thick with smoke and my eyes stung.

Setting my bow down on the grass, I started toward the flames when Saffron pulled me back. "Running into a fire won't do anyone any good."

"We can put this out." Madame Lyndsey shouted. She and Master Flanders stood in their sorcerer stance and called water. I stood next to them, following their movements. Celeste and

Ashton joined us. Together, we managed to pull water from a nearby stream to the house. We'd worked with water a lot in my lessons, but there wasn't enough in the stream to quench the flames.

Frustrated, I shook out my hands. There had to be a better way to extinguish these flames. We needed more water. Clapping my hands together, I glanced at the sky. Instead of calling to water, I'd create it. I turned to Celeste. She was the only member of our group that aligned with air and she commanded it with ease. "Celeste, help me bring more clouds."

Gusts of wind brought great clouds and I concentrated on making those clouds heavy with water. Thunder rumbled through the darkening sky. I closed my eyes, imagining the water falling onto the burning building. Rain began in earnest, then picked up to a downpour, drenching us through in seconds.

The flames subsided, leaving a soaking, steaming pile of rubble. We ran to the home and began to search for any of the inhabitants.

"A family of five lived here. They had three children," Saffron called. Her voice was filled with anguish as she tossed aside boards and moved piles of debris.

Anger welled up inside me and I felt the pull to the Darkness that was becoming all too common. Startled, I stepped away from the rubble, catching my breath and forcing myself to calm down. I wasn't any good to anyone if I let my emotions get the better of me.

Master Flanders narrowed his eyes at me as I stepped back. I shook out my hands and walked in a small circle away from the home willing myself to send the Darkness away. Once I felt like I'd regained control of myself, I joined the others in the search.

"Etta," Master Flanders called to me. "Go check the barn." He pointed to a building nearby that had been spared from the flames.

A jolt went through me. *Please, please, please be in the barn.* I ran as fast as I could and slid open the huge door. The barn smelled of animals and hay. I looked around and saw a lone horse restlessly tapping the ground with his hoofs in his stall. Above me was a hayloft. If I were hiding, that is exactly where I'd be.

"Anybody in here?" I asked. I didn't want to startle anyone who was hiding and I didn't want them to try to hurt me thinking I was an attacker. "My name is Etta, I'm here to help you."

No response. I stood at the base of the ladder to the loft and listened. The only noises were the whinnying and hoof beats of the horse mixed with the patter of rain. Butterflies filled my stomach as I climbed the ladder. *Please be up here, please be safe.*

I stopped at the top of the ladder and looked around. The hayloft was full of neatly bundled bales of hay, a good place to hide. "I'm coming up, but I'm not here to hurt you. I want to help."

A small rustling sound came from the other side of the loft. I rested my hand on the dagger in my belt and slowly approached. Peeking over a large stack of hay bales, I saw two children huddled together, a boy and a girl. They both had dark hair and brown eyes and were close in age, but the girl looked to be older. They were scared, but didn't look hurt. I let out a breath. *Thank the gods.*

They stared at me with wide eyes then scooted back away from me. I removed my hand from my dagger and knelt down in front of them. "I'm here to help. It's going to be okay. I'm a friend of your parents, do you know where they are?"

The girl pushed her brother behind her and straightened. "Our parents sent us here to hide. Are you really here to help us?"

I offered a hand to the girl. "Yes, I am."

She looked from my hand to my face. "The guards had a sorcerer with them, how can you help against a sorcerer?"

I smiled at her. "Because I'm one, too. Not all sorcerers are bad."

She tilted her head to the side, nose crinkled in disbelief as she studied me. "A lady sorcerer?"

"Yes, and I brought help. There's more of us down there and we will keep you safe."

She took a step back from me, shrinking away.

"It's okay," I said. "I promise I won't hurt you."

After another pause, the girl put her hand in mine and let me pull her up. She turned to her brother and pulled him up.

"I think they killed our parents," the girl whispered.

I winced at her words and worked to keep my reaction from showing through. The last thing I wanted to do was scare these children any more. "Did they stay in the house?"

She nodded. "They saw them coming and sent us running. They stayed. Then we heard lots of loud noises."

"Is it just the two of you?" I asked, remembering that I was told there were three kids in this family.

Her eyes filled with tears and she shook her head. Her brother looked down at the floor.

"It's all right, we don't have to talk about it." I felt a connection to these two youngsters. Like me, they'd had their family ripped away. "You're safe now. We're going to take care of you."

I was tired of living in a kingdom full of orphans. It was too late for their parents, but I had to make sure these kids were safe. The Ravens would watch over them, like they had watched over me and Ashton and who knows how many other orphans. It was time for that cycle to end. The king needed to pay.

MASTER FLANDERS HANDED a red coin to Madame Lyndsey. "This will get the three of you back to the camp."

She nodded and held on to the children's hands as they teleported away. Once Madame Lyndsey saw that the children were in safe hands, she'd join us so we could continue on to Greenville.

I retrieved my bow from where I had set it on the ground then sat down on the damp grass in front of the barn. Tracing the carvings on my bow, I let my mind wander. This had been a message aimed at me. And only one person would have known where this safe house was. How badly did Max want to hurt me? He'd already tried to take Ashton from me and now this? Was he the one responsible for the destruction of the city? Maybe it wasn't the king at all. Maybe Max wanted to send me a message.

Saffron sat down next to me. "We found the parents and a younger sibling in the house. We burned the bodies so the king can't control them. They are at peace now."

I balled my hands into fists. "That's the only way to find peace, isn't it? Death. Then fire."

"Don't talk like that. We're going to beat him."

I tucked my hair behind my ears, trying to remember all of the people who had died for the cause. I didn't even know most of their names. "This wasn't the king. You know that."

Saffron stared straight ahead, unblinking. "I know."

We sat in silence for a moment, an unspoken understanding passing between us. I knew I was wrong to doubt her loyalty to our cause but I couldn't help but wonder what she'd do if she saw Max.

Ashton walked over and offered a hand to both Saffron and me. "Madame Lyndsey is back, we should get going."

I took his hand and he hoisted me up, then he helped up Saffron. The rest of the group was gathered a few feet away, waiting for us to join them. The first mile of the walk to

Greenville was quiet. We had prepared ourselves to see the damage in the city, but none of us had expected to find the destruction we had at the safe house.

Knowing that Max had shared its location took away any last vestige of hope I had for his redemption. I knew Max wanted the throne and I knew he was willing to see me dead to achieve that. Going after innocent people who just wanted to live a better life went too far.

I couldn't keep making excuses for him in my head. He'd sent Ashton's essence from his body and was learning how to use dark magic from the king. I stopped walking and the group around me paused.

"What is it?" Ashton asked.

"We should split up," I said. "I think you're right, they're trying to draw us in. Max or someone that works for him took out the safe house because they knew we'd come. They're waiting for us."

"Maybe we should go back," Ashton said.

I shook my head. "No. We have to save Calder's family and we have to find out what happened in Greenville."

"You mean you want to know if it was Max," Saffron said.

I didn't respond. She was right. I wanted to know if the king had taken all the dead from the city to find out if he had the power of the Skystone behind him, but I needed to know if Max was responsible for the destruction. Was it possible to share the same blood with someone who had that much Darkness?

"It couldn't be just him, right?" I watched her expression for any clues. "Even if it were Max, he couldn't possibly be powerful enough to destroy an entire city."

Saffron looked away for a moment, then back up at me. "I once watched him destroy an entire camp of king's guards alone."

I stared at Saffron in stunned silence as the vision from

earlier replayed in my mind. Max yelling into the darkness, hands ablaze. How had I never heard this before? "When was this?"

"Doesn't matter right now," Saffron said. "What does matter is that he's more powerful than you could ever imagine. If he's waiting for us there, splitting up isn't going to help us."

I swallowed, thinking of how I was going to phrase the words. "It helps us because I send most of you in as bait."

"What do you mean?" Ashton said.

"We might not want to parade around town anymore, but we have to get to Calder's family. I can go with Calder and we can get them back to the barn. It'll be easier for us to blend in if it's just two people. The rest of you can go in the opposite direction. Your faces are well known, you'll draw attention. If you run into trouble, you can teleport out. You'll be out of there before they notice I'm not with you or they'll think you left me behind. We can meet back up at sunset and teleport everyone back to camp." I looked around at my friends, trying to read their reactions.

"Makes sense to me," Calder said. "I'm in."

"Take me in your group," Madame Lyndsey said. "That way you have an extra sorcerer if needed. I'm not as familiar a face as the others."

"Etta, you know how dangerous this is," Ashton said. "There is no way we're going to let you do this."

Celeste set her hand on Ashton's arm. "I think it's a good idea. Calder knows the city. It's worth a try. Besides, Madame Lyndsey can teleport all of them out in a second."

I knew I didn't need permission to split up the group, but I didn't want my friends to worry. I locked my eyes on Ashton's, hoping he'd see how important this was to me. "Just give me a few hours. We'll be back at the barn by sunset."

Ashton's brow furrowed. "Please be careful."

Saffron looked to the sky. The sun was already getting low.

"Alright. Keep your hood on and stay out of sight. No going in and showing off who you are. Stay hidden. If we haven't returned within an hour of sunset, you go back to camp."

I opened my mouth to argue with her, but her glare told me she was not going to back down. I nodded.

Ashton leaned in to me. He tucked my necklace under my collar. "Stay safe, please."

I kissed him on the cheek. "I will if you will."

He squeezed my hand. "We should teleport in and start showing our faces around town. Etta's group can walk in and probably won't draw much attention."

Saffron held out her hand to Ashton. "I'll need a ride."

He let go of my hand and took hers then looked at Master Flanders and Celeste. "Town gates?"

Master Flanders nodded.

"Sounds good to me," Celeste said.

"Good luck," Ashton said to me.

Madame Lyndsey, Calder, and I stood there as the gray smoke swallowed our friends. Once they were clear, I started walking. I hoped I'd made the right decision.

6

ETTA

I adjusted the quiver on my belt, not caring that it caused my dress to wrinkle in ways that would make Lady Genevieve cry. My bow was slung over my shoulder and I tucked my pair of daggers inside the hidden pockets of my skirts. Pulling my hood over my head, I kept my gaze down as we approached the gates of Greenville. It hadn't been long since I'd walked through these gates with Celeste. It had been my first and only visit to the bustling city and we'd only stayed a few hours. This time, the once proud Greenville resembled so many of the destroyed towns I'd seen.

A torn blue banner hung from the gate. I froze. These were the remnants of the few weeks the city had kept the king's guards away and flown my family's colors. I couldn't remember a time when blue flags were flown in place of King Osbert's red. The change washed over me as if I had been thrown into an ice-cold lake. The tattered ends blew in the breeze, shredded and scorched like the rest of the city.

My stomach twisted with guilt. I never asked the people to step up to the king. I didn't want the people of Illaria to go through any more than they already had. Glancing over to the other side of the gate, I noticed a brand new red banner hung with the king's crest embroidered on it in bright gold thread. The contrast between the two was clear. My family's color had been left as a warning.

Calder moved closer to me. "It's not going to be like this for much longer. Soon, we will never have to look at those red banners again."

My throat tightened as I gave the tattered blue banner one last glance. It was the first time I'd seen my family's colors flown and this was how I had to see it. My mind was a tangle of emotions that I couldn't place. Clenching my fists, I nodded at Calder. Now wasn't the time.

I picked up the pace, careful where I placed my footsteps on the uneven ground. My heart sank as we passed through the gates. Most of the buildings resembled the destroyed farm house we had just left behind. The few buildings that weren't in pieces didn't look like they'd be standing for long.

With each step I took, my heart pounded faster. I had to know who did this. The king made it clear that he had no concern for human life. Did he take the bodies away with him? I had to know if this was his doing, or if someone else could take the blame. How many people died in his brutal attack? With each step, I could feel the pull of the Darkness, urging me to let it in. I took a deep breath and focused on clearing my mind. *Stay in control.*

Laughter sounded from ahead of us, sending the hair on my arms standing on edge. Nobody should be laughing in these streets right now. My fingers tingled with the telltale sign of magic. "Sorcerers. Hide"

We darted behind a crumbling two story building. Two of the walls were still mostly standing. I brushed against one of the walls and my sleeve came back covered in black soot. I looked around again and noticed that all the buildings seemed to be stained black. Whoever had done this had clearly used sorcerer fire. It was getting more difficult to hope that Max hadn't been involved. Had it been him and the king? Or Max's Order of the Dragon? Or had they combined forces? A bead of sweat rolled down my cheek. The thought of the king's sorcerers and Max's fire sorcerers working together was terrifying. I wiped my brow with my sleeve. My heart was still beating too quickly. The sooner we got out of here, the better.

Calder led us through narrow pathways between the rubble, taking us deeper into the heart of the city. I was grateful for his guidance. In the destruction surrounding us, my sense of direction was failing me.

We passed people who were walking through the rubble. Glassy eyed and ashen faced. They dug though the mess or called out the names of their loved ones. Nobody even looked at us. They were too focused on themselves and I couldn't blame them. I hoped the cart of supplies we sent could help some of them.

Reaching into my pocket, I found the full purse that Sir Henry gave me. With one hand, I loosened the string and grabbed a few coins. I started passing coins into the hands of the people we passed. Some of them stared at me with blank expressions, too numb to respond. Others thanked me or bowed their heads.

Madame Lyndsey threw me a warning glance but I continued to pass out the coins as we walked. It was a large bag, and I wanted to do something to help people. I needed something good to come from all of the destruction around me.

Calder stopped in front of a crumbled building. His shoulders dropped and the color drained from his face. I moved closer to him, worried he was going to pass out.

"This used to be my parents' house," Calder said.

The pile of debris in front of me was indistinguishable as

anything other than a crumbled structure. Looking around, I tried to find a way inside, a way to make sense of what had been here.

"Maybe they weren't home," Madame Lyndsey said.

Calder stood there, unmoving, unblinking.

"Calder?"

I turned to see Holden, Calder's friend that I met on my last visit to Greenville running toward us.

He pulled Calder into an embrace. "Thank the gods you're alive."

"My family?" Calder asked.

Holden looked down, then shook his head. "I came right after it happened but they were all gone."

"No chance my father was out on business?" Calder asked.

Holden's expression confirmed my fears and I covered my mouth with my hand. My throat burned as tears threatened.

Calder stumbled backward, out of Holden's embrace. "My sister?"

Holden remained silent for a moment. "I'm so sorry."

I couldn't hold back anymore. I moved over to Calder and wrapped my arms around him. "I'm so sorry."

It felt like I was spending a lot of time apologizing to my friends for the destruction following in my wake. The only reason Calder lost his family was because I continued to challenge the king.

Calder looked at me with a hint of the wild-eyed madness he'd worn when we first met. Nostrils flaring, jaw tense, he stepped away from my embrace. "When you kill him, I want him to suffer."

A lump rose in my throat and I felt the tendrils of the Darkness wrapping themselves around my insides. I knew exactly how he felt. I wanted the king, Max, the Oracle, everyone who wronged me to suffer. "We will make them all pay."

For a moment, I relished the feeling of the Darkness, it was as if it gave me permission to want revenge. Then, I caught myself. It wasn't worth it. I couldn't let it in, even for this. Taking a deep breath, I sent the Darkness away.

I turned to Holden. "Did you see what happened?"

He shook his head. "I didn't see it, but I've heard the stories."

I lifted my eyebrows. "And?"

"It was a whole group of sorcerers here. All of them using fire. All dressed in black. Rumor is that the Order of the Dragon works for the king now." His forehead creased. "That true?"

I nodded.

Holden's shoulders dropped. "It's over, then, isn't it?"

"Don't you say that," Calder said. "It's even more important that we fight this."

"Since when did you become a revolutionary?" Holden turned from Calder and pointed at me. "This girl is the reason your whole family is dead. The king left us alone until she came along."

I took a step back from Holden as the destruction around me assaulted my senses. He was right. Last time I'd been here, this had been a thriving city, full of life. Now, it was the smoldering remains of something out of a nightmare. All this because of me. I looked over at Calder, waiting to hear his response. Part of me wouldn't be surprised if he wanted to scream at me right here in the middle of the rubble.

"No," Calder said. "She's the reason I'm alive. The king wasn't ever going to leave us alone. And it won't end anytime soon. It's about to get a whole lot worse."

The tension filling me lessened at his words, but it wasn't enough to wash it away. I was determined to put an end to this destruction but I had no answers for what would happen before we gained our victory.

Holden spun in a circle, arms extended wide. "How can it get worse than this?"

Madame Lyndsey had been silent the whole time, just watching our exchange. She stepped in front of Holden. "The Darkness is on its way to Illaria. The barrier between the realm of the living and the realm of the dead will vanish and the king, a necromancer, will bring back anyone he wants. The dead could outnumber the living."

She stepped away from him and stood next to my side. "Still think she's not worth fighting for?"

Holden looked at Calder. "The Darkness is a myth. We use it to scare children."

"It's not a myth," I said.

Calder moved closer to Holden. "I've seen what it can do. I've seen the undead. Trust me. This is just the beginning."

The mention of the undead sent goosebumps down my arms. I recalled the mass of bodies moving toward us through the trees. The rotting corpses that came at us even after we lit them on fire. I glanced around, half expecting to see them coming after us. That was when I realized I didn't see any bodies. "Holden, why aren't there any bodies? Where are the dead?"

I could feel Madame Lyndsey and Calder tense up beside me. They knew where I was going with that question.

"I haven't really seen any," Holden said. "I suppose families must have taken them."

"Have there been any burnings?" I asked. "Piers? Funeral rites?" I already knew the answer the question. The scent of burning flesh was not something that faded quickly from your memory and it was a smell that we had not encountered in Greenville.

"I don't think so," Holden said.

Glancing around at the destruction, I realized exactly how

much danger we'd put ourselves in. There had to be thousands of people dead. What would the king be able to do with an army that size? Had he raised them all and sent them away or were they hiding in the streets, waiting for us? "We need to get out of Greenville."

"Yes, we do. I'm not prepared to fight off the undead." Calder turned to Holden. "You coming with us?"

"I can go with you?" he looked to me.

"You want to help us take down the king?" I asked.

He looked around at the rubble around us. "I've got nothing left here. I'm in."

I turned to Madame Lyndsey. "Can you teleport three?"

"Wait a minute," Holden said. "I have to bring my wife. I can't leave her here."

"Where is she?" I asked.

"Married?" Calder's mouth dropped open. "You and Anna? When did this happen?"

Holden smiled. "Yesterday. Figured the world is ending, might as well make it official."

"We'll celebrate later," Madame Lyndsey said. "Right now, I want to get all of you out of here."

Holden nodded. "Follow me." He took off at a jog through the streets.

"Guess we're going this way," I said to Madame Lyndsey.

"If he tries anything, I'm teleporting you out. Calder's on his own," she said.

Holden had his chance to turn me in weeks ago when he helped us find horses. I was pretty sure he wasn't about to do it now. "Sounds fair."

After about ten minutes, we reached a part of the city that had not been touched by destruction. People flooded the streets, seeking refuge in one of the inns or a moment of escape in one of the overflowing taverns. Holden stopped in front of a tavern. The sign had a picture of a dragon with a circle of stars over its head.

"What is this place?" I asked.

"The Dizzy Dragon Tavern. My wife runs this place, give me a minute." Holden pushed open the door and disappeared inside.

"How well do you know this friend?" Madame Lyndsey asked Calder.

"He's my best friend. He'd never do anything to hurt me and he's never had love for the king."

"What about this wife of his?" She asked.

"He's been seeing Anna for years. Honestly, though, I'll be surprised if she agrees to go with him. She took over this bar for her aunt and uncle. She loves this place."

Just then, the door swung open and Holden stepped back out, hand in hand with a woman who could only be, Anna. Her dark hair was pulled into a messy bun and she wore a dirty apron over a faded dress. She had a bag slung over her shoulder.

Anna stopped in front of me. "You really the lost princess?"

I looked from her to Holden. It had been a while since someone treated me so informally when they first met me. Looking back at her, I nodded.

"Any proof?"

I raised my eyebrows. What kind of proof was she expecting? "I'd show you proof, but it could just as easily be stolen."

She lifted her chin toward my bow. "Where'd you get the bow?"

"I made it," I said.

"You must have had a great teacher."

"He was the best."

"Alright," she said. "I'll go with you."

She turned and walked away from the bar. I wasn't sure what had just happened between us, but somehow, I had passed some secret test I wasn't aware I was taking.

"Can you teleport yourself to the barn?" Madame Lyndsey asked.

Nervous flutters filled my stomach and I swallowed back a lump in my throat. So far, I'd only teleported from one end of the Raven camp to the other. Master Flanders had insisted that any distance that didn't involve an ocean was possible with the limited training I had. "I think so."

"I'll take the others and meet you there."

"Sure you got this, Etta?" Calder asked.

"Only one way to find out." I smiled at him. "See you there."

7

ASHTON

Ashton followed Master Flanders, Celeste, and Saffron through the rubble of Greenville. The path they chose went through the most damaged part of the city, making the sight of others a rare occurrence. Their footfalls made strange echoes through the abandoned streets.

The black scorch marks of sorcerer fire stretched across the remains of the buildings. There was no denying that fire sorcerers had been at work here. Ashton wondered how many of the king's sorcerers aligned with fire. A wave of nausea rolled through him. How much of this damage had Max caused? He knew Max was powerful, he'd watched him complete his trials when he applied for the Order of the Dragon, but there had been little opportunity for Max to test his full strength. Ashton's jaw tightened. It was possible that he was strong enough to destroy most of a city. Was all of this just his way of testing his power?

Ashton forced his thoughts back to the present and looked around the debris for any sign of trouble. A sound like thunder reverberated from behind him and he turned to see a badly damaged building collapsing to the ground, leaving a cloud of dust in its wake. He stood, frozen for a moment, then turned to look at his companions. "Should we go check it out? Somebody could be hurt."

"Look around, Ashton," Celeste said. "We haven't seen any other people for the last ten minutes."

Aside from the shifting and settling of the building, the only sound Ashton heard was his own heartbeat throbbing in his ears.

"It's too quiet," Saffron said.

Ashton looked over his shoulder and saw sun was low in the horizon, bathing the ruins in a warm glow. The last rays of light mixed with the smoke had turned the sky a violent shade of red, a testament to the destruction they were seeing. "Maybe we should turn back."

"It looks like all the sorcerers are gone," Celeste said. "Master Flanders, what do you think?"

The older sorcerer stood with his face lifted toward the sky, eyes closed. A breeze blew the gray strands of hair that hung loose around his face. He lowered his head and looked around at the group. "I'm not sensing sorcerer magic, but I fear something is out there. We'll walk back to the gates to make sure we gave Etta enough time. But stay focused."

Ashton could feel his senses prickling in anticipation at Master Flanders' words. Every sound, every breath of wind, every smell seemed magnified. After walking so easily into Max's trap and losing his essence, he had learned his lesson about dropping his guard. Just because they couldn't see danger now, didn't mean something wasn't lurking out there, waiting for them.

"Come on." Saffron drew her sword and moved to the front of the group, retracing their path back to the gate. On the way here, they had decided she should keep her sword sheathed so as to not scare any locals they may encounter. But Celeste had made an excellent point, beyond the first few blocks inside the gate, they had seen no other people. Where was everyone? Had they all fled the city already?

Another thunderous collapse sounded as a building a block in front of them crumbled to the ground. A cloud of dust rolled through the street, eliminating their visibility. The group hesitated, waiting for the dust to settle before they progressed.

Through the brown haze, Ashton could just make out new shapes on the road in front of them. His whole body tensed as the shapes took on a human form. For a moment, he cursed himself for being so careless in his observations. They'd walked through a city of ruins. The streets should be full of the dead bodies of the victims or they should at least see some funeral piers remaining. Instead, they'd encountered a handful of living people and empty streets.

The king had left behind the dead and he had made them rise.

"It's the undead. Fire. Now." Ashton was the first to react. He charged into the settling dust where the graying, dead-eyed bodies of the dead were coming into clearer view. Calling to fire, Ashton launched a wave of flames at the approaching masses. A gust of wind flew past him and he knew Celeste was adding her magic to his, working to cause more damage with his flames.

Several of the bodies collapsed to the ground, charred and blackened from the fire. Saffron was quick to thrust her blade into the chest of one that kept moving, despite its charred exterior.

Master Flanders rushed by in a flourish of sweeping robes, going right into the middle of the onslaught. A moment later, the ground shook and an arm pulled Ashton back as a crack ate its way through the dirt.

Ashton stood frozen next to Celeste and Saffron as they watched half of the street rise until it was taller than them, forming a cliff that dropped off into a gap between the two halves of the road. Master Flanders stood on the raised part of the road, using wind to push the bodies of the dead into the crevice.

"Help him!" Ashton moved to the lower part of the street where the undead were regaining their bearings after being knocked down during the quaking earth. Ashton launched a fireball at a group of them, then Celeste used wind to push them into the opening in the earth.

Ashton continued to throw fire at the creatures and just when he thought they were nearly finished, a new wave came from the direction of the town gates. Had the king been hiding them all over the city? Who was commanding these creatures?

Ashton spun around, nearly colliding with Saffron. She looked up at him, red-faced and sweaty as the new hoard approached. With a battle cry, she ran toward the oncoming foes, sword raised. He knew she wouldn't go down without a fight, but how could they win a battle where the enemy never gets tired and more join in for every one you destroy?

With a deep breath, he called to fire again, ready to run toward the new wave of monsters. Then, the hair on the back of his neck stood on end and he glanced over his shoulder. His blood ran cold. There were thousands of undead streaming in from the other side of the city, the streets were completely full.

"Ashton!" Celeste called as she ran over to him. "We can't fight them all."

Saffron was backing up now, her wild expression replaced by one of worry. "Any bright ideas?"

Something grabbed hold of Ashton and pulled. He went down, landing hard on his back, head smacking down against the ground. For a moment, his vision went black, then white spots appeared and he saw a blurry figure looking down on him. Before he could react, he was being dragged into the throngs of reaching, cold, dead hands. He covered his face with his hands and rolled, trying to break free of their grasp.

With a scream, Ashton lost all control, igniting his fire in a way he hadn't done since the accident he had as a child. He let his magic rush through him, pouring out of him without concern for what it did or where it would land. His tunic went up in flames and a shriek sounded from the creatures surrounding him. They scurried away like insects and he emerged, breathing heavy, teeth bared, ready to take them all down.

Heart racing, he launched fire in all directions in a frenzy of anger, determined to kill as many of them as he could. After a moment, he realized what he had done. Looking around, he noticed that he had created a perimeter of fallen bodies and he closed his hands, letting his fire die, then patted out the flames eating away at his scorched tunic.

In a flash, Master Flanders had his hand around Ashton's and grey smoke rose around them. Ashton squeezed the older sorcerer's hand, and let some of the tension release from his body as they teleported away.

We arrived at the barn after the sun had set. Madame Lyndsey created two fire orbs and sent them into the center of the barn to illuminate the space. I looked around for any signs of the other group but found the barn empty. Were they on their way back? It was my idea to send them in as bait, if anything happened to them, it would be my fault.

Holden and Anna settled themselves in a corner. Madame Lyndsey performed a protection charm to conceal us in the barn. I paced around the empty space, stopping on occasion to listen for any indication of a group approaching us.

"Etta, why don't you sit down. There's nothing we can do right now." Calder gestured to the corner where Holden and Anna sat. "Come on."

Reluctantly, I followed Calder and set my bow on the ground before sitting down across from Anna. I looked over at the doorway and saw Madame Lyndsey bent down to stare through a hole. Feeling too restless to sit, I stood. "Maybe I should go see if she needs help."

A tug on my sleeve brought my attention back to the group

on the floor. Anna was pulling me back down. "I have to tell you something."

Curious, I sat back down. "What is it?"

"Your bow." She nodded to the ground where I had set it down.

"Why are you so interested in it?" I asked.

She opened her bag and removed a small, wooden box then handed it to me. I saw it before I even had it in my hands. Carved on every side of the wood was the flower pattern Sir Edward had carved on the bow he made for his granddaughter. The bow I had learned how to shoot with. I traced my fingers over the flowers. "Where did you get this?"

"My grandfather made it for me."

My mouth dropped open and I blinked a few times, stunned into silence as the meaning of my archery master's note became clear. After all this time, I'd given up on Master Edward's message. I never expected the girl whose name was written on that note to find us. "Annalise?"

She nodded.

"What's happening here?" Holden said.

Anna turned to him. "My real name is Annalise. I haven't gone by it for years." She looked back at me. "My grandfather sent me to live with my aunt and uncle. And he gave me this box. He told me that one day I'd need to give it to you, the rightful queen of Illaria."

I pictured the rolled parchment that Master Edward had left for me with the words *Annalise Sutton, Greenville.* Tears blurred my vision. I'd given up on finding that girl. We'd sent our best scouts and they had failed. "We looked for you. I wasn't even sure if you were real."

She sniffed and her words came out choked. "I'm real. I've been waiting a long time."

I ran my hand through my hair and stared at Annalise, trying to find the words. "I'm sorry I didn't come sooner."

"Somebody please explain this to me," Calder said.

Feeling giddy, I laughed. As relieved as I was to have found her, I couldn't help but feel stunned and a bit light headed. After the destruction of Greenville, the loss of Calder's family, and all the stress of not knowing where the rest of our party was, here was the girl I was sent to find. "Annalise's grandfather was my archery master. He left me a message before he died with just her name and Greenville written on it. We sent scouts, but they never found her. I can't believe it."

Anna's face fell. "He's really gone, then?"

The initial elation eased and my shoulders sunk. I hadn't even thought of the fact that she wouldn't know about his death. I leaned closer to her and rested my hand on top of hers. "I'm so sorry. He passed a few months ago. He was a great man."

She wiped tears from her cheek. "I'm surprised he lived that long, really, but it's still difficult to hear."

"We should return to camp soon," Madame Lyndsey said.

I passed the box back to Anna and stood, crossing the barn to the front door. "What is it?"

Madame Lyndsey shook her head. "I'm not sure, but I have a bad feeling. I don't think it's safe to stay here much longer."

"We can't leave yet, the others haven't returned," I said.

"If they aren't here soon, we should go. We agreed to an hour after sunset. We shouldn't wait much beyond that time."

I nodded. It wasn't safe to stay in one place for so long, even with a protection spell around the barn.

Pacing again, I wondered what Ashton and the others were up to right now. Had they run into trouble? It was well past sunset and the longer we waited, the worse my imagination got. I pictured my friends surrounded by black-robed sorcerers or being overrun by a hoard of undead.

Calder joined me on my pacing. "It's going to be fine. They'll be here any minute. Come sit down."

I glanced at the front door where Madame Lyndsey still stood vigil. There wasn't anything I could do while we waited so I relented, finding a seat next to Anna and Holden. After a few minutes of silence, I turned to Anna. "What is in the box?"

"It's a map, I think." She turned the box around in her hands. "It's supposed to show where the king hid the Stone of Morare."

A chill ran through my whole body and I stared at Anna in disbelief. "Are you sure?"

She nodded.

I recalled my encounters with the king's Reapers, nose crinkling as I recalled the stench. They were terrible creatures who were often sent to target individuals the king wanted to eliminate. So far, I'd managed to use my arctic fire to send them away, but it wasn't without a price. The energy required for me to gain that kind of power took its toll on me and I ended up unconscious from the effort. I didn't even want to think what happened to most people when they were ambushed by the monsters.

The Stone of Morare. If we could get that stone, we would finally have an advantage. The king might have the Skystone, but we could take his Reapers away. We could destroy those monsters.

"Another stone?" Calder looked a bit green. "How many of those stones are there? And what terrible thing does this one do?"

Calder had helped us try to find the astral projection stone. Instead, we'd found the dragon stone, which was of little use to us. I looked at him, feeling sympathetic. He'd only been with us for a few weeks but after all we'd been through together, I felt like I'd known him for years. "There's five different stones. The Stone of Morare controls the Reapers."

The color drained from Calder's face. "As in, those monsters the king sends after his enemies?"

I nodded, then turned to Annalise. "Wait, wouldn't the king just keep that stone with him?"

The dragon stone we had found was on a chain and Celeste wore it all the time. It seemed the safest way for us to keep track of it.

"He used to," she said. "But people kept trying to steal it from him. He figured it would be safer to hide it, I suppose."

"How do you know where it is?" Calder asked.

"I don't. I just know the map in the box shows where it is." She tucked the box back into her bag. "I'm the only one who can decode it now that he's gone." She busied herself with the ties on her bag, seemingly finished talking for now.

I could almost feel Anna's pain as she struggled to keep it off of her face. She was forcing herself to be strong, it was an expression that was too common in the faces of those I met. Everyone in this room had lost so many they cared about. I glanced over at Calder. He was staring blankly in front of him, eyes unfocused. He'd lost all of his family in the last few weeks at the hand of the king and he never stopped to grieve. None of us had. I pried his fist apart and laced my fingers between his, squeezing his hand. He looked over at me, then looked away again.

"Get ready to go," Madame Lyndsey walked over to us. "We have to head out in the next couple of minutes."

"No, it can't be time already." My pulse raced. Ashton wasn't back yet. After everything we'd been through, there was no way I was going to lose him again. "Not yet, they have to be coming soon."

She frowned. "I know how you feel, I do. But something doesn't feel right."

My stomach turned as visions of Ashton, Celeste, Saffron, or

Master Flanders hurt and alone filled my head. "Maybe I should go after them."

Madame Lyndsey lifted an eyebrow. "What good does it do anyone for you to go out after them?"

"What if one of them is hurt and they need help?" I never would have sent them away if I thought they would encounter danger. I thought that if they saw trouble, they'd teleport right back here. If they weren't here, something was wrong.

"Then perhaps they are resting in the woods or waiting a few hours before they come here. Maybe they were followed and chose to go straight back to camp," she said.

My shoulders dropped. She was right. It was possible that going after them could end up doing more damage if they were in a bad situation.

"Etta, they can take care of themselves. I mean, they have Celeste with them," Calder said.

"That's true." I smiled at Calder. He'd never seen the others in action and though I would consider Celeste to be the least powerful sorcerer of the group, she was a force on her own. That thought helped ease my mind. "I'm sure they're fine. They probably just got held up somewhere."

Out of nowhere, a faint tingle began in my fingers, the same feeling I got when magic was being used near me. My heartbeat quickened.

I jumped to my feet. "Somebody is here, and they're using magic."

Madame Lyndsey bolted back to the door and peered through the hole in the barn. She turned to me and placed a finger over her lips. My heart beat faster and the uncomfortable prickle of fear radiated from my chest. The tingle was stronger now, spreading up my arms.

I looked back to Anna and Calder, mirroring Madame Lyndsey's motion for silence. Anna had both hands on her bag, gripping it so tightly that her knuckles were white.

I tip-toed across the barn to the hole in the door where Madame Lyndsey was standing. She shifted so I could look. When I peered through the hole, my insides felt like they had ice running through them. Max was outside of the barn. A sharp pain shot into my fingers and traveled up my arms, taking my breath away. I stepped back from the hole and took a moment to catch my breath. The tingling settled as the most intense reaction to magic I had ever felt.

My breathing was rapid as I looked back out the hole, already knowing what I would see. *Reapers.* All four of them were floating around the barn with Max. I stepped back and nodded toward the hole. Madame Lyndsey looked through quickly then pulled back, face drained of all color.

Madame Lyndsey grabbed my hand and led me to the center of the barn then let go of my hand. She motioned for Anna, Holden, and Calder to join us. They stood, and walked to the center of the barn. The building shook as someone worked to break through the ward Madame Lyndsey had set up. The ward only had one sorcerer worth of magic so it wouldn't last long.

Madame Lyndsey pulled a red coin out of a pocket and held it in her hand. She looked at me. "You have your coin? Think you can take someone with you?"

My stomach twisted and nausea overtook me. This would be the farthest I'd ever teleported and it would be the first time taking someone besides myself. I found the coin I had hidden in a pocket and held it out for her to see. The barn shuddered as magic hit it again. There wasn't time to worry.

"Annalise, Holden," I whispered. "Hold on to Madame Lyndsey's hand. Don't let go no matter what."

They nodded at me and each took hold of one of her hands.

"You first," Madame Lyndsey said.

I swallowed against the lump that had risen in my throat. *You can do this.* Reaching my hand out, I grabbed Calder's.

He nodded. "It's going to be fine. You have been training for this."

Calder had heard stories of my shaky first attempts at teleporting. If he was still willing to take a chance on me, he either really believed in me, or he was really worried about the Reapers. Either way, it was our only choice. "Hang on."

"Dropping the ward now," Madame Lyndsey said. "Go!"

The room around us shuddered as the protection charm was dropped. The door to the barn exploded in a mass of flames and black smoke, heat causing me to turn my face away.

I closed my eyes as I called to my magic, focusing on the Raven camp, imagining the two of us dissolving into nothing and reappearing. Heat rose around me, the flames had to be getting nearer. Too afraid to open my eyes, I let out a little breath of relief as I felt the tugging sensation take hold. Focusing on getting us home, I squeezed Calder's hand. When my feet touched down on solid ground, we both tumbled forward, Calder landing on top of me, knocking my breath from my lungs.

He moved off of me and started laughing. "You did it."

Struggling to catch my breath, I looked around. We were on solid ground. "I did."

A moment later, Madame Lyndsey landed gracefully next to us with her two charges.

"You just need to work on your landing," Calder said.

My head was spinning as I processed what had just happened. We left so quickly I didn't have a chance to consider the consequences of our actions. We ran away, leaving an ambush for the other group. For a moment, I considered teleporting right back there, then I realized how stupid that would be. There was no way that Madame Lyndsey and I could have taken on Max and the Reapers alone. I had to hope that my friends would see the destruction of the barn before they were too close. Maybe they'd teleport straight here instead of going back.

I had to keep myself together, focus on my responsibilities and take care of the people here with me. With the discovery of Anna and the map to the Stone of Morare, things had changed.

"Is everybody alright?" Madame Lyndsey asked.

"I'm here, but I think I'm going to be sick," Anna said.

"We won't have to do that again, will we?" Holden asked.

I couldn't help but smile as I remember my first time teleporting. "It'll pass, you actually get used to it after a few times."

"I don't think I want to try it again," Anna said, clutching her bag with both hands.

"Don't let her fool you, it's still awful and I've done it a few times," Calder said.

In the starlight, I could just make out the dummies we used for archery practice. We were back at camp. Nobody was out here in the dark and I was thankful for the moment of peace. I focused on taking deep breaths and pulling myself together.

"Where are we?" Anna asked.

"Welcome to the camp of the White Ravens," I said.

Madame Lyndsey took a few steps toward camp then turned to look at me. "They'll be waiting for an update from you, I'm sure somebody will have noticed our arrival by now."

I looked toward the darkened camp. People were settling in for the night, but there would be enough lamps still lit to notice us walking through. "We'll have to wait until morning. The others should be back by then and I'm sure our guests are tired."

Madame Lyndsey nodded. "Why don't you get some rest, your highness. I'll check in with the watch, make sure everything is normal."

"Thanks." I was grateful that Madame Lyndsey had chosen to

stay and help us after the trials. She and Ashton were the only fire sorcerers we had on our side and we were going to need their power to stop the king. "Please come and get me if you need me. I'm going to find Anna and Holden a place to sleep."

As we walked toward the camp, I realized I didn't know where to put the two of them. We'd need to make a tent for Anna and Holden if they were going to stay with us long term. In the end, I led them to my tent, it was the largest one in the camp and we'd all be meeting there in the morning, anyway.

"Where are you going to sleep?" Calder asked after we closed the tent flap on his friends.

I glanced to the tent across from mine. It was empty right now because I'd sent its occupant off as bait.

Calder walked over to Ashton's tent and silently lifted the flap for me. I paused at the doorway, fighting back the worry that was occupying my mind.

Calder gave me a kiss on the cheek, then nudged me toward the tent. "Get some rest, Etta."

I walked into the darkened space and the flap of the tent dropped closed behind me. Somehow, I found my way to Ashton's bedroll and curled up into a little ball. *Please come home soon. Please be safe.* I wrapped his blanket around me, breathing in the smell of him.

9

ASHTON

Ashton collapsed on the ground when he landed. He blinked a few times, trying to clear the double vision and regain his balance. It took all of his willpower to force himself up. He took a few tentative steps then turned to vomit in the bushes behind him. He wiped the sweat from his brow then wiped his mouth with his sleeve. He stood straighter, feeling a little better, though still fighting for his balance.

"Are you alright?"

Ashton turned to see Saffron and Celeste staring at him. He smiled at them to try to hide the screaming pain in his head.

"I'm fine," he said, "just a bump on the head."

Ashton looked around in the twilight. The sun was already below the horizon line, it would be dark in minutes. Was Etta already waiting for them? He looked through the trees, expecting to see the barn in the distance. All he saw were trees. "Where are we?"

Master Flanders was speaking quietly to Saffron. He paused in his conversation and turned to Ashton. "We're about two miles away from the barn. I didn't think it wise to show up right in front of it, we'd draw too much attention."

"I guess we better get walking," Ashton said. "The rest of the group has to be there by now."

Master Flanders shook his head. "Not yet."

Ashton narrowed his eyes at him. "What do you mean? We have to get back to them. They won't wait long."

Master Flanders rested his hand on Ashton's shoulder and guided him to a fallen tree. "Sit, I'll heal you first, then we can go. If we run into trouble, I need you to be able to fight."

"You're not going to be able to help anyone if you're in the bushes throwing up," Celeste said.

Ashton wanted to argue, but he looked at the little group around him. They had a powerful master sorcerer, two sorcerers who had only passed their first round of trials, and a warrior. If they ran into a group of sorcerers or more undead, they needed him to be ready. Reluctantly, he sat on the log. Celeste sat down next to him.

Master Flanders lifted his hands and moved them through the air, hovering around Ashton's body. Ashton felt warmth travel through him as Master Flanders worked. The pain in his head began to lessen and his vision cleared. A wave of relief washed over him.

"Thank you," Ashton said.

Master Flanders smiled. "You're lucky it was just a bump on the head."

Ashton reached behind his head and felt the area where the lump had been. His hand ran over his hair, sticky and matted with drying blood. The bump was gone. He shook his head. "That's amazing."

Master Flanders smiled at the younger sorcerers. "You two did well considering," he said. "When we have some time after this mess, let's work on your training. I think I can get you two ready for the next round of trials."

"Better?" Saffron walked over to the group of sorcerers. Her blonde curls were a tangle of blood and dirt, her face scratched and bruised. Ashton was guessing he looked about the same. The sooner they could get Etta to Gallia to get that army and end this war with the king, the better. Ashton shivered as he recalled the touch of the gray hands of the dead. He could happily go the rest of his life without seeing another one of those creatures. Facing off against sorcerers seemed easier. At least with them, there weren't more crawling out of buildings and flooding the streets.

"Let's get back home," he said.

They walked silently with careful footsteps through the dark woods. The progress was slow in the faint starlight. They couldn't risk illumination for fear that it would alert their enemies to their location.

In the distance, the trees looked to be thinning and Ashton's heart leapt at the sight. The barn was located in cleared farmland next to the woods. They had to be close.

In front of him, Master Flanders stopped walking and put his arm out to stop everybody's progress. Ashton was just about to ask what was going on when he felt it, the unmistakable tingle of magic began in his fingertips and quickly spread though his whole body. There was magic at use nearby, lots of it. A bright light illuminated the darkness. *Sorcerer Fire.*

His heart began to hammer wildly in his chest and panic rose inside him. *Etta.* Ignoring Master Flanders and the others, he ran toward the fire.

Ashton shielded his face with his arm from the intense heat as he ran toward the burning barn. His heart was in his throat as he yelled Etta's name. There was no time to think about strategy, his passion took over, blinding him. When he reached the barn he jumped through the flames, searching inside for any survivors. A frantic horse nearly trampled him as he ran through the barn.

She's not here, he thought. He struggled to regain control of his emotions as the sense of panic lessened. Reality began to sink in. Sorcerer fire was climbing up the walls of the barn, Max had to be here. His pulse raced. *Max tried to kill Etta.*

Ashton felt the heat rise from within him, forcing his fire to surface. Flames licked at his palms, as if they had a mind of their own. He was pure anger and passion. Not stopping to consider what Max could do to him if he let his emotions get the better of him, he charged in.

As he reached the doorway, the flames faded. A startled horse barreled past him into the night. The only illumination came from the fire emanating from his own hands. In the glow, he could make out a form. His lip raised in a snarl. This had gone on long enough. Somebody had to teach Max a lesson. He took a few deep breaths, aware now of his emotions running wild, and tried to reign them back in before he faced his opponent.

Then, the figures multiplied. Suddenly there were four. Ashton froze. He hadn't been looking at Max. The figures floated unnaturally. Mingled with the scent of the fire was the rotting corpse smell of the Reapers. The dark hollows under their hoods where their faces should be were all facing him. His stomach tightened. Swallowing back his fear, he raised his arms. All he could do was hope he could make enough fire to send them away long enough to escape.

Fire was their only weakness, but he didn't know how much it would take to scare them away. Every time he'd faced the Reapers, he had Etta with him. Her arctic fire was so much stronger against the undead creatures.

He took a deep breath and just as he was going to let loose his flames, the ground shook, sending him tumbling to the ground and extinguishing his flames. He pushed himself upright and reignited his fire, turning in the direction of the

Reapers. They were no longer moving toward him. They were floating away toward a new target, somebody of greater importance than Ashton.

Ashton remembered that the Reapers were usually sent after specific people. It appeared they weren't here for him. They were after somebody else. If Etta's not here, they were after somebody in their group. Who did the king want dead enough to send his Reapers?

A memory flashed through Ashton's mind in a second. He was four years old. The little princess was in his grandmother's arms. An old man stood over her, long grey hair tied in a tail at the base of his head. He was only there for a few minutes before he vanished in a cloud of smoke. A shiver ran down his spine. The old man had to be Master Flanders. He must have been casting the protection spell on Etta before she was smuggled into hiding. He'd tried so long to suppress the memories of that day that he never stopped to think about the details. Master Flanders was the key to Etta's survival. Ashton ran toward the Reapers.

Ashton's breath came out in heavy pants and he squinted to see better through the darkness. There were two people surrounded by Reapers and the monsters were closing in. He raised his hands, calling his fire from deep within and released.

The Reapers made an inhuman scream as his fire burned their robes. They turned away from their victims and floated toward him. Sweat beaded on his forehead as he continued to push fire through his hands.

A rush of wind hit him and he lost his balance. Ashton turned to the direction of the wind and saw a dark hooded figure walking toward him. *Max.* Ashton's whole body tensed and his nostrils flared as Max's form came into clearer view. The last time he'd seen his old friend, Max had almost killed Ashton by sending his essence to the Astral Realm. Now, Max was after

Etta. For a moment, Ashton considered charging Max, ignoring the rest of the threats around them. But he'd been trained too well to make decisions based on anger.

Ashton looked between the Reapers who had turned their attention away from him, to Max. He didn't know where he should be aiming his attack. Before he could make a final decision, another figure emerged out of the corner of his eye.

In a blur, a dagger flew through the air, just missing Max's shoulder. Ashton realized Saffron was standing not far from Max, sword drawn. She was waiting for him. Max gave one last glance at Ashton, then turned and walked toward Saffron.

Glancing away from Max for a moment, Ashton saw Master Flanders and Celeste battling the Reapers, both of them creating weak flames to try to fend them off. Neither of them were aligned with fire so their magic was gaining them little progress against the monsters.

The sound of steel on steel rang out and Ashton looked over to see that Saffron and Max were engaged in sword-to-sword combat. Ashton hoped Saffron was ready to take on Max and turned away, racing toward the Reapers. Despite the power Max held, Ashton thought the four Reapers closing in on his other friends were an even greater threat. As he closed in on the fight, he threw a fireball at the Reaper nearest him, just missing. The fire caught on the ground, spreading quickly, illuminating the darkness.

Ashton leapt over the burning ground and slid between two of the Reapers surrounding his friends. The three of them were now surrounded by the creatures. They would have to work together to send them back to their master, or wherever it was the Reapers retreated to. Ashton wished there was a way to kill them but other than the theory about Etta's arctic fire, they hadn't found another way.

"Celeste, use your air to feed Master Flanders' fire," Ashton called out. Next to him, Master Flanders released a modest flame and Celeste fed it with a burst of air. The flames grew until they rivaled one of Ashton's own.

Ashton turned to face the Reapers who were on the other side of them, launching fireballs at them without pausing for breath. He was getting tired but the adrenaline flowing through him was helping to mask some of the fatigue.

The ground rumbled again and a large piece of earth shot up under one the Reapers, sending it flying. Ashton turned his fire on that Reaper, hoping it let its guard down enough for his flames to get through. The fire caught on its robes and flames engulfed it. It let out a haunting scream that echoed inside Ashton's head. He had to fight back the urge to cover his ears. The flames turned to black smoke, and the Reaper was gone. They'd managed to send one of them away.

Ashton's spirits rose. If they did it to one of them, they could get rid of the rest. "Again!"

Master Flanders called another piece of earth up from the ground, throwing a second Reaper skyward. Ashton released his fire and Celeste threw air behind his flames. It burned so bright, it looked like daylight for a moment as they lit up the sky. The Reaper was instantly engulfed in orange and yellow, vanishing in the same black smoke as the other one.

There were only two Reapers left now. Ashton narrowed his eyes and took aim, throwing his fire at them with everything he had. Celeste and Master Flanders both sent air behind his flames, strengthening them beyond anything Ashton could ever imagine. He had to turn away as the flames grew white-hot.

He had to let go of the flames to catch his breath. When he looked back, the Reapers were gone. Wiping the sweat from his brow, he glanced down at his destroyed tunic. In all the years of using his magic, he'd never called this much fire in one evening. He'd been training his whole life to do defensive magic, to be able to fight against the king and those under his command. Tonight had been the most he'd ever used it. He wasn't as proud of himself as he thought he'd be. There was something hollow in fighting the dead but that feeling would have to wait. The battle wasn't over yet.

10

ASHTON

Spinning around, Ashton searched the darkness for the fight he had left behind. "Where's Max?"

"There!" Celeste pointed.

Max and Saffron were silhouetted against the blaze of the barn. Neither party looked to be showing any signs of weakness as they attacked each other with steel. Ashton hesitated for a moment, eyes narrowed on his old teacher. Max wasn't using any magic in his fight with Saffron. He'd always told Ashton that there was no point in learning how to use a sword, sorcerers were their own weapons. Ashton couldn't even remember ever seeing Max practice with any weapons in all the years they'd lived in the same camp. Saffron, on the other hand, was an expert swordsman. She should have no problem defeating Max.

They were both holding back. It was the only explanation for what he was seeing.

"We should help her," Celeste said.

Ashton put his arm out to stop her. "No, I don't think they'll hurt each other. If we go over there, it could make it worse."

"I'll get her out of here," Master Flanders said. "You two, tele-port to the old Raven camp. I'll meet you there."

Just as Ashton opened his mouth to protest, Master Flanders yelled, "Now!"

Celeste reached out and gripped Ashton's hand. "I don't know where that is, you'll have to take us."

Ashton closed his eyes and imagined the archery range at the old camp. The place where he first kissed Etta. A tug in his stomach pulled at him as his feet left the ground.

They landed hard on uneven ground, knocking them both down. Ashton helped Celeste up and they both brushed the dirt off of their hands as they looked around. They were back at the old camp. The place where Ashton had grown up. The place where he had fallen in love.

He shook the nostalgia from his mind. It wasn't the time to dwell. He turned to Celeste. "You alright?"

"I'm fine," she said. "Do you think it would be safe to get some light here?"

The thick trees blocked the starlight, making it darker than it had been in the other woods. Ashton conjured a small fireball in his hand and held it out to Celeste. Her face was bruised and covered in scrapes. He pushed her hair off of her forehead and lowered his eyebrows in concern. "You sure you're alright?"

She batted his hand away. "I'm fine. Just a few scrapes." She looked around the abandoned archery range. "So this is where you grew up?"

He nodded. "This is it, my old home."

She looked at the archery shed, he followed her gaze. An ache filled his whole body when he saw the place where he had first kissed Etta. He didn't want to look at it anymore.

"Come on," Ashton said. "We should probably go wait in the common area. That's the most likely place they'll teleport."

"Why'd you teleport here?" She asked, then caught herself. "This is the archery range, isn't it?"

Ashton nodded and started to walk away.

"That's where you first kissed Etta," she said.

He stopped walking and turned to look at her. "How'd you know that?"

"GIRLS TALK ABOUT THINGS, Ashton. Etta's my friend." She gave him a sly smile. "I bet I know more than you realize."

Ashton shook his head. He was happy Celeste and Etta got along so well, but it was strange to know they discussed him when he wasn't around. "Great, now my girlfriend and my best friend are talking about me behind my back."

Celeste patted his shoulder as they walked. "Don't worry, it's a good thing. She's madly in love with you, you know."

Ashton smiled. He knew that, already, but in the midst of all of the changes going on in their lives, it was nice to think that Etta had shared that with someone else. His smile faded. "I hope she's safe."

"Me too," Celeste whispered.

They rest of the walk to the common area was silent, both of them too lost in their own heads to speak. As they approached the clearing, they heard voices. Ashton picked up his pace and Celeste followed suit.

"Thank the gods," Celeste said as Master Flanders and Saffron came into view.

Saffron had an arm across her chest, holding on to her shoulder. Her face was distorted in pain.

"What happened?" Ashton asked. He held the fireball up so he could see her more clearly.

She winced in pain and turned her face away from the light. "Don't worry about it let's just get back."

"It will take me a few minutes to make a new coin to get us into the camp," Master Flanders said. "Celeste, check on Saffron's wound."

Celeste moved to Saffron without hesitation and the two women walked to one of the tables.

"Ashton." Master Flanders lifted his chin. "Come over here. I want to show you how to do this just in case I'm not around to help."

Ashton wondered what was going on inside the old man's head as he hurried to catch up to him. "I thought you couldn't learn to make these coins until you passed the next round of trials."

Master Flanders led the two of them to the space previously occupied by the blacksmith. The only remnants of its previous inhabitant were a few workbenches and a large fire pit. He set a wooden circle the size of the other coins that were used for tele-portation on the edge of the fire pit, then looked at Ashton. "If we don't stop the king soon, there won't be any guild to monitor those rules. Now, pay attention."

"Wait," Ashton said. "Before you start that, can I ask you something?"

He looked at Ashton and waited in silence.

"That day." Ashton took a deep breath. He'd never told anyone the story of the day his grandmother had smuggled the princess away from her home. Until he had the flash of a memory during the battle, he had almost managed to convince himself that it wasn't real. "The day Etta was brought to my house. You were there, weren't you?"

"I wondered if you even remembered that. You were so young." Master Flanders sighed. "How much do you recall?"

For the first time in a long time, Ashton let the memories wash over him. He clenched his teeth as he pictured the guards breaking down his door. His hands squeezed into fists as he recalled his mother's fire being swallowed up by the Reapers that dragged her body away. "All of it. After my grandmother took the princess, the guards came. They brought the Reapers. My mother..."

Master Flanders set his hand on Ashton's shoulder. "I hoped you'd forgotten it all. Your mother was a very powerful sorceress and your father fought valiantly at the Battle of the Dead. They would be so proud of you."

Ashton cleared his throat. He didn't want to remember any of it, but he had to know. "You're the one who cast the protection spell, aren't you?"

Master Flanders nodded, his face serious. "Yes, Ashton. That's why it's so important for you two to learn as much as you can from me in the time we have left."

"Why do you keep saying things like that?" Ashton shook his head. If Master Flanders dies, the protection spell is broken and the king himself can kill Etta.

"Ashton, I've lived a long life. Even if the king wasn't trying to kill me, my days would be numbered. But he suspects that I'm the sorcerer who cast the spell and you can only outrun the Reapers for so long before your luck runs out."

He touched his index finger to the wooden circle. "It's time for me to make my peace and make the most of the time I have left."

Ashton felt a mix of sadness and anger rise up inside him. "How can you just give up like this? You are the most powerful sorcerer I know. Surly you can stand up to the king, to his Reapers. We did it tonight."

Master Flanders smiled at Ashton. "We did well tonight. But I'm tired and I'm not as young as I used to be. We'll talk about this more later."

Ashton sighed and fixed his eyes on the wooden circle, he knew better than to try to argue with Master Flanders. And he was ready to go home. "I'm ready to learn."

"Good. First, you need to know the location that you're going to make the coin for. If it's like our camp, and it has a ward or other magical protection, only those who helped to create the ward can make a coin." He glanced at Ashton. "When we get back, we'll have you add a layer to the protection so you can make coins if you need to."

Ashton nodded and watched as Master Flanders pressed down on the wooden circle. "You'll need to gain the strength of all the sorcery elements. You need to find a way to channel each element within you, and hold them all at once. Once you've done that, tell the coin where you want it to go."

Knowing how to make these coins would be a huge benefit. The coins not only allowed one to gain entry to a protected location, they could also be useful for a quick exit if the sorcerer using it was too tired or weak to focus properly. They took much of the burden off of teleportation. Ashton made sure he was completely focused on every movement Master Flanders was making.

The old man closed his eyes and lifted his face toward the sky. He let out a long, slow breath then lowered his chin toward his chest. He lifted the coin with both hands, then pulled it up to his mouth, cupping his hands around it. Then, he whispered into his closed hands. Opening his eyes, he pulled his hands away from his face and held out an open hand for Ashton to see.

In his palm was a glowing red coin. "You have to explain the location to the coin," Master Flanders said, tossing the coin to Ashton.

Ashton stared at the newly created coin in his hand. Master Flanders had a way of making things seem easier than they actually were. He wasn't sure he'd be able to channel all four elements at the same time. What kind of power would that take? Ashton now understood why so few people could create this type of magic.

Master Flanders turned away and Ashton followed him. The

two sorcerers walked back to the common area to find that Celeste had stopped the bleeding on Saffron's shoulder.

Ashton held the coin up for them to see. "Let's go home."

"Wait." Saffron stood and looked at the group. She had a hand pressed against her injured shoulder, holding down a bandage that Celeste had applied. "There's something you need to know before we go back. Something Max told me."

Ashton's brow furrowed. "What is it?"

Her gaze turned hard and her mouth pressed into a tight line. "He told me the princess is with child. He's marrying the king's daughter."

Silence fell over the group as the weight of the words sunk in. Ashton squeezed his hands into fists as rage seeped in through him. How could Max have done this to Saffron? Ashton had watched them together most of his life. He couldn't even remember a time when they hadn't been viewed as an extension of one another. Ashton couldn't imagine how he'd feel if Etta left him for the king. It was a betrayal beyond forgiveness. "I'm so sorry, Saffron. I promise, we're going to make him pay."

Celeste stood and walked over to Saffron, pulling her into a hug. "We're here for you. And Ashton's right. We're going to make Max pay."

A true smile crossed Saffron's face. "And then we kill the princess."

The hair on the back of Ashton's neck stood on up. He had never seen Saffron look happy discussing someone's death. She'd never even had that look when talking about the king. This was personal for her; this was revenge. He was sure it was going to make her a more difficult adversary in their fight for the kingdom, but he wasn't sure he liked this Darkness in her. Was that what they were about now? Killing women and unborn babies? Even if it was the king's daughter and Max's child. Was that right?

He had a feeling that Etta wouldn't support that. But then again, she wouldn't want to have to prove her legitimacy against this child when it was older. He pushed the thoughts away. It would have to wait. For now, he just needed to get back to Etta. "We should go."

11

ETTA

Sunlight filled the tent, bathing the room in a soft glow. I could almost feel Ashton next to me. *I must be dreaming.* My back was hot, as if somebody warmer than me was pressed against it. Blinking, I realized I wasn't dreaming.

My heart raced as I turned to see who had joined me in bed. Tension washed away from me as I stared at Ashton's sleeping form. I pushed his hair away from his eyes and kissed his forehead. He was here, he was breathing. My vision was distorted by tears. I let out a half-laugh, half-sigh and threw my arms around him.

He fell back on the bedroll, pulling me down with him. Strong arms held me tight and I didn't want him to let go. In a perfect world, I'd stay here just like this all day. We held each other for several minutes, neither of us speaking. How many more times would we have to endure separation and concern for each other's safety? It had been my idea to send my friends into the city, but it was the only way I could think of to get out of there quickly. I ran my fingers through his hair as I moved in closer to kiss him, then froze when my hand caught on what could only be dried, matted blood.

My breath caught in my chest as I brought my hand to my face, some of the sticky blood on my fingers. I sat up. "What happened?"

"Don't worry," Ashton's said. His voice was hoarse. He cleared his throat and pushed himself up onto one elbow. "I'm fine. We had a run-in with some undead in Greenville."

"Celeste? Saffron? Master Flanders?" I stared at him, wide-eyed, heart pounding.

"We're all fine, though. Don't worry."

I pressed my eyebrows together, worried about him and all of my friends, but also worried about what finding undead in Greenville meant. "How many undead?"

"A lot. We ended up having to teleport out. I think we have to consider that the king probably has the Skystone."

I closed my eyes, then covered my face with my hands. For every piece of good news we got, there was bad news close behind.

Ashton lowered my hands from my face. "How about you? Any undead?"

I shook my head. "No, but we had to leave the barn because Max and the Reapers showed up. I was so worried that you'd arrive while they were still there."

Ashton sat up. "We did run in to Max and the Reapers."

I looked away from him for a second as guilt swept through me. "I'm so sorry. I didn't want to leave, I should have come back to help you, I shouldn't have sent you in the first place."

Ashton pressed his index finger over my lips. "You did the right thing. If you had stayed, you could be dead. I'm glad you left. I'm glad you didn't come back for me. Every once in a while, you have to let me be the hero."

I smiled. "You know that I'll fight by your side always, right?"

"I know that. But sometimes, you have to take a step back and let other people help you. You can't do it alone."

He was right, of course. It was still difficult trusting people after everything I'd been through. I still wasn't sure that all of the Ravens who had stayed with us were loyal to me, but I was determined to earn their support. Greenville declaring their allegiance to my reign was a huge boost. We'd seen an influx of new members in the last few weeks and our numbers had grown larger than they had been under Max. My stomach twisted at the thought of my brother. Out there destroying cities and helping the king. "What happened? Max? The Reapers?"

"We were able to fight them off." Ashton's brow furrowed. He seemed to be lost in thought.

"What is it?"

He looked up at me. "Something Max said to Saffron." He paused, as if trying to decide how to form the words. "He told Saffron that he's marrying the king's daughter."

I gasped, covering my mouth with my hand. Was this his plan the whole time? Was that part of his deal with the king? "How did this happen?"

"I'm not sure," Ashton said. "I used to think I knew Max, but I've realized I never really did."

"I don't think anyone did." My thoughts traveled to Saffron. I wondered what the two of them had been through together and how Max could give it up so easily. "How's Saffron?"

"She's trying to be strong." Ashton took a breath. "There's more. The princess is pregnant."

For a moment, I stopped breathing. If Max married the princess, he was next in line for the throne and he was already bringing in an heir. He was doing everything he could to prevent me from stepping up to the role I was born for. I pressed my lips together as the shock wore off, anger stepping in to replace it. Max had betrayed us all and he was better at playing this game than I was. "He's going to kill the king." I looked up at Ashton. "He's still playing for the throne."

"It's the only thing he's thinking about," Ashton said. "When we figure out a way to take down the king, we're going to have to deal with Max, too."

My thoughts around Max always seemed so jumbled. He was my brother, but he'd sided with the king. While I wanted to believe there was a way to bring him back to us, a way to salvage the only family I had, it was getting harder to ignore the terrible things Max was doing.

Reluctantly, I moved away from Ashton's arms and sat up. As much as I wanted to stay here forever, there was too much to do. "We're going to have to fight them both. When we get the army from Gallia, we have to make sure neither the king, nor Max survive."

Ashton sat up. "How did things go in Greenville?"

My shoulders sunk. "We were too late for Calder's family."

We were both quiet for a moment. It had been the reason for our visit, yet we hadn't come back empty handed. "There is some good news, though."

"I could use some good news," Ashton said.

"We found Annalise. And she knows where King Osbert hid the Stone of Morare. He doesn't keep it on him to control the Reapers." I stood up and offered my hand to Ashton, helping pull him up. "I'm going to round up the council. We have a stone to steal."

***

Ashton left the tent in search of water to clean the blood from his head while I went to find the other members of my council. It wasn't long after sunrise but the Raven camp was teeming with activity. The air smelled like baking bread and as I walked further from the tents, I could hear the sound of steel on steel.

I found Calder and Saffron already running a training

session with a group of newer Ravens. Everyone lowered their weapons and bowed to me when they noticed my arrival.

"Your highness," Saffron said. "Glad to see you're doing well."

"I'm glad to see you keeping this one busy." I nodded to Calder. "Did he tell you what you missed?"

"He did." Saffron glanced from me to Calder, then back again. "We had breakfast with Sir Henry and Madame Lyndsey."

"Where's Celeste?" I asked.

Saffron lifted an eyebrow and turned to Calder. "Yes, where is Celeste? I didn't find her in her tent when I stopped by this morning."

Calder's face turned red. "I wouldn't know. Perhaps she's working with Master Flanders in the sorcery training grounds?"

I narrowed my eyes at Calder and Saffron. "Am I missing something here?"

"Council meeting?" Saffron asked.

I looked at the two of them again and decided not to press the issue. There were few secrets in the Raven camp. Everything eventually came out in the open. It was pretty clear what was going on, but at the moment, I figured it might be better to allow for the illusion of privacy. "Yes, my quarters."

She turned away from me and handed her sword to one of the men who was standing nearby pretending not to listen to our conversation. "Take over for me, will you? I'll be back later."

"I'll go see if I can find Celeste," Calder said, walking away before I could respond.

Saffron and I walked away from the training grounds. I glanced at her. "Do I want to know?"

"They're still figuring it all out," she said. "Best we leave it for now."

I nodded. It wasn't my place to pry but I did wonder what it meant for Celeste's friend back home in Gallia. I stopped walking. "You know, if we can find that stone, it will be another way to show Gallia that we really can defeat the king."

Saffron shook her head. "Who would have thought that after all this time, we'd find a way to finally hurt him. Things are going to change when we get that stone, Etta. I can feel it."

She put her arm over my shoulder. "We won't have to keep hiding for much longer. We will finally be safe in our own homes."

Saffron had been at this much longer than I had. She'd lost everyone she loved, just as most of the people here had. It was hard to imagine a time when we no longer had to worry about the king and his guards. An image flickered through my mind. A quiet afternoon sitting outside, not hiding. All my friends were gathered and we ate and drank and sang too loud. Was it possible that we could finally be free of the king? Finding that stone sure felt like a step in the right direction.

12

ASHTON

Ashton walked through the tents toward the stream that ran right outside the ward. Despite fighting Max and everything he'd been through, he felt like things were looking up. He'd managed to help fight off the Reapers, and the Ravens were going to be able to stop the king from using them once they took that stone.

He had faith Etta would gain the favor of Gallia when she visited and everyone seemed to agree that with an army, they could defeat the king. He let out a long breath. Everything in his life had led to this moment. He'd been fighting against the king as long as he could remember. What would it even be like when they didn't have to hide anymore?

A white-haired older man with a red face approached him. "You must be Ashton."

Ashton stopped walking. "I am. I'm sorry, have we met?"

"Not yet, but I've been looking forward to having a talk with you. I'm Sir Henry." The older man extended his hand.

Ashton straightened his posture and shook the older man's hand. He knew Sir Henry had been a member of the court and had worked with Etta's father. Ashton's experience with nobility had been limited and he wanted to make a good impression on the man Etta held in such regard. "Nice to meet you."

"My tent is just over here, could I trouble you for a private word?" He gestured behind him. "It won't take more than a minute."

Ashton wanted nothing more than to rinse the blood off his head and get back to Etta. He considered asking the man if they could meet later, but he know how much Etta trusted him. "Alright."

Sir Henry pulled the tent flap aside and Ashton ducked in after him. There were two chairs and a bedroll in the room. A wooden trunk sat at the end of the bedroll. Ashton took a seat in one of the chairs as Sir Henry did the same.

The older man's lips were drawn into a thin line. He looked like he was holding something back.

"What is it?" Ashton asked.

"You aren't going to like what I'm going to say, so I'm just going to say it." Sir Henry took a deep breath. "You need to end things with Etta."

Ashton glared at Sir Henry, sure he had misheard what he was saying. Why would Sir Henry care about their relationship? "Excuse me?"

"Word is starting to get around about the two of you, it's time to end things before people make assumptions."

Ashton felt like he'd been punched in the gut. His breath hitched and his face grew hot. It took him a moment to figure out how to best respond. Opening and closing his mouth, Ashton tried to form words to react to what he had just heard. They wouldn't come.

"As long as she's with you, she's going to be making decisions with her heart instead of her head. You're a distraction."

He stared at the old man in disbelief. "You don't even know me. I would do anything for her."

"I don't doubt your dedication to her. I know your story. I know you could have just as easily followed Max. But this isn't about you. It's about her."

"How can you say that?" Ashton stood, looking down at Sir Henry. "She can make her own choices. She's the rightful queen."

"Exactly." Sir Henry remained calm. "And she spent several weeks chasing down a cure for you when you were injured. What's to stop the king or Max using you against her again? What's to stop her from throwing everything we've all worked for away because of you?"

Ashton slowly sat down on the chair. Etta had sacrificed so much for him, too much. "I've told her not to come after me."

"You think she'd listen? When it comes to you, she makes stupid choices. Choices that could cost her the crown." Sir Henry's expression looked sympathetic. "It's not only her poor decision making when it comes to you. You realize that as long as she's with you, she's giving up her only bargaining tool: a marriage alliance."

"Who would she need to marry?" Ashton said. "She's going to convince Gallia to help her and then she'll be queen."

"She needs a powerful man by her side. Not an orphan without a title. That is how it works for royals. You know that. Everyone knows that. They just didn't want to break your hearts. Why do you think her father didn't marry Max's mother? He had to marry for an alliance. Why do you think Max is choosing to marry the king's daughter? Marriage is the way the royal houses are built."

Sir Henry's words were true but how could he expect Ashton to give her up? Ashton felt like the life was being sucked from his body. Like he was back in the Astral Realm, watching something he couldn't control. How was he supposed to do this? Etta was his whole world. "I can't do it. I love her."

Sir Henry leaned forward. "If you really love her, you'll let her go."

13

ETTA

A feeling of peace settled over me as I looked around the table to see my entire council assembled. There were few people I trusted and all of them were gathered here in one place. Without them, I would feel lost and overwhelmed with the decisions that have come with stepping up to this role. Even our new additions, Holden and Anna, felt comfortable in this room.

"As you all have heard by now, we encountered bad news in Greenville." I looked down at my hands on the table and took a deep breath. I glanced at Calder, then quickly looked away from him. "We were unable to find any survivors from Calder's family and it does appear the king has taken the bodies of the dead."

The room was silent as I spoke. "It's possible that the king has found the Skystone. If he hasn't, he has recruited and trained more sorcerers to aid him in raising the dead."

I let the words sink in for a minute, still processing everything myself. The prospect of coming across a group of undead as large as the deceased population of Greenville was terrifying. I took a few breaths to steady myself to keep my voice from shaking. Though I knew the people in this room would support me, and were likely as scared as I was, I wanted to maintain my composure.

"We also returned with good news." I nodded to Anna. "Master Edward sent us after his granddaughter, Annalise. We didn't expect to find her, but we did. She brought some very valuable information with her. Anna?"

Anna set her bag on the table and opened it carefully. I realized her hands were shaking. She had worn a brave face since we met, but leaving behind everything you knew after surviving an attack on your city had to be hard.

She pulled out the small box she'd shown me earlier and slid it over to me. "It's a puzzle box," she said. "Inside you'll find a map to the Stone of Morare."

All eyes around the table were glued to the box. They had all heard the news of Annalise and what she brought with her but this was the first time we were going to find out the details.

"How does it open?" I asked.

She stared at me for a long moment then finally spoke, "You have to promise that you're going to destroy the stone, not use it."

The room was silent. I set the box back down on the table and looked at her, brow furrowed. "Why would I want to use the stone? I've seen the destruction those creatures can do and I want no part of that."

"What are you going to do with it?" She asked.

I stared at her, unblinking. "We will destroy the stone or the Reapers or both. Whatever it takes to make sure those monsters cannot hurt anyone else."

She took the box from me and proceeded to twist, turn and spin the various sides until it made a popping noise and then one of the sides came off. She folded down the other sides until it was flat on the table. On the inside of each of the squares that made up the box was a series of numbers and letters, a code.

"I can translate it if you get me a quill and some paper," she said.

Madame Lyndsey was across the room pulling the items out of a box near my bed before I could ask. She passed them to Anna.

Despite the bright sunlight outside, the tent was still dim. I moved a lit candle closer to her so she could see better while she scrawled letters out on the paper. After a few minutes, she set the quill down and pushed the paper over to me. I read the paper carefully several times before I slid it across the table to Sir Henry.

His face grew pale. He looked from me to Anna. "Are you sure about this?"

She nodded.

He pressed his lips together in a tight line. "This makes things very difficult. No wonder he's not worried about somebody going after the stone. It's not even in Illaria. The Montage Castle is just across our border in the mountains of Sardinia. That explains his desire to form an alliance with them."

I tapped my fingers on the table and thought about what this meant. The journey to the border wasn't going to be quick and it was sure to be dangerous. While I wanted to make sure we got this stone and I hated the idea of sending others into such a challenging task, I knew it would be irresponsible to leave the camp again so soon after my trip to the Oracle.

There was also the problem of the stone not actually being in Illaria. There was no way I could cross into Sardinia. They had already declared their alliance with the king, making me their enemy. I closed my eyes and took a deep breath. *How are we going to get to the stone?*

Conversation erupted as people made suggestions for how we could claim the stone. I listened to the ideas being tossed around the table, my eyes darting back and forth. Most of the arguments involved what to do with the stone once we had it. Very little conversation was taking place about how to actually get the stone.

Sir Henry stood and looked around at the people seated at the table. As everybody noticed him standing the room began to quiet.

"We know what needs to be done," he said. "The stone must be retrieved before the king realizes that we know its location. We can figure out how to destroy it after we have it safely in our possession."

There was a murmur of agreement. Sir Henry locked eyes on me and raised his eyebrows, urging me to speak.

I cleared my throat and stood. Sir Henry sat down and smiled at me.

"We need send a group right away."

"Who's going to get the stone?" Calder asked.

"It must be someone we trust completely." I looked around the table, knowing who I should send, but afraid to say it aloud. I didn't want to risk losing Ashton, but out of all the people here, he was the one I trusted the most.

My hands tightened on the edge of the table. I sat back down and looked at Sir Henry. "How long will the journey be?"

Sir Henry unrolled one of his maps across the table. "If they can get there before winter gets too bad, it should take about two weeks each way. If the snow is bad, it could be as long as a month each way."

"And what do we know about the location the stone is hidden in?" I asked.

Master Flanders spoke up. "The castle is likely abandoned, but I'm sure the king left something to protect it."

I looked to Master Flanders. "What do you think he's using as protection?"

Master Flanders' fingers were steepled under his chin. "I

would expect that he's using dark magic. Possibly even the undead."

The hair on my arms stood on end. *Undead.* When I had encountered those creatures on my trip to the Oracle, the most effective thing against them was fire. Sorcerer fire was even better. "We'll need a sorcerer on this trip."

"It has to be me," Ashton said. "You can't afford to send Master Flanders or Madame Lyndsey. It has to be me."

"I can help, too," Celeste said.

My chest tightened. *This is what I was afraid of.* I knew they were the best people I could send to retrieve the stone, but I worried about being away from them. *Maybe we could go together.* I gripped the table even tighter. I couldn't be gone from camp for a month. I couldn't put off meeting with Gallia for that long.

"We'll get the stone for you," Ashton said. "We can leave at first light, try to beat the winter storms."

I fought to keep my face impassive, but I'm sure my hesitation was obvious to the group. These were my friends, my most trusted advisors, and the people who knew me best. They knew why I was struggling to find my voice. They turned away when I snuck into Ashton's tent, kept quiet when we walked through the camp hand in hand, and knew that whatever they said to one of us would find its way to the other. Since his return from the Astral realm, we hadn't hidden our relationship.

"Master Flanders," I said, finally finding my voice. "Do you think the two of them would be enough against the magic the king left at the castle? Or should we send a larger party?"

"Sorcerers are likely the only ones who could get through the protections that the castle will hold," he said. "Sending a larger party will just draw unnecessary attention."

"Have either of you been to Canton or any of the towns along the border?" Master Flanders asked.

Ashton and Celeste looked at each other and their shoulders sunk. Sorcerers could only teleport to places they'd been to before. From the looks on their faces, neither of them had traveled to that part of Illaria.

Their reply came back in unison. "No."

"It's alright," Madame Lyndsey said. "They can ride in, and teleport back."

That helped ease some of my tension. Celeste and Ashton could return more quickly than a party of non-sorcerers. Perhaps everything would go well and they'd be back in two weeks. That wasn't such a long time.

"Very well." I nodded at Ashton and Celeste. "You two will leave at first light. Please meet with Master Flanders for any advice he can offer prior to your departure."

I looked around the silent room. "Is there anything anybody would like to add before I close today's meeting?"

The seriousness of the upcoming departure seemed to weigh heavily on those assembled. Nobody spoke. The room felt far too small all of the sudden. I needed to get out of there. I needed to run, scream, shoot something, anything to take my mind off of the fact that I was sending Ashton into danger again.

I kept my face straight as I looked around the table at each person seated there. Internally, I was screaming. "Meeting adjourned."

Everybody stood. I looked at Ashton, trying to read his expression. He looked focused, strong. If he was nervous about leaving, he wasn't showing it.

The members of the council filed out of my quarters, leaving me completely alone for the first time in days. I didn't want to depend on others, but Ashton was the only person who knew how I felt before I did. I'd come to rely on him for so much.

I tied my long hair into a knot at the base of my neck and

walked out of my tent and through the camp. Once I was a few feet away from the furthest tent, I took off at a run.

I didn't slow down until I reached the edge of our camp, the place where the ward protected us. The tingle of magic ran up and down my arms. Tentatively, I pressed my fingers through the shimmery surface that separated us from the outside world. It was cold and sent a shiver through me. Sliding a hand into my pocket, I felt for the coin that would allow me to re-enter the ward if I left. My fingers closed around it.

Glancing behind me, I saw that I was alone. Taking a deep breath, I stepped through and started running again, through the woods that surrounded our camp. The feeling of being free of the camp's protection was heady. I felt like I was back in my woods, sneaking out of my grandmother's house, breaking the rules.

You're the queen. You don't have to follow the rules like the others. I stopped running and took several deep breaths. My lungs were on fire. *That's true. I am the queen. I make the rules.* I shook off the thoughts, they weren't like me at all. I valued the counsel of my friends and those who had more experience than me. Of course, I knew being outside of the camp was reckless, but there wasn't a rule about it.

You could keep him here, you know. Send Madame Lyndsey, Saffron, anybody else. Do what you want. What's the point of being queen if you can't get what you want? I grabbed at my pendant and rubbed my thumb and forefinger over the metal surface. *That's true. Everything you've done has been about everybody else. So what if you did one thing to benefit yourself?*

I tucked the pendant back under my blouse. *No.* I will not be a selfish queen. I have to do what's best for my kingdom, for my people. *What about what's best for you? What do you think is going to happen when Ashton and Celeste spend a month alone together?*

You think he'll still want you when he gets back? I'm sure she'd be willing to give him things you won't.

I covered my face with my hands and knelt down on the ground. *What is happening to me? Where are these thoughts coming from?* Ashton loves me and Celeste is my best friend. I trusted both of them and I knew they were the right ones for the job.

My breath caught in my chest. These weren't my thoughts. The Darkness—it was getting worse. A flicker of panic rose inside me. What did that mean? Taking a deep breath, I focused on staying calm. *It's going to be fine. You can control this.* I stood and brushed a few loose strands of hair away from my face, tucking them into the knot of hair.

I closed my eyes and felt the wind on my face, listened to the sound of the birds. *Focus.* These thoughts needed to go away before I went back to camp. *Focus. You are a good queen. You do what is best for your people.*

Opening my eyes, I looked up at the tress, taking in one last moment of calm before walking back to camp. In the branches above me, I saw a huge black raven. Its eyes followed me as I moved. The bird seemed to be making notes of me. It looked like the bird that brought me the note from the king. I narrowed my eyes, searching its legs for any signs of being used as a messenger. *It's just a raven.*

Turning away from the bird, I took a few steps toward camp. Glancing behind me every so often, I noticed that the bird was tilting its head from side to side as if trying to figure out where I was going or what I was doing. That was enough to get me running again. My heart pounded as I ran, more from fear than the act of running itself. When I crossed the barrier into our camp, relief washed over me but it only lasted for a moment as I realized the potential danger we were in.

If the king had Ravens outside of our camp, then he knew where we were.

I FOUND Ashton and Celeste with Master Flanders in the clearing where I worked on my sorcery training. They were engrossed in a lesson, mimicking his moves and listening to his corrections. I stood at a distance, taking in the sight of my friends.

My gaze went to Ashton. I noted the way his hair was tucked behind his ears, how his brow furrowed in concentration. His movements were quick and confident. His tunic was slightly open at the top, revealing part of his muscular chest and I briefly imagined us intertwined. I looked away for a moment, clearing my head.

Ashton caught my eye and waved to me. I smiled at him, thankful for the distraction from my own thoughts. The lesson seemed to be over. Master Flanders, Celeste, and Ashton started walking toward me.

The Raven. That's why I had come here. "Master Flanders, there was a raven in a tree outside the ward."

Master Flanders stroked his chin. "Did it approach you?"

I shook my head. "It just sat on a branch and watched me. It seemed like it was paying attention to what I was doing. It wasn't acting like a normal bird. Do you think it could be one of the king's birds?"

"It's very possible," Master Flanders said. "I think we should assume the king knows where we are. We'll need to be extra vigilant. Nobody should leave camp alone."

"I'll make an announcement at dinner." My mind replaying the dark thoughts that had found their way into my head. I wasn't in control yet and wondered if I should tell Master Flanders.

"What's wrong?" Ashton asked.

I smiled at him, doing my best to hide how I really felt. "I'm fine. I'll come find you in a few minutes, alright?" I turned to Master Flanders. "Do you have a minute?"

"Of course," he said.

"Please join me in my quarters." Without waiting to explain my request to Ashton or Celeste, I walked away.

Master Flanders closed the tent flap behind him and looked at me, forehead creased in concern.

"It's getting worse." I started pacing the room. "At least I think it is. These thoughts just keep entering my mind. It's like this nagging voice that inside me that speaks my fears or ambitions. Or maybe it's just me? Am I turning into my brother?" I was speaking too quickly, my mind struggled to keep up with the words pouring out of my mouth.

Master Flanders placed his hand on my elbow, stopping my pacing. "I'm feeling it, too, the Darkness is getting stronger. You're going to have to work even harder to keep it away. Take a few minutes to meditate, then go back out there. It'll get easier every time you fight it."

I watched Master Flanders walk out of the tent and collapsed into a chair. How was I supposed to fight this off when it grew worse all the time? Was Max facing the same thing? What would happen to me if I didn't learn how to manage the Darkness? Closing my eyes, I took a few deep breaths and concentrated on clearing my mind. After a few minutes, I managed to send away all the distracting thoughts. It was getting easier, but it only lasted a few minutes. Deciding I could work more on it later, I stood and left my tent.

"I've been looking everywhere for you," Celeste called to me as s

he grabbed my hand. "I need you for a bit."

Celeste dragged me behind her, not letting go of my hand. "What's so urgent?" I asked.

"I need you to take care of something for me, you're the only one I trust."

We entered her quarters and she dropped my hand. "You haven't seen this yet, I'm still not sure if it's totally ready, but I don't want it in the wrong hands."

She lifted an upside-down crate that was in the corner of her tent. I had to shield my eyes from the bright light that filled the room. After a moment, my eyes adjusted and I was able to see the object under the crate. A new orb. It was larger than the first one, about the size of my head.

My mouth dropped open. "Is it finished?"

She lifted her eyebrows. "Close. It shows promise as a healing tool but I have yet to get it to amplify a user's magic. I was hoping we'd be able to strengthen your power enough to take out the Reapers once and for all, but if we get that stone, we won't need to worry about it."

I reached toward the orb. "Can I touch it?"

She nodded. "Go ahead."

I touched the orb with my fingertips. It hummed in response to my touch and I felt the tingle of magic transfer from the orb into my fingers and run through my arm. "It's amazing, Celeste."

"Thank you." Her wide smile faded. "But it's also dangerous. Can you imagine this in the wrong hands? If Max or the king had something like this, they might even be able to improve on it. Make it stronger." She shuddered.

"I won't let anything happen to it," I said. "I'll make sure it's safely hidden. Who else knows about this?"

She shook her head. "Just us and Master Flanders."

I was surrounded by amazing, intelligent people. *Good thing she's on my side.* "Celeste, what am I going to do without you?" My shoulders dropped.

She covered the orb and held it with both arms wrapped around it. "I know, I'm going to miss you, too. But it'll go fast." She took a deep breath and smiled. "And don't worry, I'll bring him home safe to you."

"I need both of you back home safe," I said.

"We will. And when we do, we'll be that much closer to defeating the king."

"When you say it like that, I believe you," I said.

"Things are looking up for us, Etta." She passed me the wrapped-up orb. It now resembled a bundle of fabric.

I took it from her. "I'll go hide this in my tent. We'll meet up again before you leave, okay?"

The day was quickly slipping away. It wouldn't be long before I'd have to see my friends off again. After hiding the orb under a much too formal dress in the chest in my tent, I left my quarters for Ashton's. If we were going to be apart for a few weeks, I wanted to spend as much time with him as I could before he left.

"Ashton?" I peeked my head inside his tent. He was shoving something into a bag. My chest tightened. He was going to be gone in the morning. Last time we'd been apart for more than a few days, I had left camp to save his life. This time, we'd be on separate missions. He'd be the one going off into danger while I stayed at camp and traveled to Gallia.

I went into the tent, closing the flap behind me. "Sorry for the wait, Celeste had something she wanted me to watch for her."

He shoved something into the bag he was packing and looked up at me. "What was it?"

I considered telling him about it, but why ruin a good conversation for the road. "She can tell you all about it while you're traveling."

"Besides," I stood close to him and ran my hands from his wrists up to his muscular shoulders. "I don't really want to talk about Celeste."

One side of his mouth turned up in a smile. "What do you want to talk about?"

"I don't know if I really want to talk at all." I draped my arms over his shoulders.

He pulled me into him until my chest was pressed against his, then leaned down and kissed me. My whole body felt alive, his touch sent a shock through me as he moved his hands from my waist to my shoulders, then down to my hips.

Suddenly, he stopped and stepped away from me. He pushed his hair away from his face, letting out a long breath.

I started to move toward him, then hesitated. I studied his expression, expecting to see some sign of playfulness. Instead, his forehead was creased and he stared at the ground. He looked like something was upsetting him. Had I done something wrong? My body craved his touch. I wanted to feel the weight of him pressed against me. Instead, he was pulling away. "What's wrong? Why did you stop?"

He frowned. "I can't do this."

I crossed my arms over my chest, feeling both hurt and confused. "What do you mean?"

He shook his head. "I just can't."

We had talked about the importance of not taking things too far, but I didn't think we were in that territory yet. "We were just kissing."

He looked away from me. "You know you are supposed to be with somebody better than me."

"What are you talking about?" I reached for him, to pull him closer to me.

He stepped away. "Look, we've been fooling ourselves to think we could be together. You're a queen. I'm the orphan son of a soldier. They all look away because you're not queen yet. But you will be. And I know where this is going."

"Why would you say that? You know I love you. I would die for you." *I had died for him.* Why would he doubt me?

"You were stupid. You should have let me die. It would have made it easier." His face was empty, devoid of emotion.

My head spun as his words rang through me. Ashton was the most important person in my world. He was the one constant thing I'd come to rely on. After everything I'd been through, I knew I could at least count on him. How could he not know that? How could he be so willing to give up his life when he knew how much he meant to me? "How could you say that?"

I'd never seen him like this before. My whole body was shaking and I wasn't sure if it was from fear or anger. I took a few steps backward and struggled to catch my breath. My heart was being pulled from my chest and Ashton was holding the strings. "I don't understand."

"You think I want to be like Max's mother? " He shook his head. "It's a matter of time. Your family doesn't know what loyalty is. They don't know what love is. Your father left the woman he loved for power. Max left the woman he loved for power. One day, you'll do the same to me. You know that. I'm just making it easier on you."

It felt like an explosion went off inside me. "How dare you. After everything we've been through. After everything I've done for you. How dare you say that."

"It's always going to be about you, Etta. I'm giving you a gift.

I'm letting you go free of the guilt." He lowered himself into a deep bow. "I will remain your humble servant, I will serve the Ravens."

He stood. "But when we have defeated the king, I'm going away and you'll never see me again."

"You can't be serious." I stared at him, waiting for him to tell me it was all a misunderstanding. "I know how you feel about me. Why would say this? Why are you trying to hurt me?"

"I don't want to hurt you, Etta. I've never wanted to hurt you. What we have, it's just a distraction for both of us. It isn't real love. We came together because of what we're going through. Once this is over, you'll find someone who deserves you. Someone you deserve. Someone who can love you the way I can't."

Heat surged through me and my heartbeat filled my ears. *This can't be happening.* It was like the monsters from my nightmares had come to life and I felt like my whole body was being torn apart in different directions. Darkness seeped into me, fueling the pain, turning it to anger. I struggled to catch my breath as I fought against the rising Darkness. "You can't expect me to believe that you never loved me. You are a liar." The words seemed to get caught in my throat as I spoke. "You love me. I love you. What more do we need?"

"It's over, Etta." Ashton turned his back to me.

The edges of my vision blurred as the Darkness pulled on me. Jaw clenched, I stared at the man I loved. *You're better off without him. He was holding you back.* Gasping, I turned away from him. *No.* The Darkness was not going to win. Balling my hands into fists, I fought against it. I needed to find control. Feeling Ashton's gaze on me, I turned back to him. "How could you do this to me?"

He looked down, face drained of color. He didn't look like he wanted to say these words. "I'm sorry, but it's over." He looked back up at me, green eyes meeting mine, unwavering.

I stumbled forward as I lost control over my body for a moment, then righted myself. Everything around me seemed to be crumbling. How could he look at me like that? *You don't need him.* Taking a deep breath, I glared at Ashton. *This is his fault. He is the one who is hurting you right now.* The Darkness was getting harder to fight off and worse, it was starting to feel right. Shaking my head, I gave one last glance at him before I left his tent for my own.

Alone in the dark, I collapsed onto my bed, pulling myself up into a ball. My whole body felt numb. Like whatever I had been through wasn't real. Like it was part of a nightmare. *You're stronger than him. You're stronger than all of them. You don't need him You can make all the pain go away.* The Darkness spoke like a warm caress, so enticing. For a moment, I breathed it in, letting it comfort me. *No.* I wasn't going to go down that path, even if it was easier. Even if it could make the pain go away. Struggling to clear my mind, I fought against the call of the Darkness. It wasn't going to win. As I regained control of myself, tears rolled down my cheek. The longer I sat there alone, the harder the tears fell, until I was curled up in a ball, shaking from the sobs. Somehow, I managed to cry myself to sleep.

15

ASHTON

Celeste secured the saddle to her horse. "Where's Etta? I figured she'd be here until we left. It's not like her to skip goodbyes."

Ashton tightened his saddle and turned his face away from Celeste. Etta would probably never want to speak to him again. His eyes still stung from the tears he'd shed last night and he was already feeling like there was a hole inside him where something was missing. He knew he'd never love anyone the way he loved her. "She's not coming."

Celeste stopped what she was doing and walked over to Ashton, hands on her hips. "What happened?"

"I don't really want to talk about it."

She tilted her head and stared at him. "You know, we've got a month together, I'll get it out of you now or later. Choice is yours."

"Fine," he sighed. "It just wasn't working out. We had to end it."

Celeste pushed him. "What are you talking about?" Her eyes narrowed. "What did you do?"

Ashton looked up at her. "I did what I had to do. You do know how dangerous this mission is, don't you? You know there's a very good chance we won't make it back."

He went back to the strap of his saddle. "I don't want her pining over me forever. I want her to be able to move on if something happens to me."

Celeste rested her hand on Ashton's, stopping his progress. "And what happens when we come back, alive and well? And she can't even look at you because you broke her heart. Then what?"

He swallowed and looked away, unsure of what he'd do. How would he handle seeing her again? She wasn't the type of girl you stopped loving. "By then, she'll have moved on, found somebody worthy of a queen."

Celeste shook her head. "I don't know why you're fighting it. You should go apologize. Don't make her think you stopped loving her."

"Leave it, Celeste. I did what I had to do." He glanced at her. "Besides, you're not in the position to judge me about my love life, not with what you've done. I saw you and Calder, looks like the two of you are getting to know each other *very* well."

Celeste closed her mouth and went back to her horse. "Fine. Have it your way."

In the quiet darkness of early morning, Ashton couldn't keep his mind from replaying the scenes of last night over and over in his head. His eyes stung with tears, but he fought them away. He hated himself for what he did to Etta. But if giving her up was the only way to protect her, that was the risk he was willing to take.

He wouldn't allow their relationship to cost her the crown, or her life. Ashton knew how powerful Max was and he had a feeling if they ran into him again, he wouldn't hold back this time. It had been too easy for Max to send Ashton's essence from his body. Was there something even worse he could do to threaten Etta? Ashton knew all too well that Etta would give up her own life if it meant saving his. But if she thought Ashton had given up on her, maybe it would keep her safe. Maybe she wouldn't risk her own life to save him.

"You two almost ready?" Master Flanders was standing in the doorway of the stables. He hadn't made any noise when he approached.

"Just about," Ashton said.

"Almost," Celeste called out.

"Where's Etta?" Master Flanders asked. "I figured she'd be here."

Ashton felt sick. He didn't want to talk about Etta, his heart was already shattered as it was.

"Ashton broke her heart last night," Celeste said.

Ashton glared at her, though he couldn't blame her after his stab about her complicated love life.

Master Flanders raised an eyebrow. "Being noble? Think you are sparing her of pain if something happens to you?"

"Something like that," Ashton mumbled.

Master Flanders shook his head. "I think you underestimate the girl's feelings for you."

Ashton's jaw tightened. A memory flashed through his mind of a kiss under the shed at the archery range. His stomach twisted, he felt nauseous. The feel of her lips against his was burned into his very being. No matter what he did, Etta was going to be part of him. But he was a nobody, the orphan son of a soldier. She could do better.

"Look," Ashton said. "You know this had to happen eventually. She can't marry me. Everybody knows that, they just looked the other way. Dragging it on was just going to make things worse." He mounted his horse. "It's better this way."

Master Flanders frowned. "You do love her, though, don't you?"

Ashton shook his head. "What does that matter? Love? It isn't a magic fix for anything. Love doesn't save you from the Reapers or protect you from the king."

Celeste mounted her horse and called down to Master Flanders. "Can you tell her goodbye for me?" She glanced at Ashton. "And tell her that Ashton thought he was doing the right thing but he's an idiot."

Ashton's stomach clenched. He needed to go before he changed his mind. He was doing the right thing. "We'll see you in a few weeks, Master Flanders." Ashton prepared to move his horse forward.

"Wait," Master Flanders called. "What should I tell her? If she needs to hear it, what should I tell her?"

A lump rose in Ashton's throat. He knew what Master Flanders was asking. If Etta started to slip toward the Darkness or something worse happened, what would Ashton tell her?

He reached into his pocket and pulled out a silver ring, he tossed it to Master Flanders. "Give her this." Then he pulled up on the reins and led the horse away.

ASHTON AND CELESTE rode in silence along the road as the sun began its ascent. In the gray light of dawn, the roads were empty and their breath came in out clouds. Ashton drew his hood closer around his face, trying to keep the cold away.

Celeste moved her horse up alongside him. "Ashton?"

Ashton turned toward her.

"Did you really mean what you said back there? About not being good enough for Etta?" She pulled her eyebrows together. "You can't really be giving up on her."

"I had to, Celeste."

"No." She shook her head. "You didn't. She would never give up on you."

"What if Max or the king try to use us to get to her? It's the only way she won't risk her life for ours if that happens."

Celeste sighed. "Oh, Ashton, she'd come for you no matter what. You know that."

Part of Ashton hoped she was right. For a moment, he imagined that Etta would wait for him, then he pushed the idea away. He'd spent his whole life trying to get the king off the throne. And Etta deserved to be queen. She was the best chance for peace in Illaria. If this was the sacrifice he had to make, it was worth it. "I had to try, Celeste."

"You need to stop trying to protect her from everything. She's the queen. She's more powerful than both of us put together. Honestly, if we were captured, I'd want her coming after us. Have some faith in her."

Ashton turned back to the road. "You know, you're just making me feel worse."

Neither of them spoke until the sun broke the horizon. They lowered their hoods to try to block out the blinding rays.

"What's with the ring?" Celeste asked.

"It's just something I had made for her for her birthday." He didn't want to talk about it. It was taking every bit of his willpower to not turn the horse around, to not go back to Etta. He made a decision, and it was the best one. He had to keep telling himself that.

"Come on, let's pick up the pace, we want to get to the safe house soon." He squeezed his legs against his horse and they took off at a gallop down the road. The cold wind on his face helped him stop thinking. He focused on his breathing and the sound of the hoof beats over the dirt road. *I did the right thing.*

As the sun climbed, the road grew more crowded, forcing

them to slow down. They'd covered a lot of ground in a short time and the horses were growing tired.

"We're about a mile away," Ashton said. "Let's slow it down, we made good time."

They were approaching a town and Celeste dropped behind Ashton so they took up less space on the crowded road.

The village was small, with a few shops and a tavern but it was only a half-day's ride to a much larger town so it saw its share of visitors during the day. Ashton and Celeste didn't even warrant a second glance as they rode through.

"There it is," Celeste called to Ashton as they neared the blacksmith's shop. They tied their horses to a post nearby and walked toward the shop. It was an open structure and they could feel the heat of the fires as they approached.

A muscular man in an apron stood over one of the fires. His skin glistened with sweat. He pulled a horseshoe out of the fire with clamps and dropped it on an anvil. He started to hammer at it, the sound echoed down the street.

Ashton and Celeste approached with caution. After the destruction of the barn, they were weary to use any of their contacts, mostly for fear that it would end badly for them or their families. In the end, they decided they would only stop at a safe house if there were no children living there.

The smith stopped his pounding and turned the shoe over with his clamps. Then the pounding started again. It rang in Ashton's ears.

Ashton and Celeste stood a few feet away from him, watching him work. The man stopped mid-swing and turned his eyes on them. He set the hammer down and stood to his full height. He was a large man and Ashton could sense Celeste flinch as he turned toward them.

"Can I help you?" he asked, wiping his hands on his apron.

"We are in need of your unique services," Ashton said. He

reached into his pocket and pulled out a small circular piece of leather. The circular snake eating its own tail, the ouroboros, was burned into it. He passed the leather circle to the man.

He took it and lifted it near his face to inspect the symbol. His jaw tightened and he glanced up, looking out into the busy street.

Passing the circle back to Ashton, he removed his apron and gestured toward an open door. "Come on in."

The two sorcerers followed the blacksmith inside a small room with a table and a few low stools. The blacksmith motioned to the stools, and they each took a seat.

"I wasn't expecting company," the blacksmith said. "I haven't heard any news in a long time, but I've heard rumors."

"What have you heard? We can tell you if it's true," Ashton said.

The blacksmith rested his arms on the table. "I heard that they found the princess. That true?"

Ashton's stomach tightened. *Everything in his life would always take him back to Etta.* "True. Any more?"

"I heard that she's in charge now, that Max isn't the king's son."

"Close," Ashton said. "He was illegitimate. Etta has taken over the claim for the throne."

"Never been a queen in charge before, who's she gonna marry?"

Ashton opened his mouth to speak, but didn't know how to respond. His heart was pounding as he considered the true weight of Etta married to some prince. Wasn't that what they needed her to do? It was why Ashton had given her up, but the words stung.

"She's the rightful heir to the throne. It doesn't matter who she marries," Celeste said.

The blacksmith looked at Celeste. "A woman sorcerer?"

Celeste tensed. "What makes you think I'm a sorcerer?"

He shrugged. "Both my parents were sorcerers. Don't have the skill myself, but I can sense those that do."

"Never thought I'd have two sorcerers visiting me. I joined up with the White Ravens right after they were formed. Lived in the woods with you all." He smiled at Ashton. "I remember you as a little kid."

Ashton didn't remember this man, but there had been a lot of people in and out of the camp over the years. Though, most people who left did so because they died for the cause.

"What made you leave?" Ashton asked.

"Same reason any man gives up everything." He looked away from them. "I fell in love. Saved her from a town the king's guard destroyed. Brought her to camp to fix her up, fell in love. She didn't like the life, so I gave it up for her."

He gestured around the space. "This was her father's shop, they took me in, taught me the trade."

"Did she know you kept in touch?" Celeste asked.

He shook his head. "I didn't. My wife died a few years ago and my son went to study at the University. He was such a smart boy."

He sniffed and cleared his throat. "They hung him in town square. Not even sure what he did wrong. I got nothing left to live for. I'm willing to give the last of what I have to see that king dead. Nobody should outlive their child."

"I'm so sorry." Celeste covered her mouth to mask a small cry.

"That's why we're here," Ashton said. "What we're doing, it's going to help take down the king."

The blacksmith studied Ashton for a moment. "I suppose you won't be giving me the details of what you're doing, what with the king's abilities."

"I'm sorry, but it's safer for all of us that way," Ashton said.

The blacksmith held up his hand. "I don't want to know. I don't want to be the one who hurts the cause." He rested his chin between his thumb and forefinger. "I'm going to call you sorcerer and girl sorcerer."

He reached his hand out to Ashton. "I'm Thomas." He shook Ashton's hand then Celeste's.

Thomas led the group to his home, a modest stone building with two glass windows. It was well made and had been cared for over the years. What was it like for Thomas to come home every day to an empty home that was once filled with the people he loved? Ashton wondered if his life was going to turn out the same way. He couldn't imagine spending his life with anybody other than Etta. The thought sent his stomach into knots. *What have I done?*

The house was furnished with wood furniture in warm colors and had blankets hanging over every piece. It was warm and comfortable. Ashton had a hard time imagining Thomas here alone.

They walked past a large dining table and Ashton noticed it was covered with a layer of dust. He supposed you didn't really need a large dining table if you were eating alone.

"Up here," Thomas said, leading them up the stairs to the second level. He opened a door and ushered them into a small room. It contained a desk with a chair and a wooden chest. Ashton's heartbeat quickened. *Was this a strap?*

Celeste backed toward the door, she must be thinking the same thing, and positioned herself in front of the open door, preventing it from closing.

Thomas didn't seem to notice their concern. He slid the chest across the room and started to remove the floor boards where the chest had been. Ashton relaxed a bit but Celeste didn't move from her place by the door.

Thomas pulled out a large object wrapped in blankets then set it on the ground. He knelt down next to it then looked up at Ashton and Celeste.

He raised his eyebrows. "I'm not going to hurt you." He lifted his chin toward Celeste. "You can come into the room. Trust me, I have no ability to use the magic inside me. You two could finish me off in a second if you wanted to."

Ashton sat on the ground next to Thomas and nodded to Celeste. She stepped slowly into the room and knelt down next to the object.

Thomas started to remove the blankets, pulling back several layers to reveal an unimpressive looking sword. It was dingy, the shine long gone. Thomas rubbed at the sword with one of the blankets. "I can clean it up for you before you go."

Ashton wondered why he went to so much effort to hide a sword. He reached his hand out to touch it. As soon as his fingers brushed against the cool steel, a shock ran through him. He pulled his hand away, then reached out again, slower this time. He ran his fingers along the blade. It hummed inside his head. This was no ordinary sword. "Where did you get this?"

Thomas smiled. "Told you, both of my parents were sorcerers. They fought for the true king. My dad made this, it's enchanted with something that can kill the undead. I don't understand it, I just have a feeling that you two might need it wherever you're going."

Thomas held out the sword and set it in Ashton's hands. "I think he'd want you to have it."

"You have no idea how much this will help us," Ashton said. "Thank you."

"Like I said, anything I can do to see that demon killed." Thomas lifted the sword back out of Ashton's hands. "I'll take it to my shop, get it cleaned up for you. You two are welcome here as long as you'd like."

"Thank you, Thomas," Ashton said. "But we'll need to head out in the morning."

Thomas stood and lifted the sword over his shoulder. "I'll have this ready for you before you go."

16

I rolled over onto my back, blinking up at the fabric of the top of my tent. My eyes were still stinging and my throat was dry. I groaned and rubbed my eyes. *Please tell me that was all just a bad dream.*

Birdsong sounded from outside my tent and I could hear the mumbled conversations of people going about their business. *No.* I sat up and ran outside. Bright sunlight blinded me and I lifted my arm to shield my eyes. *No.* My stomach churned.

It was late morning. Ashton and Celeste were planning to leave before daybreak. Something must be wrong. He would have said goodbye. Last night's fight couldn't be the last memory I'd have of him for a month. *He didn't mean it.* It had to be stress, something. *It isn't how he really feels.*

Running through tents and around people, I reached the stables to find them short two horses. Ashton's brown steed and Celeste's spotted mare. *So this is what heartbreak feels like.* I leaned against the wall and slid to the ground. I didn't have any tears left after last night so I sat there staring blankly ahead of me.

He was really gone. He didn't even say goodbye. Maybe he

really meant it. I hugged my knees to my chest and rested my forehead against them. Celeste didn't even come say goodbye. She was his friend before she was mine. Had I lost her, too?

I don't know how long I sat on the floor in the stables. Time seemed to stop. If it weren't for our horse master finding me while completing his chores, I might have stayed there all day. I forced a smile on my face when he asked me if I was alright. I stood and smoothed out my clothes. "Just needed a quiet place to think. Thank you for your concern, Travis."

Travis bowed at me. "You're welcome here any time, highness."

"Thank you, I may take you up on that. It's very out of the way here."

"Sure is, good place to be alone and think." Travis shifted the heavy bag of feed in his arms.

"I better let you get back to work." I waved to him and walked back to camp.

Travis was a good reminder that no matter where I went, people were always watching me to see how I reacted. They looked to me as an example, as a sign of strength. I pushed my shoulders back to straighten my posture as I walked and held my chin high. I couldn't let this get to me. I had to stay strong, no matter how broken my heart was.

It was nearly lunch time already. I couldn't remember a time I had ever slept through breakfast. The lack of sleep over the last few weeks had caught up to me. I glanced around as I walked, looking for members of my council. If they had let me sleep instead of starting on our work for the day, then they must already know about Ashton.

Our camp was too small for secrets. I'm sure everybody knew by now. *Even more reason for you to be strong. Don't let anybody know you are upset.* My stomach grumbled. I couldn't remember the last time I ate. Facing the whole camp for lunch was the last thing I wanted to do, but was probably the quickest way to show everybody that nothing was wrong. I took a deep breath in and let it out, then turned around and headed toward the common area.

Saffron was seated at a table with Calder and Master Flanders. They were already eating their lunch. She stood when she saw me and walked over to me, hugging me before I could stop her.

"I'm fine," I said, surprising myself with the steadiness of my voice.

She narrowed her eyes at me, inspecting me as if I should be showing visible signs of my heartbreak on my face. His gaze softened. "You don't have to be fine, you know."

I waved her away. "Everything is just fine. In fact," I said as I walked toward the lunch table, "I've never felt better before in my life."

She walked with me, unable to drop the subject. "Etta, we know what happened. Ashton shouldn't have done that to you. I'm sure he still cares."

I stopped and turned to her. My heart felt like it had been ripped from my chest and I didn't think I could handle re-living the whole thing. "Look, don't blame Ashton, it was me, I told him it was over. Didn't make sense to keep dragging it on. If he told you otherwise, he was just being noble."

Saffron pursed her lips and didn't say anything more.

I walked over to the food and added some bread and cheese to my plate. When I arrived at the table where my friends awaited me I spoke before they could ask anything. "I don't want to talk about it. I'm not upset. It was my idea and we all knew it was going to happen anyway. So please don't ask me about it."

I sat down and bit into the bread, chewing slowly.

My friends looked from me to each other, then down at their own plates. We ate in silence for several moments.

"Want to go for a ride later, your highness?" Calder asked.

Did I ever. How wonderful would a ride be? The wind in my hair, my heart pounding, the thunder of the horse's hoofs to shut up the thoughts inside my head.

"She can't today," Master Flanders said. "She's got lessons with me."

I sighed. *The Darkness.* While I still struggled to fight against it inside the wards of the camp, it seemed to be stronger if I left them. It was safer to stay. Riding would have to wait. "That's right, maybe another day, Calder?"

"Sounds good," he said.

"Lessons all day?" Saffron asked. "You haven't done that in a while. Learning something specific?"

"Just getting caught up on things she's missed with all of the excitement over the last few weeks," Master Flanders said.

I nodded along, my mouth full of food so I didn't have to join in on the conversation.

"Council meeting this evening, then?" Saffron asked.

I swallowed. "Yes, right after dinner. We need to discuss Gallia."

"Off to the training fields. Classes for a few new recruits today." Saffron stood. "I'll see you after dinner."

"I'll go with you," Calder said. "Maybe I can help."

I waved to them as they walked away and finished my food in silence. Out of the corner of my eye, I could see Master Flanders watching me.

My mind was a tangle of thoughts and emotions. I focused on pushing away the anger, but that was harder than I thought it would be. Ashton's words kept resurfacing in my mind. The look on his face kept haunting my vision. *I'm nothing like my brother. Why would he say something like that?* I pushed my plate away, unable to eat any more.

"You ready?" Master Flanders picked up my plate with his.

I nodded and followed him away from the common area. Doing anything with magic was going to be challenging today. For magic to work best, you needed to be completely focused. A clear mind and even temperament. How was I supposed to keep my mind clear today?

When we reached the clearing we used as our practice space, Master Flanders sat down on the fallen log we used as a bench. He patted the space next to him and I sat.

"I think I have an idea of what happened last night," Master Flanders said. "Do you want to talk about it?"

I fidgeted on the log, unable to get comfortable. "No, I don't think that's a good idea."

"We both know it wasn't your idea," he said. "Are you doing alright?"

I stood up. "I just want to focus on me for a while. Can we get started? I'd like to be able to leave camp again."

Master Flanders nodded and pushed himself to standing. His movements were slow and deliberate. He was really starting to look old and I worried about losing him. A stab of sadness went through me at the thought. I've lost too many people close to me already. Did my father go through the same thing? Was this just part of being a ruler?

Ashton's words from last night rang through my ears again. *Your father, your brother, they both chose power over love.*

"Master Flanders?" I wasn't sure I wanted to know the answer to the question in my mind, but it was beginning to gnaw at me. I had to ask. "Did my father give up Max's mother to marry my mother? Were they in love?"

Master Flanders eyebrows pressed together in concern. "Is that what Ashton said?" He shook his head. "Oh, Etta. Your father and Max's mother were in love, but they were young. They both knew it wasn't the best thing for either of them to stay together."

I could read between the lines. Just like Ashton had said, my father had left my mother to gain power. My shoulders sunk. Was I destined to follow in his footsteps? Would I have done the same thing to Ashton? "He did leave her for power, then."

"It's not as simple as that, Etta. Max's mother was already betrothed. Your father could have overturned it, but he didn't. I don't know why. We may never know all of the pieces that went into that decision. Everybody who was involved is dead so we can't ask." He paused. "What it is that's really bothering you?"

I sighed. *Might as well tell somebody.* "I'm worried that I'll turn out just like Max. That I won't be able to resist the pull of power. Especially with the Darkness. What if it's in my blood?"

"It's not." He patted my shoulder. "Your father was a good man, a great king. The decisions he made were in the best interest of his kingdom. If he wanted to keep himself alive, he would have agreed to marry you to the Duke, secured a bloodless transition that would have resulted in a tyrannical king. He took a chance, tried to stop him, at the risk of losing his crown and his family."

"How am I supposed to do this on my own?" I said. "Even my father couldn't take down the king when he had an entire army."

"You aren't on your own," Master Flanders said. "You won't gain your crown until you learn to start trusting people and believing in the power that you have. The people want you to lead them."

I remembered the runs in Greenville. The smoke rising from the ashes of a once great city. "So far all I've done is hurt the people of Illaria."

"You've done so many great things, and you will continue to do great things. I believe in you."

"The Oracle made it sound like the fates were against me." I'd never shared that with him before. Master Flanders didn't seem to want to talk about the daughter that had helped the king to trick me into opening a portal to the Darkness. "What if I can't do it."

"My guess is she can no longer see your fate at all." Master Flanders stood, knees cracking. "You are carrying the Darkness with you all the time and visions of the future can change in an instant. The only things we can rely on are prophecies and those are few. If anything, you carrying the Darkness may help us in that sense. She cannot predict what you will do and report it to the king."

I perked up a bit at that news. While I would have done the same thing every time if it meant saving Ashton's life, I'd spent a lot of time wondering if there had been another way. A way that would have not resulted in me being a way of helping the Darkness enter Illaria. For once, there was something almost good to come from my mistake. I took a deep breath. "Are we going to practice some magic today?"

Master Flanders smiled. "Ready to do some more work with fire?"

I took my sorcerers stance and prepared for the lesson.

17

ETTA

The council meeting didn't feel right with the empty chairs where Ashton and Celeste usually sat. Saffron, Master Flanders, Sir Henry, and Calder sat around the table. They all looked at me as if I were something fragile perched on an unsteady ledge. Or maybe that was just inside my head.

"I'm sorry." I walked over to Celeste's usual chair. "I just need to move these out of the way, the table feels too empty with these." I picked up Celeste's chair and moved it to a corner of the tent.

Before I could get to Ashton's, Calder had it in his arms and carried it outside the tent. I bit back a smile, appreciating the gesture.

"That's better." I nodded to Calder. "Thank you."

I turned my attention back to the group. "Thank you all for joining me. We have a few items to address today. First, we need to discuss what we are going to do to help Annalise. She's put herself in danger by keeping this information safe for us and she can't return home. Saffron, you were going to talk to her, what did she say?"

Saffron set her hands on the table in front of her and

straightened in her chair. "I think we have a very easy solution for the time being. She's asked to stay with the White Ravens until you have taken back your kingdom."

"That does make things easier," I said.

"Just wait till you hear the best part," Calder said.

Saffron shot a glance at Calder. He pressed his mouth shut and raised his eyebrows.

Saffron turned back to me. "As Calder indicated, she did have a request from us. She'd like to open a tavern for the camp. Says she doesn't feel right if she's not contributing and would like to start brewing ale for everybody."

I laughed. "Yes, I think that would be appreciated by everybody here. Calder, can you help her find the things she needs in town?"

"I'd be happy to," he said.

"Well, since that's settled, let's move on to our favorite topic. What are our next steps for eliminating the king? I'm traveling to Gallia soon. With any luck, they'll offer use of their army. Will that be enough?"

"If Gallia gives you some of their army, we can win," Sir Henry said.

"I think we need to continue to build up our alliances. What if Gallia isn't enough?" Madame Lyndsey said. "We aren't strong enough yet. There are other sorcerers who are prepared to join us when the time comes, but I don't think we can overpower his army, alive or undead."

Master Flanders stood. "You need the support of your people more than anything else. While I can't deny that gaining the support of Gallia is vital, I have to remind you, if you don't have the people of Illaria, we can't do this."

Sir Henry stood across from Master Flanders and narrowed his eyes. "Battle strategy has never been your strong point, sorcerer. Do we need to revisit the Battle of the Dead?"

I wondered what had happened between the two men for them to mistrust each other so much. Turning my attention to Master Flanders, I tried to read his expression. He remained impassive as he looked at Sir Henry. "What is he talking about?"

Master Flanders looked at me. "It's a long story."

"You think you'd learn your lesson," Sir Henry said. "Your highness, with all due respect, do you think it wise to send unarmed, untrained citizens into battle against the king? Why risk further Illarian life? Haven't we lost enough. Do we need a repeat of Greenville? If we aren't careful, this will be just like the Battle of the Dead. Thousands dead. We need trained soldiers."

"The people can fight the king," Master Flanders said.

"Stop." I stood up and looked at both men. "Master Flanders, you know I value your counsel, but I can't ask the people of Illaria to sacrifice more than they already have. We need to convince Gallia we are worth supporting."

"Agreed," Sir Henry said.

Heads nodded around me. I took a deep breath. I'd never gone against a suggestion from Master Flanders, but it felt like the right thing to do. Making decisions was starting to feel more natural. *Maybe I can do this on my own.*

Both men sat back down.

"We need to discuss proposed strategy," Saffron said. "When you go to Gallia, they will ask for our plans."

"Do we know the date of Max's upcoming wedding?" Sir Henry asked.

"Just that it's going to be soon." I glanced over at Saffron, then turned away from her. "According to Max, the princess is pregnant. They won't want her to show before the wedding."

"I'd guess we have less than four weeks, then," Sir Henry said. "This isn't her first wedding and if this one is even half the party the last one was, nearly all of the king's loyal friends will be there and they will stay the night, too drunk to go home until the next day."

"That's when we need to strike. The morning after the wedding. We won't have much time." I turned to Master Flanders. "Can you send a White Raven to Gallia? Ask if we can move our meeting up. After what happened in Greenville, I don't want to involve any more innocents."

The meeting seemed to last for hours as we discussed our best plan of action. By the time we finished, I was feeling overwhelmed. I needed to do something to clear my mind. My first thought was to find Ashton. As the members of my council stood and prepared to leave, I walked over to the corner where I kept my bow. "I'll be at the archery range if anyone needs me."

"Etta, wait up!"

I turned to see Calder jogging after me. I stopped walking and waited for him to catch up. When he reached me, I started moving again.

"You doing okay?" he asked.

"I'm fine. We're going to meet with Gallia, they're going to help us, we are going to beat the king."

He set his hand on my arm, stopping my progress. "Not about that, Etta. How are *you* doing?"

Frozen in place, I stared at him. I didn't want to talk about Ashton. "I told you, I'm fine."

"You saw me after I lost my wife. I was in a dark place. You, this group, saved me. I know what you've been through for him. I can't imagine how you're feeling. We all need help sometimes," he said.

My heart sunk. Ashton had hurt me worse than I ever thought possible, and I didn't think I'd ever repair the hole I felt inside me. But he was alive, he hadn't been ripped from me. Calder would never see his wife again. At least I would see

Ashton. I would know if he was safe. "I'm so sorry, Calder. What you went through was so much worse."

"You died for him, Etta. I know how much he means to you. And I have a feeling he feels the same way. I still can't figure it out. It still doesn't make sense."

"He doesn't want to be with me," I said. "He's free to make his own choices."

"You don't really believe that, do you?" Calder asked.

I started walking again and he kept pace beside me. I hadn't told anybody what Ashton had said to me. I considered telling Saffron, but she'd known him longer than she'd known me. She was practically his sister and Ashton had brought her and Max up. How could I ever tell her that?

I gripped my bow tighter. "Ashton told me he was done with me because he didn't think I'd stay with him."

"How could he say that after everything you've been through?" he asked.

I bit down on the inside of my lip to keep the tears at bay. "Because it's what my father did and what Max did. He thinks I'll leave him for power."

Despite Master Flanders' reminder that I wasn't the same as Max, part of me still wondered if Ashton was right. I loved Ashton more than anything but hadn't my father and Max felt the same way about the women they left behind?

"That's not you," Calder said. "You aren't them. They made their choice. Life is about choices. You made yours. If you wanted power over Ashton, you would have let him die or you would have joined the king. You are taking the harder path, the right path. You're going to save all of Illaria."

My lower lip trembled. It was too much. I felt more confident about the tasks I needed to complete when I had Ashton and Celeste by my side. "I feel so alone. How can I do this, Calder?" My words caught in my throat as I fought the tears.

I took deep breaths, trying to steady myself. Arms encircled me as Calder pulled me in for a hug. His body pressed against mine was comforting and I relaxed into the hug, appreciating the human contact. "I'm sorry."

He let go of me and held me at arm's length. "Don't be. What you are doing is hard. Even for somebody older who was trained since birth. You're young, you were thrown into this. You are allowed to break down every so often. Just do it when you're alone or with people you trust. I'm sure even your father had his moments. You can do this. And you're not alone. After what I saw you do to save Ashton, I will follow you anywhere."

Calder had been wild, overwhelmed with the idea of revenge when we first met. He'd helped me save Ashton and stayed on to help us take down the king. Over the last few weeks, he'd even seemed almost happy. If he could recover from what he'd been through, I could, too. I placed my hands on top of his. "Thank you."

He smiled and dropped his hands. "Now, I heard a rumor that you're one of the best archers in the kingdom and I've never shot a bow. Feel like giving me a lesson?"

I picked my bow up. "I think that can be arranged."

18

ETTA

My fingers were numb with cold but I didn't want to stop shooting. While I went through the repetitive motions of loading up my bow and releasing arrows, I didn't have to think about anything else. It was an even better distraction than usual because I was explaining my process to Calder or taking breaks to watch him line up his shots.

I laughed as another of his arrows failed to reach the target. "I really have never seen anybody as bad at archery as you are. Good thing you have other skills."

He propped his bow against his legs and rubbed his hands together. "I'm going to blame the cold. I think we'll have snow any day now."

I looked up at the gray clouds hiding the sun. Fall was giving way to winter. My thoughts traveled to Ashton and Celeste as they made their way to the mountains. My chest tightened. *Was I ever going to stop thinking of him so much?* How much time would need to pass before my mind didn't wander to him?

Calder reached out and cupped his hands over mine. "Your hands are freezing. We should go in."

We walked silently back to my quarters. Calder pulled open the flap of my tent but remained outside.

Stepping inside, I turned back to face him. "Thanks for listening, Calder."

"Any time." He smiled, then turned to walk away.

The tent flap fell, leaving me alone. Out of the corner of my eye, I caught sight of the chair that Ashton used to sit in. Someone had moved it back inside my tent. Suddenly, I felt very tired. I collapsed into the nearest chair and couldn't take my eyes off of Ashton's empty chair. *What's he doing right now? Is he safe? Does he miss me? Is he even thinking about me?*

I rubbed my eyes and swallowed a few times to try to clear out the lump that had risen in my throat. I needed to find a way to get over this. Calder didn't seem to think Ashton had meant what he said, but I couldn't sit here holding on to the hope that Ashton still cared. Dwelling on the past wasn't going to help me in Gallia. I needed to be strong on my own if I was going to defeat the king and Max. My hands clenched into fists in my lap as I thought of my brother. How could he do this to us?

His hunger for power was so clear, even when I first joined the Ravens. In my confused state of trying to figure out who I was, I missed all of the signs. If I had been more observant, if I had paid attention to the details, maybe I would have had some warning. I covered my face with my hands and my heart sunk. *Ashton was a distraction.* I was so wrapped up in the emotions and excitement of our relationship that I missed things.

I stood so quickly that the chair I had been sitting in toppled to the ground. I didn't pause to pick it up. Instead, I marched over to Ashton's chair and picked it up. The chair was heavier than it looked and I grunted with each step as I carried it toward the entrance of my tent. Chair first, I pushed through the tent flap and dropped it once I was outside.

An older man who had been with the White Ravens longer

than me was walking by as I struggled with the chair. He jogged forward and took it from my hands. "Let me help you, your highness."

I let out a breath as he took the burden from my arms. "Thank you."

He smiled and held the chair easily in his arms. "What would you like me to do with it?"

I waved a hand in front of my face. "I don't really care. I just need it out of my tent. I don't have space for it any longer."

He lifted the chair higher and looked at it before lowering it again. "It's a nice chair. Do you mind if I take it back to the men's quarters?"

"Not at all. I'd like to see it go to good use." *Firewood might be a better use.* I winced at my own thoughts then quickly fixed a smile on my face. "Thank you."

"Any time, your highness." He walked away.

My stomach twisted as I watched the chair make its way towards the men's quarters. It was the only thing in my room that reminded me of Ashton. Regretting the decision, I almost chased after him. Instead, I found my way to Ashton's tent. Taking a deep breath, I pushed through the flap.

Over the last few weeks, I'd spent a lot of time in here with Ashton. Sometimes he'd show me simple spells I could try, or we'd play cards. Celeste and Calder sometimes joined us and the four of us would stay up late into the night talking and laughing.

Then there were the private moments with just the two of us. They were rarer than I would have liked. The tent still smelled like him. My fists clenched and unclenched as I stared at the nearly empty space. *How could you do this to me?* After everything we'd been through, hadn't I proven myself to him?

Overcome by rage, I kicked the bedroll, sending it up against the side of the tent in a pile. "Why did you leave me? Why did you make me love you? I hate you!" My voice sounded like it was coming from somebody else as I shouted at nothing.

My chest rose and fell quickly as I caught my breath. I rubbed my forehead and my shoulders sunk. *Why are you letting this get to you?* My cheeks burned with embarrassment and all of my senses piqued. Had anybody seen me go in here? Had they heard my outburst? I turned away from the bedroll. *How could you be so stupid?* I shook my head. To think of the things I almost gave up for him. I risked too much by being with him. Taking a deep breath, I closed my eyes and focused on calming myself.

The throne. That was what mattered. Defeating the king. Eliminating Max. Ashton was a distraction that had kept me from reaching my full potential. The ice inside me started at my fingers and ran its way through my arms to my chest. I imagined it filling my chest and forming a barrier around my heart. *Nobody else gets in here.* Any relationship I had would be for the benefit of my kingdom and my people.

Lifting my chin, I left Ashton's tent without looking back. There were more important things to do than to dwell on a girlish fantasy. It was time to find an army. All of my energy needed to be focused on Gallia and getting them to support us.

Anticipation mixed with fear and I swallowed back my nerves as I pulled out clothes for the journey. *You can do this.* I thought back to Lady Genevieve's lessons and knew I'd only get one chance at a first impression. Only this time, I didn't need people to believe that I was a princess, they needed to believe that I was a queen.

MASTER FLANDERS TOOK my hand as we prepared to leave for Campari, from there, we would take a ship to Gallia. Teleporting across the sea without a teleportation coin or a magic object like the Oracle's key was dangerous. But our ability to teleport to Campari would cut down on the length of the journey.

Was I ready for this? I laughed to myself. Had I been ready for anything that I'd been through in the last few months? Was I ready to be a princess? A queen? A leader? A sorceress? How hard could it be to meet the uncle I'd never met and convince him to let me borrow his army? My stomach twisted into knots. He might be my uncle, but he was the King of Gallia. A kingdom that prided itself on its neutrality. They'd never taken sides in a war before but it was vital to our cause that I convince him. Somehow, I had to act like the queen I was claiming to be. I had to do this.

Master Flanders eyed me with a tilted grin but didn't comment on my nervous laughter. "You ready?"

I took a deep breath and nodded. *Here goes nothing.*

Smoke began to circle my ankles. In a burst of energy, my breath left my lungs and I squeezed my eyes shut. As the nausea crept in, my feet touched on solid ground. Opening one eye at a time, I watched the smoke dissipating from around us.

We arrived at the dockyard in Campari, bypassing the city gates. Last time I had been here, we'd struggled to secure passage to the Sacred Island so I could visit the Oracle. This time, we'd used our resources and contacts to gain us a place on a supply ship taking goods to Gallia.

I wore trousers and a tunic and had my hair tucked up inside a hat. My best dress was packed into a bag slung over my shoulders. The clothing choices were more for comfort than to hide who I was since the owner of the ship knew who he was transporting.

Master Flanders and I cut through the crowds. The sound of seagulls and sailors shouting filled the air and I breathed in the smell of the sea. Just a few weeks ago, I'd only seen the sea once in my life. Now, I was about to board a ship for the second time.

Our crossing to Gallia would take several days and I hoped my stomach wouldn't be as unhappy with the journey as it had last time I'd sailed. The crowd thinned as we neared the end of the docks.

"There it is." Master Flanders lifted his chin toward a large ship in front of us. On the side of the ship the word *Destiny* was painted in blue lettering. It was an appropriate name for a ship considering the weight of this trip. If I succeeded, I could reclaim my throne, my birthright. If I failed, there was no way we would be able to defeat the king. Either way, this trip would seal my fate, it will determine which path my destiny would take.

19

ETTA

A s our ship arrived in Gallia, I was greeted by the sight of a bustling city. A carriage awaited our arrival, a coat of arms carefully painted on the door. Disembarking, we walked toward the royal carriage. As we approached, the footman climbed down and greeted us with a bow. I was thankful I'd decided to change into the dress when we were near land.

"Your highness." The footman stood then lowered his head as he greeted Master Flanders. "Master. We are honored to have you in Gallia."

He reached for my bag and gestured with his arm toward the carriage. "If you will."

We followed him and settled inside the comfortable space. As the door closed behind us, I took in the sights of the luxury I was surrounded by. Every surface was covered with a shiny, blue fabric. Gold embroidery covered the walls in an elegant pattern of crowns and wings. I traced my fingers over the surface.

During our boat ride, I'd been treated kindly and the members of the crew fought over who got to entertain me or bring me meals. Now, we were being greeted like royalty and being taken to the castle as honored guests. I hoped this was a sign of things to come.

The castle was a short ride away and neither Master Flanders or I spoke as we watched the Gallic countryside flash by the windows. We rode past lush, rolling green hills and the sea was nearly always in view in the background. Gallia was beautiful.

The carriage rolled to a stop in front of a large wrought iron gate. Guards in matching blue uniforms stood at the entrance, tense and ready. One of them peeked through the bars, then waved us through. The gates parted and the carriage moved again. My body tensed as we rode through. "What if I can't do this?"

Master Flanders smiled. "You can. Your uncle is a kind man and he will see that helping you will benefit Gallia as well."

He has to. I nodded at Master Flanders. It was my job to show him how important this was to Illaria and prove to him that it was worth it for him, too. *You can do this.*

The carriage came to a halt, and the door swung open. The footman bowed as he offered a hand to help me down. I took it and stepped onto the gravel driveway outside of the royal palace of Gallia. My eyes traveled up the pale stone of the facade. It was larger than any other building I'd seen and the architecture was so different from home. Sweeping lines and jagged points topped the palace. Circular stained-glass windows lined the front. This building was a work of art, nothing like the drafty gray dungeon like castle the king called home.

A man in a velvet tunic trimmed in gold approached. He had dark hair, flecked with gray and the same tan skin Celeste had.

His smile caused wrinkles around his eyes and mouth. "Niece, you cannot even imagine what joy it brings me to see you alive."

"Welcome to Gallia." He wrapped his arms around me in a tight hug.

I stiffened under his embrace, unused to being greeted so intimately. When I cleared my throat, he pulled back and stared at me, one of his large hands on each of my shoulders.

I curtseyed. "Thank you for having us, your majesty. It's an honor to be here."

"Please, no need for all that. We're family. Call me Gaius."

"You have the same face as your mother." He ducked down to look into my eyes. "It's a shame you got your father's pale complexion. Does your face turn red when you're embarrassed as his used to?"

I felt my cheeks flush at his question and tried to will it to stop.

He grinned at me. "Looks like it does."

Master Flanders took a few steps forward and bowed. "Your majesty, thank you for allowing us to move up the meeting."

My uncle removed his hands from my shoulders and turned to greet Master Flanders. "Thank you for your help keeping my niece safe."

Gaius returned his attention to me, setting a hand between my shoulder blades. "Come, let us go inside. We have much to discuss."

We walked toward the large, open double doors of the castle.

Gaius smiled at me. "Your mother and I were so close as children. She sent me white ravens every week after she moved to Illaria. Even when things got bad, she found a way to keep in touch. You being alive brings me so much happiness."

The way he talked about my mother was so genuine. I started to relax a little. As we reached the doors, the tingle of magic raced through my veins. When we stepped through the doors, we were no longer alone.

There were four men on either side of the doors. On one side, all of the men clad in armor, standing at attention with one hand resting on the hilt of a sword that was holstered at their waist. The other side of the door was attended by four men in long, dark green robes. Their posture wasn't as strict as the soldiers opposite them.

All of their eyes followed me and the tingle inside me surged to a level I had never felt before. I jumped and my uncle stopped in his tracks.

"What are they doing?" All manners lost, I turned on the sorcerers and pulled my tingling arms across my stomach, trying to quench the rising vibrations inside me. "It's too much."

Gaius looked from me to his sorcerers. "Enough." He raised a hand. "I don't think it's necessary for you to use any more of your detection spells on her."

My breathing was ragged as I struggled to overcome the magic being thrown at me. *So this is what it feels like to have four sorcerers casting spells at you at the same time?* The tingle started to ease. It hadn't been painful, but it was overwhelming.

Now that I had caught my breath, anger spread through me. *How dare they use that much magic on me?* I marched up to the tallest of the sorcerers and stood right in front of him. "You are not to use magic on me without my consent. Is that clear?"

The man's jaw dropped and he looked to his king.

Ice ran through my veins. *They should not defy me.* The ice was turning to fire as it traveled through me, causing little sparks to begin to form in my palms. "I am the rightful Queen of Illaria, you will not disrespect me in such a way."

The man swallowed and bowed his head low.

"Etta," Master Flanders rested his hand on my shoulder. "Deep breaths. Clear your mind."

My whole body wanted to turn on him and scream but before I acted on it, a small voice inside reminded me that I wasn't in control. *The Darkness.* Closing my eyes, I squeezed my palms into fists to hide the sparks as I took a few deep breaths. "Forgive me," I said. "I've never felt that much magic at once."

I opened my eyes and found the sorcerer watching me, his brow furrowed as he studied me. "You can feel it already, can't you?"

"Feel what?" I had a feeling I knew what he was talking about, but I didn't want to explain to them that I'd accidentally opened a portal to the Darkness.

"The Darkness. Some of us can feel it already," he said.

I swallowed and glanced at Master Flanders. He nodded.

"I'm working on controlling it."

"You must be very sensitive to magic," he said.

I nodded. "I am. Why were all four of you using magic on me at the same time, anyway?"

I turned to my uncle. "You thought I was an impostor?"

"I had to make sure it wasn't a trick. Forgive me." He bowed his head. "Once I saw you, I knew you were my sister's daughter, but I didn't call off my sorcerers. I don't have the same skills you or your mother had. I forget the response that magic can elicit."

"My mother was like this?" I asked.

He nodded. "She was very sensitive to magic. I believe that to be part of why she wanted to live in Illaria, where magic is rare. Here it's so common it would sometimes overwhelm her."

I blinked a few times, trying to process what he said. What must it have been like for her living here while learning how to control her powers? A million questions spun in my mind. How I wished this was a social visit. That I could spend the days here learning about my family and Gallia. But that wasn't to be. At least not on this trip. "I would really like to learn more about my mother and my family, but I fear this trip has to be focused on business. We've just received word that the king's daughter is going to marry Max."

"That does change things, doesn't it." Gaius bent his elbow and nodded for me to take it.

I obliged and we crossed the threshold into a long hallway

with a white marble floor. One side of the hallway was lined with windows taller than me. The other was lined with mirrors, giving the space the illusion that it was glowing. My eyes darted around the hallway. The sight left me momentarily breathless. "Your home is beautiful."

"Thank you, your highness," Gaius said.

"Please, call me Etta."

"As you wish," he said. "Please know you are welcome here any time. And know if things shouldn't go the way we would like them to in Illaria, you always have a home here."

His words hit me like I'd been thrown from a horse. *Home.* I hadn't truly felt at home since my grandmother died. And that had never really been my home. How easy would it be to let Max take Illaria and stay here in this luxury? I wouldn't have the burden of ruling over a kingdom or the expectation of marriage. I'd be a favored family member. Maybe I could even train with the sorcerers here, visit the library. It would be easier to stay here. But what about everybody who was counting on me? *No. Living in Gallia isn't an option.* I was going to take back my rightful home.

20

ASHTON

It had already been five days since their last hot meal at Thomas' home. Ashton dreamed of a cup of tea or some warm porridge. The pre-dawn morning air was crisp and cold. Most of the leaves had fallen, winter was threatening to begin. The cold air made his cheeks sting and he pulled the hood of his cloak tighter around his face.

Traveling before dawn had become habit for Ashton and Celeste. There was something peaceful about those early hours of the day and they brought clarity to Ashton, though sometimes they gave him too much time to think. His mind had drifted to Etta as it often did when it was quiet. He tried to focus on his surroundings, find anything to distract himself.

The sound of their horses crunching over the gravel road echoed through the cold morning air. Celeste's horse was in sync with Ashton's making the sound louder. He considered talking to Celeste, but wasn't sure what to say. They'd never had trouble talking in the past, but since leaving the camp she'd kept their conversations minimal after Ashton made it clear that Etta was not a subject he was willing to discuss. Celeste seemed to be withholding conversation as a form of protest.

He let out a long breath and shifted in the saddle. The sword Thomas gave him moved with him from its holster on his back. It was an unusual burden that made him uncomfortable. He'd never trained in using a sword. All of his time had been spent learning to use magic. He'd likely need the sword when they reached the castle where the Stone of Morare was hidden. Ashton shivered at the thought of the undead that they might encounter.

His breath caught in his chest and the image of a woman flashed before his eyes. He hadn't had to relive that night in a long time. The night when his mother was killed in front of him, her lifeless body dragged away while he hid behind a chair crying out for her. When he had these dreams, they felt so real. And every time he had the dream he was helpless to fight back. He'd stand there frozen in fear, unable to save his mother.

He shook his head, trying to push the memory back into the depths of his mind. Ashton's childhood nightmares had resurfaced since the trip to Greenville. He wondered if it was a result of his visit to the Astral Realm or the impeding Darkness. Neither would surprise him.

He pushed the hood of his cloak back, relishing the shock of the cold air on his face. Taking a deep breath in, the vision of the dream faded. He wrinkled his nose, then sniffed the air. Something was burning.

"Do you smell that?"

Celeste lifted her chin and sniffed. "Something's burning." She wrinkled her nose.

"Let's get off the road. Wait for sunrise so we can see the smoke." Ashton turned off the road and headed into the woods, Celeste followed behind.

They tied their horses to a tree sat on a large rock while they waited for daylight.

"You've been quiet on this trip," Ashton said.

"I'm still not sure why you did it, Ashton."

"The things I said." His shoulders dropped. "I can't ever take them back."

"What did you tell her?"

Ashton shook his head. "I told her she was just like her father, just like Max. That she'd eventually give me up in exchange for power. It was awful."

"Oh, Ashton." Celeste put her arm around him and rested her cheek on his shoulder. "I'm sure she'll forgive you when we return. She'll know you didn't mean it."

Ashton shrugged away from Celeste. "I don't think I want her to forgive me."

In the gray light of dawn, Ashton could see the confusion on Celeste's face.

"She needs to be able to marry for the good of the kingdom. She'll never do that if she has me. I don't want to be responsible for preventing her from gaining or keeping her throne. I won't do that to her. To the kingdom. So many people have sacrificed so much for this. My parents, her parents. We have to sacrifice, too. She'd never do it if I didn't break her heart."

Ashton stood, rubbing his hands together to warm them. "There's enough light to find the smoke now. We should go."

Celeste wore a frown on her face, not even trying to hide her disappointment. She took a deep breath and stood, then silently mounted her horse.

Ashton's throat burned as he recalled the look on Etta's face when they last spoke. How could that really be the last memory they'd have of each other? *This is for the best. Everybody has to make sacrifices.* He mounted his horse and rode out of the woods toward the road.

When they reached the road, they saw a massive cloud of smoke rising above a small town that looked to be less than an hour's ride from where they were. The smoke was thick and dark, like a storm cloud.

"What should we do?" Celeste asked. "Keep riding or check it out?"

Ashton narrowed his eyes at the cloud, wondering if it was worth the detour. The town wasn't on their way to the mountains and they weren't on a mission to rescue people from fires. What good would two sorcerers be, anyway?

The cloud started to glow, a reddish-gold color. The hair on the back of Ashton's neck stood on end and his whole body tensed. "Celeste?"

His hands were trembling and he turned to see Celeste staring wide-eyed at the cloud, her body visibly trembling.

Slowly, she turned her head toward Ashton. "Ashton, why is the smoke doing that?"

He looked back at the glowing cloud. Only one thing made smoke like that. *It's not possible.*

"It has to be something else, a sorcerer trick," Ashton said.

Celeste nodded. "Must be."

Ashton clenched his jaw. "We better go check it out."

Celeste swallowed. "Are you sure? What if it's not a sorcerer?"

"Then we'll need to send a message to the White Ravens." Ashton was pretty sure they were both thinking it, but neither of them wanted to say it out loud. *Dragon.*

It took some convincing to get the horses to head toward the glowing smoke, but once they started moving again, they made quick progress. Ashton glanced behind him at Celeste. She was wearing a frown on her face. He didn't blame her. If there was a dragon, chances are it was gone by now, so they weren't in harm's way. But if there had been a dragon, everything would change.

Dragons hadn't been in Illaria or any of the neighboring kingdoms in over a thousand years. Nobody knew what happened to them. They vanished when the Darkness took hold of the kingdoms. With the impending Darkness, it made no sense for the dragons to return.

Ashton had been fascinated by the creatures as a child. He grew up listing to campfire stories about them. His favorites were the stories of brave men who would ride on their backs. Dragons were intelligent creatures who often stayed to themselves. But every so often, a few would allow themselves to be part of human groups, sometimes joining armies or settling near a town.

They couldn't be trusted, though. They were wild and had minds of their own. So for every story of a good dragon, there were stories of dragons who would take out whole villages in a fiery attack for no reason at all. Some dragons just liked to cause destruction.

If there was a dragon who had returned to Illaria, Ashton hoped it was the first kind. The kind that liked being around people. Not the type that liked to watch things burn. As they drew nearer to the town, the dense smoke obscured their vision and his heart sunk. He had a feeling this wasn't the good kind of dragon.

21

ASHTON

The town was in chaos as Ashton and Celeste rode through the gates. The wall they passed through was crumbling in places and nobody stood guard as they entered. Smoke hung thick in the air, the red glow still clinging to the clouds.

Ashton covered his mouth and nose with his sleeve to try to filter out some of the smoke. Several people ran in front of his horse, startling her, nearly throwing Ashton from his saddle. Rather than risk being thrown, he dismounted and led her by the reins further into town. Celeste rode cautiously behind him. She was a better rider and stayed on her horse.

Buildings around him were still smoking, blackened from fire and crumbling. Ashton's throat was tight from the smoke and he found swallowing nearly impossible due to the dryness in his mouth. As they moved down the street, his boots crunched over debris and fallen stones. None of the people running around seemed to pay any attention to the strangers in their town. They carried valuables, children, and tools over their shoulders as they did what they could to salvage their homes or businesses.

Turning down a side road, they found a town square where less damage had been done. The cobblestones lining the courtyard in a diamond shaped pattern were coated with a thin layer of ash from the sky. Ashton led his horse toward a storefront that had a place for him to tie her.

The store was still standing, perfect condition, aside from the ash that coated it, darkening the otherwise cheerful stone exterior. It was a tiny, single story building that appeared to sell books and parchment. Ashton tied up his horse. Celeste dismounted and tied hers as well.

"Do we have any water left?" Ashton asked.

Celeste dug through her saddle bags and found a water skin. She tossed it to him.

He drank, then closed it and threw it back to Celeste. "I'm going to see if we can find some answers. You want to wait with the horses?"

She paused mid-drink and wiped her mouth with the back of her hand. "Sounds good. I'll be right here."

Ashton entered the book store, hoping he'd be able to find somebody who had seen what happened. He pushed open the door and looked around the dim room. The only light came from the single window. It was larger inside than it appeared from the outside. The space was filled with shelves of books and baskets of rolled parchment. He had to turn sideways to move between the crowded shelves as he searched for the proprietor.

"Hello?" he called, "anybody here?"

The sound of a clearing throat from behind him sent Ashton spinning around with a jolt. In front of him stood a small, hunched old man. His back was curved in a hump and he stood nearly doubled over from the deformity. He had a full head of bright white hair and a bushy white mustache.

"What can I do for you today, son?" His voice was clear and

strong. It didn't seem like it belonged to such a frail looking figure.

"I was passing through and saw the smoke," Ashton said. "Wondered if somebody could tell me what was going on."

"You stopped by to see if anybody saw the dragon, more like."

A chill ran down Ashton's spine. "So it was a dragon?"

"Yes," the old man said, "frightful creature. One of the larger ones, based on my research. Terrible temper. Seemed to be angry at the town for no reason."

Ashton tried to remember what he knew about the size of dragons. In all the stories he heard, he just remembered that they were big. He couldn't imagine what a larger than normal dragon would be. "What do you mean, larger?"

"I've read a lot, son." The man gestured to the book shelves around them. "From what I've read, most dragons are about the size of six or so horses put together. This one, looked at least twice as big. Though it's hard to know if any of what I've read is true. A thousand years is a long time."

This was going to change everything. If the dragon decided to side with the king, they wouldn't stand a chance. Or it could just go around Illaria randomly attacking towns, which wouldn't make their lives any easier. Why couldn't it just be one thing at a time?

"Do you know where it came from?" Ashton asked.

"From the west, but it headed east when it left," the old man said. He lifted a bushy white eyebrow. "You fixing to chase after it? Be a hero?"

Ashton shook his head. "No, I'm not a dragon hunter."

The old man squinted and looked Ashton up and down. "No, I suppose you're not. But you are hunting for something."

"I'm just passing through, and really should be going," Ashton said as he turned toward the door.

"Young man, wait a moment."

Ashton considered ignoring the request, but manners prevented him from doing so. *He's just a lonely old man.* He turned around slowly, intent on telling the old man goodbye but didn't see him anywhere in sight. *Crazy old man.* He headed toward the door again, only to be intercepted by the man.

"Here." The old man held out a wooden box with a sturdy lock. "Take this with you."

Ashton put his hands up, trying to deny taking the object. "That's not necessary. Really, you don't even know me."

The old man lifted an eyebrow. "No, but I've heard about you. You know my brother. Goes by the name Flanders."

Ashton's head moved back in surprise. "How?"

"White Raven the other day. Told me to keep an eye out in case you passed through. Never thought you would. You'd think I'd have learned that my brother is never wrong by this point." He pressed the box into Ashton's hands.

Ashton held the box and lifted it to look at the lock more carefully. "What is it?"

The old man smiled. "Honestly, I'm not sure. My brother left it with me years ago and asked me to keep it safe. I suppose you'll have to ask him."

Ashton held the box at arm's length, worried it might contain something dangerous. What could Master Flanders have kept in a locked box with a brother he'd never told anyone about?

"Don't worry, it won't bite," the old man said. "You best be off. Before that dragon decides to return. And don't worry about getting a message along. I'll send it for you. You just get on with your mission."

Ashton lowered the box and narrowed his eyes at the man. "How do I know what you are saying is true? How do I know this isn't a trick by the king?"

"You'll have to trust me."

Turning back to the door, Ashton held the box closer. It was yet another reason to find the stone and return to the Raven camp.

"Wait a minute," the old man called out. "I almost forgot."

Ashton turned to look at him.

The man shuffled along the floor to a desk that Ashton hadn't noticed before. He pulled out a drawer in the desk and removed a folded piece of paper. He shuffled back, his left leg dragging as he walked. Handing the paper to Ashton, he waited.

Ashton opened the paper and a small silver ring fell into his hand. His stomach tightened. It was the ring he left behind for Etta. With shaky hands, he read the note. *If you see Ashton, give him this.*

Ashton turned the ring over in his fingers. Was this a trick? It looked like the same ring. Why would Master Flanders send it so far away when he didn't know if Ashton would even stop here? Ashton froze and looked up at the old man. "You've been sending White Ravens to Master Flanders, haven't you?"

He nodded. "Been keeping in touch with my brother for years using our birds. I wasn't fit to be part of the fighting but I do what I can to keep the Ravens informed of things on this side of the kingdom."

Ashton held up the ring. "What does this mean? What am I supposed to do with this?"

The old man shrugged. "I stopped trying to figure out why my brother does the things he does years ago."

Ashton's shoulders sunk. This was supposed to be Etta's ring. It was supposed to be saved for Etta in case the worst should happen. Why had Master Flanders sent it to him? He knew that Master Flanders didn't do things accidentally. Everything had a purpose. Shouldn't Etta be engaged to some Gallic noble by now? His breath caught in my chest. Maybe the Gallic king didn't want a marriage alliance after all. *Maybe she said no.* If they lost that army, he didn't know how they'd take on the king. But if she wasn't going to marry somebody from Gallia, she hadn't given up on him. Ashton laughed, unable to contain the joy rising up. The empty place inside him didn't feel so empty anymore. Was it possible he could make up for his actions? Either way, something big had happened. Ashton removed the simple chain he wore around his neck and threaded it through the small ring. He no longer cared what Sir Henry thought, Etta needed him and he needed her. As he slipped the chain back around his neck he vowed that he wasn't going to give up on her until he had her back.

Gripping the box under his arm he headed toward the door. "Thanks." He nodded at the old man.

"Good luck, son."

Ashton returned to the horses to find Celeste staring out toward the smoky remains of the town with a frown on her face. The cloud of smoke was smaller than it had been when he entered the shop.

"Looks like they're containing it pretty well," he said.

Celeste spoke without turning to look at him. "Yes, but I wish we could do something to help them."

Ashton mounted his horse. "We are doing something to help them. We're doing something to help everybody."

She let out a long sigh. "I suppose so."

"You didn't ask what I found out," Ashton said as he watched her climb onto her mare.

She pushed her hair away from her face. "Didn't need to. We both already knew what the cause of the destruction was. Only real question is, was it working alone or has it made friends with a human? Don't suppose you found that out?"

"No," Ashton said. "Just that it was a big one." The ring slid against his skin as he adjusted his position on the horse. He squeezed the reins tighter. "I'll give you the details later. I want to cover a few more miles before it gets dark."

"Oh?" Celeste raised her eyebrows. "There's actually something to tell?"

He lifted the reins and started to ride away and called back to Celeste as he rode. "Later."

22

ETTA

G aius led us to an exquisitely appointed sitting room. Plush rugs sunk under my shoes as I walked through the room. A large harp and several musical instruments I didn't recognize sat in the corner.

"Please, sit," Gaius gestured to an overstuffed blue couch facing a large, marble fireplace. The fabric shimmered in the light of the large glass windows. The room was bathed in sunlight which reflected off of the thousands of crystals in the chandeliers above us.

I sat down and rubbed my hands over the smooth fabric. *Silk.* A couch like this would cost a fortune. I clasped my hands in my lap, afraid to damage the fabric with my touch. The only time I'd seen the inside of a castle had been for the dinner with the king. The castle he lived in was cold and intimidating. This castle was warm and inviting, though a bit overwhelming in its grandness. What had the castle looked like when my parents lived there? Surely it hadn't been as cold as it was under the current king. Glancing around the room, I considered what I would do in my own castle. I hadn't put much thought into where I would live when this was all over, but it would make sense to re-claim the castle that should have been my home.

Master Flanders sat on the opposite end of the couch and placed his hands in his lap, mirroring my own. Gaius settled in a high-backed wood-trimmed chair topped with a deep blue cushion. All of the furniture in this room was a shade of blue. I wondered who had decorated it. They must have a love of the color.

Peeking behind me, I noticed that Gaius' sorcerers and his guard had accompanied us to the room. They stood near the door, blocking the only exit. I fidgeted in my seat, feeling trapped despite the fact that Gaius was supposed to be on my side. His guards reminded me too much of the king's guards who had been trying to kill me. It must be typical for a king to have their own guard. Yet, I traveled only with a sorcerer. Should I be building my own guard? The thought sent a shudder through me. It was difficult to separate the idea of a guard from the ones who had been hunting me.

I swallowed and turned my head away from the door, back to my uncle.

"Are the guards making you nervous, or the sorcerers?" he asked.

"I'm fine." I forced a smile on my face. "Just not used to seeing guards that aren't trying to kill me."

Gaius waved his hand toward the door. I turned to see the guards and sorcerers file out. They closed the door. Some of the tension in me released, though I was sure they were just standing on the other side of the door.

"You should consider getting your own guard, Etta," Gaius said. "In fact, I can send a squadron of mine with you to get you started. I have some young men in my army who would happily accept the promotion of being personal guard to a queen. It's a highly prized position. The men in my guard are the very best.

Only the most loyal, well trained soldiers get to protect the king. It should be the same for you."

Perhaps I should take him up on the offer, it would make me look more like a queen. "Thank you, uncle, that is very kind."

He slapped his hands on his knees. "Now, let's discuss how we are going to get your kingdom back."

This is what we were here for. I needed to negotiate for an army to support my cause. My throat felt dry. Even though this man was family, I didn't know him. He was a king and I still felt like I was playing the part most days. He lived in luxury, I lived in a tent. I gave a sideways glance to Master Flanders. He nodded.

Swallowing hard, I began, "we'd like to ask for your support in the removal of the impostor king of Illaria."

Gaius nodded. "You have our support but before we can give you resources, I need to know how you plan to remove this impostor. I need to know that if I give you men and arms, they will be put to good use. We haven't participated in a foreign war in a thousand years. I have to know that you're going to win and that the cost of life will be as little as possible."

You knew this was coming. Discussed strategies played out in my head.

"We are currently engaged in phase one of our plan to remove the king. We are in the process of gaining and destroying the stone of Morare."

Gaius leaned forward in his chair and rested his chin on his hand. "The king doesn't keep the stone on his person?" He leaned back. "Very interesting. When do you think you'll have the stone?"

My stomach knotted and Ashton's image flashed into my mind. Now was not the time to get sentimental or worried. Ashton and Celeste could retrieve the stone. I lifted my chin. "In the next few weeks."

Gaius tilted his head. "And do you intend to use the Reapers yourself?"

"No." My voice was firm. A chill ran through me. There was a cost of all magic, and I didn't want to find out what the cost of controlling the Reapers was. The Darkness was bad enough.

Gaius smiled. "That's a good sign. You're smart. It's a wonder the king's been able to control those monsters for as long as he has without them turning on him. You intend to destroy them, then?"

I nodded. "We are hoping to destroy the stone itself but we're still working out the details."

"Do you have a backup plan? I have yet to find any writings on how to destroy that stone." He leaned forward again, as if anticipating my answer. He seemed to be testing me.

I gripped the edge of the couch with my hands. "You've heard about what I can do, haven't you?"

"Rumors," he said. "But I'm hoping they're true."

"What have you heard?" I asked. What rumors had made their way to Gallia?

"That you could take down the Reapers without needing to destroy the stone." His face was serious and his eyes didn't leave my face. It was as if he was waiting for me to flinch.

"That may be true," I said. "If I can control my powers well enough."

Gaius turned to Master Flanders, "I imagine you're working with her?"

Master Flanders nodded. "Yes, she's been training as my apprentice."

"Can she do it?" Gaius asked.

Could I do it? So far, in every interaction I had with the Reapers I was able to get them to go away, but never strong enough to destroy them. And could I handle all four at the same time? Was it possible if we controlled them that they would stand there and let me destroy them? Or would they fight back? I looked over at Master Flanders, his face was impassive.

"Yes, your highness," Master Flanders said, "she will be able to destroy the Reapers once we have the stone."

Gaius clapped his hands. "Well, then. You are something special, Etta. Your mother would be very proud of you."

I smiled. It was the first time I'd heard praise from someone who shared my mother's blood. It was almost like hearing it from her.

"After you destroy the Reapers," Gaius rested his hands on his knees. "What's next?"

I straightened, trying to make myself seem more confident than I felt. This was what we came here for. We needed his army. He knew that. We knew that. It was a matter of showing him I could command an army. That I was a worthy investment.

"We'll strike the day after his daughter's wedding. They won't expect anything early in the morning after such a celebration. If this wedding is anything like her first wedding, his lords and dukes will be caught off guard due to a night of drinking too much. Most of the high lords will stay the night in the castle, far from their armies. The king will be limited to only the guard he has at the castle. He won't be able to call for reinforcements without sending his lords out of the protection of the castle." I paused, watching my uncle for any reaction. His fingers were steepled under his chin and he nodded.

"In order to make this attack successful, we'll need more men. That is where you can help us."

Gaius lowered his hands and gripped the armrests of his chair. He leaned against the chair back, and looked up at the ceiling. His lips were pursed as he considered my words. After what felt like hours, he leaned forward and looked at me.

"When is the wedding?" he asked.

"We believe it will be within the next four weeks. We are

awaiting responses from some of the lords who are loyal to us. They will send word any day now."

He leaned back again, hands interlaced in front of him. "If our sorcerers work with yours, we can build several portals large enough to get the army through right before the battle. That would maintain your element of surprise."

Excited flutters filled my chest. "Does that mean that you're going to help us?"

"It won't be without a price," he said.

My heart dropped into my stomach. *I don't have anything.* What could he possibly want from me? I quickly replaced my frown with a straight face. "Of course, though you may have to wait for payment until I've reclaimed my kingdom."

"Of course," he said.

I waited, wondering what he could want in return for an army. Gold? Resources? Gallia was so self-sustaining, I couldn't imagine what he would be after.

"As you both know, the Darkness is fast approaching. We will have to fight against it very soon. In the last Darkness, our alliance with Illaria was invaluable. Our two countries have a history of supporting one another in times of crisis. I'd like to assure that alliance continues."

My brow furrowed as I waited to hear where this was going.

"I would like to see that our houses are linked by an alliance that means something. I'd like to see you married to one of our lords. Your choice, of course."

Before I could fully process his words, my head was shaking. *No.* My cheeks burned and I stood. "No, that's not possible. I won't be married off as a pawn in somebody else's game."

Gaius stood. "This is how the game is played, Etta. You're young and unmarried. I can't have you joining with a kingdom that is a threat to me."

"You're just going to have to trust that I won't," I said. "Would a king have so little say in who he marries? Did you?"

"Yes, Etta," he said, his tone gentle. "I was betrothed as a child."

Ashton's face flashed through my mind. He'd told me he didn't want to be with me because I could turn out just like my brother, but he'd also said I should marry someone better than him. Part of me still clung to the hope that Ashton hadn't meant what he said. But if it was true, if he didn't want to be with me, I still wanted to choose who I married. I'd fought too hard against Max for the right to protect my heart. "I won't do it, I'm sorry, I can't."

Gaius pressed his lips together into a line. "I'm afraid we won't be able to offer an entire army if you can't give us something in return. And as you said, you don't have much to offer."

I glanced to Master Flanders. Surly he had a suggestion. He stood next to me with his hands inside opposite sleeves of his robes. I turned back to Gaius.

"I'm sorry to disappoint you, but I won't be making any promises of marriage to anybody. If you can offer us any resources, that would be appreciated. If not, we'll figure out a way to finish the king off on our own." I stared at him, jaw fixed, with steel in my expression.

To my surprise, Gaius smiled at me. "You drive a hard bargain, Etta. Perhaps we can come to a compromise."

Before I could start to consider what an acceptable compromise would be, the doors swung open and one of the king's guards ran into the room at a full sprint. He stopped in front of the king and bowed low. "White Raven just delivered this, sir."

The king took the small scroll from the guard and narrowed his eyes at it. He handed it to Master Flanders. "It's addressed to you."

Master Flanders' didn't look surprised to be receiving a

message. He took the scroll and unrolled it, eyes moving back and forth as he read. His face dropped, lips moving into a concerned frown.

"What is it?" I asked.

He looked up at me, then looked to Gaius. He rolled the scroll up in his fingers. "Dragons have returned to Illaria."

23

ETTA

D*ragons?* My mouth dropped open. *This can't be real.* "Who sent that?"

"It's from my brother in Canton. He only saw one dragon, but it was angry. Destroyed most of the town." His face darkened. "He thinks it may have had a rider."

"Wait, your brother?" I had recently found out that Master Flanders had a daughter, who also happened to be the Oracle. Finding out he had a brother who was in contact with him made me realize how much I didn't know about him. There were so few people I trusted and despite the news about his daughter, I had continued to trust him. But I couldn't help but wonder if he was keeping more from me. Was that something I should be worried about?

Before he could answer, Gaius reached his hand toward Master Flanders. "May I?"

Master Flanders handed over the parchment and Gaius read it quickly. He shook his head. "If there is a rider, we have a bigger problem than just a rouge dragon."

Dragon riders were a myth, at least that was what my grandmother had told me. Dragons were intelligent and independent creatures. They sometimes worked with humans if they had the same goal in mind, but they wouldn't actually let a human ride on their backs. "That's not possible."

Gaius passed the scroll back to Master Flanders, then looked over to me. "We have records in our archives of dragon riders. They were rare, but they weren't as rare as the stories would like us to believe. If somebody has formed an alliance with a dragon, we're all in danger."

Who could have formed an alliance with a dragon? I reached for my pendant and started sliding it along the chain. *What if Max or the king made an alliance with a dragon?* For some reason, I had a hard time seeing the king on the back of a dragon. But Max, with his black dragon tattoo, didn't seem out of place riding one of the fire breathing beasts. But why destroy a random town?

"What's in Canton?" I thought back to my lessons with Sir Henry, but couldn't place the name of the town on the map of Illaria in my head. "Whoever has something to gain from destroying Canton is the person who is riding that dragon."

Gaius and Master Flanders both turned to look at me. Master Flanders smiled.

Gaius tilted his head and narrowed his eyes. "You are as smart as I've been told." He took a few steps toward the door and clapped his hands twice. The door opened and a member of his guard stepped in. "Yes, your majesty?"

"Bring us a map of Illaria."

The guard closed the door and Gaius walked back to his chair and settled in. "You're right, Etta. If there is somebody on that dragon, they'd have a reason for what they did. Now, forgive me, but my Illarian geography is rusty, so I've requested a map so we can see what is near that town."

"No need for a map, majesty. I have a feeling I know what

they're after." Master Flanders sunk into the couch, shoulders slumped.

I sat next to him, throat suddenly dry. *How many days has it been?* I counted the days in my head. Canton was on the border of Illaria near Sardinia. If they were on track, Ashton and Celeste should have passed through yesterday or today. It couldn't be a coincidence that a dragon attacked there.

Master Flanders still had the rolled-up scroll in his hands. Without asking, I grabbed it from him and opened the message. As I read, my hand moved over my heart and I leaned my head back in silent thanks to the gods. The first part of the message explained the dragon and the theory that somebody was riding it. It was exactly as Master Flanders said. The second part, however, both confirmed my suspicions and eased my mind. *I met Ashton and passed along your message. He's safely on his way.*

My relief was short lived, however, as I realized what this meant. The rider had clearly been targeting Ashton and Celeste, endangering their mission. If the rider wasn't Max, it was certainly somebody working for the king.

I tightened a fist around the scroll, it also meant that the traitor was somebody in my own council. Had Master Flanders kept this note from me on purpose? Was he trying to hide something from me? He never told me that he had a brother. How was it that his brother happened to be in that exact place at that exact moment?

Gaius cleared his throat, bringing me back to the conversation I had neglected when I took the message from Master Flanders' hand. "I think I'm missing something here."

I smoothed out the crumpled scroll. "I'm sorry. The pieces just started to come together. I'm afraid Canton is only a few days journey from where the stone is hidden. And happens to be where our people were at the time of the dragon attack."

I watched Master Flanders out of the corner of my eye. After everything we'd been through, why did he still hide things from me? I had a hard time believing that he would put Ashton and Celeste in harm's way. One by one, I pictured each of the members of my council. Only the people who had been in that room and Annalise knew our plan. The timing was too accurate to have it be mere chance.

"You have a traitor," Gaius said.

"It seems that is the case. Unless by some unrelated coincidence a person who managed to align with a dragon had a vendetta against a town," I said. Part of me hoped that was the case. Perhaps it was an angry farmer.

Master Flanders rubbed his forehead then took a deep breath. "As much as I'd like that, I don't believe in coincidence. I'd say there is a good chance that if there was a rider, it was somebody who works for the king. Which means a member of your council has betrayed you."

I didn't want to believe it could be Master Flanders who betrayed me, I had to ask. "How did your brother come to be in Canton?"

"It's actually our home town. He isn't well enough to travel anymore so he returned to take over the family business," he said.

"How is it that Ashton met up with him? We didn't have any contacts in Canton. It was just listed as a possible stopping point." Something still didn't quite add up. Why had he kept his brother from us?

Master Flanders could have been angry at me. He knew I was asking the questions out of suspicion. Instead of reacting negatively, he smiled at me. "Sometimes things don't make sense. I sent a message to my brother in the chance that Ashton would pass through town. Seems their paths crossed."

"Why keep him from us? Why wasn't he on the contact list

we reviewed in our meetings?" I didn't like having so much hid from me.

"My brother was also trained as a sorcerer and is one of the few who openly opposed the king. He's retired to a quiet life and the only magic he uses is to call on his white raven to send messages to me. I didn't wish to share his location with anyone. The king wouldn't hesitate to kill him if he knew where he was."

"I'm sorry," I looked away from him, embarrassed that I questioned his loyalty. Master Flanders had been helping me learn to control the magic that would stop the king. Why would he do that if he was working for him? But if it wasn't him, there was somebody on my council who had betrayed me to the king. I'd need to figure out who that was quickly and deal with them publicly. I wasn't looking forward to that. What type of punishment did one give a traitor? I didn't want to think about it right now. I'd deal with it soon, but at the moment, my focus needed to be on finding out if the king was in possession of a dragon.

"We have to get eyes on the king," I said.

Gaius held out both of his hands, stopping me from continuing. I turned to look at him.

"Somebody who can control a dragon is a threat to every kingdom, not just yours. If the king truly has gained a dragon, there's nothing to stop him from turning his sights on us. Etta, you have your army."

I blinked a few times while the words sunk in. "What about payment?"

"We'll create a treaty between our countries. No marriage needed for a treaty," he said.

Not wanting to come across as smug, I tried not to let my smile take over my whole face. "I would like that."

He stood. "You can stay here for a few days while we work out all of the details." He offered his hand to me and I took it, letting him pull me to my feet. "I'll show you to the guest quarters. You can rest for a bit and we will meet for dinner."

I dipped into a slight curtsey. "Thank you."

GAIUS AND MASTER FLANDERS left me alone in a well-appointed suite of rooms that were larger than the house I'd grown up in. *How does one person need this much space?* I walked from the sitting room to the dining area, to the bedroom, and through a small space that could serve as a private chapel. The floors were polished marble with thick rugs in the center of each room. I ran my fingers over the velvet fabric on the couches in the sitting room before turning my attention on the huge window.

The window overlooked the sea, reminding me of just how far away we were from Illaria. A whole ocean separated us. I sank down on a cushion covered window seat and watched the rise and fall of the waves in the ocean. Looking over the sea from the top floor of the large castle made me feel so small. What was I going to do? I had a whole country to protect. People I loved and people I had never met were counting on me to do something nobody had been able to do. Now there were dragons and a traitor in my inner circle. Every time I felt like we were getting closer, that I could really succeed in the impossible, something else came in to make it more difficult.

I let out a hard breath and the glass fogged. I turned away from the window and stared into the empty room, wishing I had somebody to talk to. What I wouldn't give to have Ashton here with me. I leaned my head back against the cool glass. *Why can't I stay mad at you?*

Before I could reprimand myself for missing Ashton, a knock sounded on the door. Jumping to my feet, I ran over, eager for the distraction. Without hesitation, I pulled open the door. A girl close to my age smiled at me. She had tight, black curls pinned on her head and the same tan complexion as Gaius. She was wearing an ivory dress trimmed in pearls. It rustled in a pleasant sort of sound when she burst past me into the room.

I spun around to face her, letting go of the door. It slammed shut behind me. Her smile grew larger and she let out an excited squeal, jumping up and down. My eyes widened and I took a step back. *What is she doing?*

"I can't believe it's you!" She spoke Gallic in a shrill voice. Each word was higher pitched than the previous one.

Switching to my unpracticed Gallic, I greeted the stranger. "Hello. I'm sorry, but I don't know who you are."

She placed her hand over her heart and spoke in rapid-fire Gallic. "I'm so sorry, I am being rude. I'm Marielle, but everyone calls me Mari. I'm your cousin. I'd always hoped the rumors were true that you somehow survived, but the longer we waited, the less likely it seemed. Now, here you are."

"My - my cousin?" The words came out in Illaria as I processed what she had said. I couldn't believe I hadn't thought of the possibility before. I never even asked Gaius about his family. I let out a small laugh. *A cousin.* Maybe there were still good things happening. I had more family.

She laughed and clasped both of my hands in hers and switched to Illarian, with only a trace of an accent. She'd clearly been studying the language for years and she put my Gallic to shame. "I want to know everything about you. Start at the beginning."

Grateful for the switch, I continued in my native tongue. "I want to know everything about you first."

Her words tumbled out, "I'm boring. I grew up here. I've never been anywhere. I've never done anything. I don't even have an aptitude for magic. Just like my father. But you, you've lived."

I never considered what I'd been through over the last few months to be anything short of terrifying. I'd wanted nothing more than to be boring until recently. And still, I wondered if I'd give it all up for a chance to live a quiet life. Mari's eyes were fixed on me, expectant. To her, I was exciting.

"Well, where do you want me to start?" I asked.

She pulled me over to one of the velvet couches and sat down, patting the cushion next to her. I joined her on the couch.

She lifted her eyebrows. "What was it like growing up as a peasant?"

She really does mean everything. I took a deep breath and started to tell her about the village I grew up in, my grandmother, the woods I explored, and the simple existence I had for most of my life. She hung on every word.

She leaned closer to me. "So how did you find out you were a princess?"

Mari was a captive listener, asking questions as I told my story. As I recounted my journey, I marveled at how far I'd come. From the weak girl who went along with everybody else's plan to queen.

"So what happened between you and Ashton?" She winked at me.

I winced. I'd talked about my friends in my story, but left out the personal details. Yet, my affection for him had been clear to her. "It didn't work out."

Her brow furrowed. "The way you spoke about him, I though you must be in love with him."

My breath hitched. She was right, of course. No matter how broken my heart was, I didn't think I'd ever stop loving him. Not wanting to linger on the thought of Ashton, I changed the subject. "How about we talk about you? What was it like growing up in a castle?"

She waved her hand. "Not as exciting as it seems. Lessons

most of the day since I turned four. Nothing interesting, either. I never learned how to fight and I wasn't able to learn magic."

"Why not?" I asked.

She shrugged. "They just don't teach girls how to fight."

"Why no magic?"

"I wasn't able to channel it. Everybody has magic, as you know, but I never could gain any control over it. My dad is the same way. He used to say that your mom had enough power for both of them. They were close, our parents. Broke his heart when she died. He named my younger sister after her. She's four years younger than us and she's training to be a sorceress."

"Are you 17?" I asked.

She nodded. "Our birthdays are only a few days apart. You should come back next month and we can celebrate our birthdays together. My father has already planned a huge feast. You might even be queen by then. Think of the fun we'd have."

Her enthusiasm was contagious. I started to picture a lavish party filled with laughing people and music and a huge cake for the two of us. "I would like nothing more."

A light knock on the door sounded.

"Enter," Mari called out with practiced grace.

I can learn a lot from her about how I'm supposed to behave.

The door opened and a woman in a plain brown dress with a white apron stepped in. "Pardon me, highness, but the king has asked me to summon you for dinner."

24

ASHTON

The terrain grew rockier every second as they climbed the deserted mountain pass. Travelers rarely took this road after summer so Ashton and Celeste were the only people in sight. Ashton pulled his hood up over his head. The higher they went, the cooler the air got. He knew they had to be close to the village.

The mountain could only claim one permanent settlement, a tiny village called Round Springs, named for the spring that traveled down the mountain. It fluctuated between being small and being practically abandoned depending on how successful the summer trade routes had been. If the trades were good, the town would have enough supplies to survive the isolated winter. If the trades were poor, people would leave the town in hopes of finding work somewhere where they wouldn't freeze to death if they ran out of firewood.

Ashton hoped the trade had been on the lower end, leaving the town empty. Less people would mean less questions. It was going to be hard enough to fend off the inquiries from curious townspeople who were unused to travelers. He wondered if they should have come up with a story before they reached the town.

Too late. The first few buildings signaling their arrival emerged from the trees before he realized how close they were.

It was late afternoon and the sun was quickly making its descent behind the peaks. A few of the homes had windows filled with the warm glow of candlelight. Several of the buildings had boards nailed over the windows. He slowed his horse and glanced around, looking for something that would serve as an inn for the night. This was the last vestige of civilization they would see until they returned home.

A small, two story building had a wooden sign with a picture of a goblet swinging from above the door. He dismounted his horse and turned to Celeste who already stood next to her mare. "Might be a tavern ahead."

He led his horse to the building and tied it to the post in front. "You want to go in this time?"

Celeste eyed him suspiciously. "Something about that last place really got to you."

Ashton didn't respond.

She handed her reins to him. "I'll go."

Once she was out of sight, he checked that the ring was still attached to the chain around his neck. He didn't need to touch it with his fingers to know it was there, he couldn't stop thinking of it the entire ride here, but somehow fingers touching it made it more real than its presence against his chest alone. The door opened and he quickly dropped his hand.

Celeste emerged from the door. "Lady in here seems nice. Says we can bring our horses around back to their stables."

Ashton untied their horses and followed Celeste around back. A boy of about ten greeted them at the stables with a wide smile. "I can help you with your horses, sir and lady."

"Thank you," Ashton said.

"Yes, thank you." Celeste handed her reins to the boy.

"We don't get many visitors this time of year. You must be

very brave or very stupid to be going up the mountain this late in the fall. It'll be winter any day now."

"Thank you for your help," Ashton said. He didn't feel like coming up with a story to explain their passage through the mountains. He began to unpack his valuables from the saddle bags in silence.

"Where are you going?" The boy asked.

Before Ashton could tell the boy that it was their business, Celeste spoke up.

"We're going home to my family in Fox Creek. My sister sent a message to let me know that my father is unwell. If we waited until snowmelt in spring, we wouldn't get to say goodbye."

The boy was quiet for a moment. "I'm sorry to hear about your father. Have you been living in the city?"

Celeste nodded. "Went looking for work when I was old enough."

The boy's eyes were wide, he was glued on every word. "That's what I'm going to do. I hear the stories from travelers. I'm going to have some adventures when I'm older."

Ashton couldn't help but smile at the boy. "I'm sure you will. What's your name?"

"Edward, sir," the young man smiled.

Thanks to Celeste's quick thinking, the inn keeper, a woman named Jocelyn, didn't question their late season visit. Celeste had given the name of a town much like this one, that was located on the other side of the mountain. The quickest way to reach it would be to go over the pass. If anybody was going to risk a late season crossing, two kids who grew up on the mountain were likely to make it across unscathed.

"No children yet?" Jocelyn asked as she showed them to their room.

Ashton's eyes widened and he swallowed back the shock that had risen up inside him. The innkeeper thinks they're married.

Celeste didn't hesitate. "No, we've only been married since midsummer."

"Soon, then." She smiled at them and turned a key in a locked door. "Here's your room." Jocelyn stepped back and swept her hand toward the open door. "I'll leave you be. Blessings of the gods on you both."

Ashton nodded to her, unsure of what the correct response was to such words. The woman seemed kind and unlikely to harm them in the night. Nevertheless, he slid the single chair in the room under the doorknob to lock them in.

The room had two narrow beds, a small table, and a chair that was now propped under the doorknob. Without words, Ashton readied himself for bed. Celeste sat on her bed, watching him.

"What are you looking at?" he asked.

"Just waiting for you to start talking."

He dropped onto the other bed, facing Celeste and let out a long sigh. He ran his hands through his hair and thought about how he should proceed.

"That bad?" Celeste asked. Her dark eyebrows were pulled together in concern.

Just start at the beginning. "Turns out Master Flanders has a brother," Ashton said.

Celeste's face twisted in surprise. "Really?"

"He was the guy running that book shop. He told me about the dragon, and said he'd get a message back to him for us."

Celeste hit her forehead with her palm. "I completely forgot we needed to send a message."

"Well, it's taken care of."

She leaned forward on the bed, hands gripping the edges. "What else?"

Ashton looked away from her for a moment and blew out a

breath. He reached behind his neck to unclasp the chain and slid the ring into his palm. He tossed it to Celeste.

She pushed herself off the bed to catch it, sandwiching it between her palms. She opened them and picked up the ring to look at it more closely. Her mouth dropped open and she looked from the ring to Ashton then back again. "Is this what I think it is?"

He looked down at his hands, unable to make eye contact with her. "Yes."

"I - I don't understand." Celeste stood and walked to Ashton's bed. She sat down next to him.

"I wasn't going to do it any time soon. I mean, there's just too much going on right now, but eventually, when things got better..." The words were difficult to say. His mind replayed the last moments with Etta over and over. He straightened, thinking back to the vow he'd made to himself at the bookshop. "I'm going to get her back, Celeste."

Celeste placed a hand on his shoulder. "If you were going to propose to her, why did you break up with her?"

"I thought I had to. Sir Henry told me that it was the only way Gallia would make an alliance and he reminded me of the stupid things Etta has done because of me." Guilt swept through him. Sir Henry did have a point, but he wasn't sure it mattered. If Etta wasn't willing to marry a prince for her throne, he was willing to do whatever it took to be with her.

"So you've been carrying around the ring this whole time?" she asked.

He turned and looked at the ring, sitting in Celeste's open palm. He picked it up and slid it over the top of his finger, spinning it with his thumb. "I gave it to Master Flanders before we left. When I got to the bookshop, Master Flanders' brother had it waiting for me with a note for him to give it to me. No other explanation."

A smile spread across Celeste's face. "You're an idiot, Ashton."

He dropped his hands to the edge of the bed and turned to look at her. "Thanks for the support."

She sighed. "If Master Flanders sent this to you, he's telling you not to give up on her. Which probably means, she hasn't given up on you."

Hearing the words from Celeste made it seem like a real possibility. He closed his fist around the ring, feeling a glimmer of hope. "That's what I was hoping it meant."

"Now you just have to hope she'll forgive you by the time we get back," Celeste said.

He pressed his lips together. "I said some pretty terrible things."

"Then we better get that stone and get back quick so she has less time to think about what you said." Celeste picked up the chain that was sitting on the bed next to Ashton and dropped it in his other hand. "Keep it close to you. If things get bad, you focus on that ring and the fact that you need to get home to give it to her."

Ashton couldn't hold back the smile. What Celeste said made sense. How could he have thought that Etta would ever agree to a marriage alliance after everything she'd fought against with Max? She had traveled to the Oracle, to the underworld, even, to save him when his essence had been sent from his body. His stomach knotted, he felt so stupid for giving her up so easily. Would she understand when he returned? He was determined to earn back her trust. *Forgive me, Etta.*

25

ETTA

The dining room held the largest table I had ever seen in my life. There were twenty-two chairs on each side of the long dark, wooden table and a chair at each end. Only one end of the table was set with plates and silverware and several people were already seated. The maid that had collected me from my room pulled out a chair for me. I sat down and Mari sat next to me. I was seated to the right of my uncle, who occupied the head of the table.

Across from me was an older woman with a pinched looking face. She had straw colored hair piled high on her head and wore a red dress with wide, belled sleeves. It was an unusual design that I had never seen before. Though, I hadn't spent much time around royalty. Perhaps this was what people who lived in castles wore. She had small watery brown eyes that watched my every move. I fidgeted in my chair and shifted my gaze away. Next to the pinched faced woman was a younger girl who looked like a smaller version of Mari. I was guessing she was Lilian.

"Etta," Gaius said, "I'd like you to meet my wife, Yvette and my daughters, Mari and Lilian" He spoked in Illaria again, making it easier for me.

"We already met, father," Mari said.

He set down the goblet he was drinking from. "You did?"

"Yes, I went to her rooms to meet her. She's quite wonderful." Mari beamed.

The way she spoke was as if she forgot I was sitting right next to her. I wasn't sure how to react so I just kept my hands clasped in my lap and smiled.

Servants entered the room and set bowls of steaming, green soup in front of each of us. The people around the table picked up spoons and started to eat. Silence hung heavy in the room. I felt very out of place and longed for something that felt normal.

"Where is Master Flanders?" I asked.

Gaius slurped a spoonful of soup and swallowed. "He requested a meeting with my head sorcerer. I imagine they are still discussing whatever sorcerers talk about." He waved his hand in the air as if sorcerers didn't have anything of import to discuss.

"Head sorcerer?" I asked.

He set down the spoon. "I have much to teach you about ruling a kingdom." He smiled and seemed genuine in his words. "Every king, or in your case, queen, should have sorcerers under their employ. You choose the best one to be your head sorcerer. That person will be your connection to the sorcerers in your kingdom and will serve as an advisor to you."

He paused, and stroked his chin. "Though, I've never heard of a sorcerer ruler with the exception of the current king of Illaira. Most rulers don't formally train as sorcerers. You're apprenticeship is unusual."

"Yes," I said. I folded and unfolded the napkin in front of me. I couldn't tell if he was disappointed by my training in sorcery.

Then I remembered what Mari had said about her father. He didn't have the ability to learn magic. Maybe that was why there had been no other sorcerer rulers. It might not have been a choice.

I looked down at the table and reached for what I hoped was the correct spoon for the soup. I took a bite, surprised to find it sweet rather than savory. My eyes darted around the table as I ate, catching the stares of the women seated around me. They were all watching me. My stomach knotted as I tried to remember all of the etiquette I had learned.

We didn't have much reason for decorum at camp. I refused to let anybody serve me. I wasn't officially queen yet and the people who were fighting alongside me deserved to be treated with respect and dignity. I supposed I'd have to knight them all or something so they could maintain the status I'd afforded them.

My head started to ache as I thought of all of the elements of being a ruler that I hadn't stopped to consider. Decorating castles, maids, head sorcerer, personal guard. Who had time to organize all of these things and keep track of them all?

"Have you considered who you would appoint for your head sorcerer?" Gaius asked.

"What about that Ashton you told me about?" Mari said.

I coughed on the soup in my spoon, spitting it back into the bowl. Yvette crinkled her nose at me. Finding the napkin, I wiped my mouth. "Excuse me."

"Ashton?" Gaius asked. "Not the same Ashton who was Max's apprentice?"

I pushed the soup bowl away from me. "Yes, the same Ashton."

"Have you considered the fact that he might be the traitor you are looking for?" Gaius asked.

My chest felt like somebody much heavier than me was sitting on top of it. I hadn't considered Ashton as a traitor. Ever.

I'd put my faith in him completely. He couldn't be a traitor. He was my closest friend, but still, I had only met him a few months ago when this whole thing started. My blood ran cold. Wasn't it Max who made Ashton teach me magic? And Max sent me with Ashton to the trials. Was it possible I was being blinded by my own emotions?

Before I could say anything, a servant removed the soup bowl from in front of me and a plate of cheese and fruit was placed before me. I stared at the plate, trying to think of how to respond to the confusion in my own head.

"I don't think Ashton could be a traitor after everything you told me about him," Mari said.

I turned to look at her. She popped a grape in her mouth. "If you ask me, he sounded pretty devoted to you."

He was. The anger in his words during our last conversation still haunted me.

"Has he passed his trials?" Gaius asked, ignoring my lack of response.

"Yes," I said. "He helped us to defend the trial site during the attack. He's a brilliant sorcerer."

"I would imagine so," Gaius said. "Having Max as a mentor would go a long way for any sorcerer. I remember watching Max at his trials. Never saw such a young sorcerer put on such a show."

"I was told that Ashton's performance was nearly identical to Max's." After I said the words, I regretted saying them.

Gaius pressed his lips together and sat in silence for a moment. "Might not be the best choice as head sorcerer," he said. He glanced at his daughter. "Mari thinks with her heart first, which is an admirable trait, but it means that she always sees the best of all people. I'm sure she would even be able to find good things about the king of Illaria."

Mari scoffed. "That is not true. I could never see anything

good about that monster. But I do tend to see the good in people." She lifted her chin and looked from her father to me. "And I'm an impeccable judge of character. I've never been wrong."

Gaius pointed his fork at her. "That's true." He took a bite of cheese. "She'll make an excellent queen one day. Who would have guessed that we'd have two queens ruling at the same time?"

Mari smiled. "Father had the laws of succession changed after I was born so that our family line can continue, even if I'm unmarried."

"Though you will be married," Gaius said. "It just means that you are in charge, not the prince of Ocea."

"Yes," Mari said, "he'll have to support what I decide, not the other way around."

"You're marrying the prince or Ocea?" Ocea was a small island country that was rich in minerals and exotic fruits.

"Yes, we've been betrothed since I was born." She covered her mouth with her hand. "I'm so sorry, Etta. It must be so hard for you to not have that alliance established. I heard about what happened with the prince of Sardinia. We cut off all shipments to Sardinia when they joined sides with the king."

I lifted an eyebrow. That was news to me. Everybody always told me that Gallia remained neutral. If they were no longer trading with Sardinia, they were practically shouting their support of me.

"We couldn't support that level of betrayal against somebody who is half Gallic," Gaius said.

Mari set her hand on top of mine. "That's what family does. We look out for each other."

"Thank you." So this is what it feels like to have family. People who look out for you just because you share a history. What would it have been like to grow up with that feeling? I could have been protected and loved. Grown up knowing who I was and learning to control my magic. "Why didn't my parents hide me here?"

"I asked myself that same question every day since I got the news that you were still alive," Gaius said. "From what I can tell, your parents left you with your governess thinking they'd be able to pick you back up in a few months. When they passed, she likely thought it too risky to move you across the border." He frowned. "If we had known you survived, we would have sent men to find you and bring you here."

How different could my life have been? Would I still be willing to fight for my country if I had grown up in the comfort of a castle like this one?

"Why didn't Gallia do anything to stop the duke after he killed my parents?" I asked.

"Without a successor, it would have been difficult to remove the new king. If my sister had asked for aid before the Battle of the Dead, the whole thing might never have happened." He shook his head. "I'm not sure anyone saw it coming."

"What about the White Ravens? Did you know about them?" I asked.

"We did, and we were in communication with them at first. The original goal of the Ravens was to find you, if you were still alive. Once Max joined, they changed their goal to putting him on the throne. I knew Max's story and I didn't want him ruining your family name, so I withdrew support."

I wasn't sure if that made me feel better or worse. It was nice knowing that they wanted to support me, and help me reclaim my throne, but was Max really so bad when compared to King Osbert? I wondered what would have happened if they had rallied behind Max. What if they had gone forward supporting him? Max would probably be on the throne right now. Would I still be living in a cottage with my grandmother? I wouldn't know how to use magic, I wouldn't know the truth about my family, and I would never have met all the amazing people I've gotten to know along the way. People like Ashton. Would my life be any easier? Or would I have grown up without ever shaking that empty feeling I'd had every time I looked at the pendant my grandmother had given me. I resisted the urge to grab hold of it, trying to maintain my composure.

"That's enough politics," Yvette said. She had a thick accent that I couldn't place that made her voice sound deeper and more masculine than most women. Something about her came across as hostile. I hoped today's meal was the only time I'd have to be around her.

Gaius gave her an indulgent smile. "You're right, my dear." He looked at me. "We'll talk more later."

"Lily, you've been quiet," he said. "Why don't you tell Etta about your sorcery training? Etta aligns with water."

Lily's eyes grew wide. "I've never met anyone who aligns with water before. It's very rare. Much more exciting than boring air."

"One of my closest friends aligns with air. It's a very useful alignment." I thought of Celeste traveling through the mountains with Ashton. I felt guilty for focusing so much of my thoughts on Ashton when she was out facing the same dangers as him. "She's from Gallia, too."

"Really?" Lily's eyes lit up. "Is she helping you fight?"

"Yes," I nodded. "She's helping with some very important work for me."

"Maybe you'll have a woman as your head sorcerer," Mari said.

"Don't be ridiculous," Yevette said. "It's bad enough that she's going to be ruling a kingdom without a man at her side. We can't have women in charge of important sorcery matters, too."

Manners forgotten, I glared at her. Some of the best sorcerers I knew were women. In Illaria, it was rare to see women sorcerers, but I thought that they were highly valued members of the sorcery community in Gallia. That was what Celeste had made me believe. How could she say such a thing when she had two daughters?

"Yevette, that's enough," Gaius said. "Etta, please forgive her. She grew up in a very different place than we did."

Yevette stood and threw her napkin on the table. "I'm feeling quite unwell, please excuse me, my lord." She exited the room without looking back.

"She's not my mother," Mari said.

Gaius sighed. "She's my second wife. She seemed so agreeable when we first met. Our customs came as more of a shock to her than she expected, I suppose."

"Where is she from?" I asked.

"She's from Vlausburg."

Vlausburg was at the edge of the known world. It was said to be so cold that the people who lived there could only go outdoors during the short summer season. I'd never met anybody from there. What kind of alliance had he needed with them?

"I know very little about Vlausburg," I said. "I'm afraid my studies have been rather limited."

Servants came again to remove the plates. I set my hand on my plate to prevent the girl in the brown dress from removing it. I hadn't stopped to eat anything. Fresh fruit was a rarity this time of year in Illaria and I planned to eat it. A plate of meat with gravy and potatoes was set next to my fruit plate. I took a bite of the fruit, worried they'd take it if I didn't eat it soon.

"Vlausburg is known for their ships. We haven't been able to duplicate their naval technology. My marriage with Yvette came with several of her countrymen in tow who worked directly with my fleet to improve it. With the coming Darkness, it made sense to prepare as best as we can."

Across the table from me, Lily winced at the mention of the Darkness. I swallowed the last grape on my plate. I could hear everybody chewing their food in the silence. It was clear that this was a subject that made everybody uncomfortable. I wanted to know more about how they were preparing to fight the Darkness, but didn't like how somber the tone of the room had grown.

"Lily," I said, breaking the silence, "do you remember finding out that you aligned with air? I didn't go through the testing as a child."

Lily straightened. "A little bit." She looked over at her father. "I was only four when I went through the test. I do remember being a little bit scared when the box opened. Nobody told me what we were doing, they just asked me to play with the boxes. What happened for you?"

"Oh, I don't know if I want to share my story. It isn't one of my finest moments."

"Please, share," Lily pressed her hands together.

"Yes, I want to hear," Mari said.

I glanced at Gaius. He was smiling at his daughters. The mood of the room had lightened since Yvette left. It was more comfortable.

"Well, it involved lots of failure, my first drink, and almost being killed by the king's guards," I said.

The girls' leaned forward in their seats and I laughed at their eagerness. I told them about sneaking out to the village and drinking my first glass of ale before finally getting an element box to open. They laughed as I recalled the story.

"Then what happened?" Lily asked.

"Well, that's when three members of the king's guard found us."

"What did you do?" Lily rested her chin in her hands, elbows on the table.

"I didn't do much of anything other than hide behind Ashton. He aligns with fire. I'd never seen a sorcerer use their power before that night. He created a wall of flames and took care of all of the guards. It was terrifying and exhilarating all at the same time."

"He took out three guards by himself? Before his trials?" Lily's mouth dropped open.

Ashton and Max were the only fire sorcerer's I knew, I never thought of what they could do as special, but from Lily's expression, I might be wrong. "Yes, this was a few weeks before his trials."

"Wow. All of the fire sorcerers I have trained with couldn't do anything like that. Even right before their trials. Mari's right, he might be a good head sorcerer."

"Isn't it sweet how he saved her life?" Mari said. "He's done it more than once, too."

I flushed. She was right, of course. Ashton had saved my life on multiple occasions.

"Where is Ashton now?" Gaius asked.

My eyes darted around the room. I wasn't sure if I should be giving the specifics of our plan to retrieve the stone.

The hesitation was enough for Gaius to put it together. "I see," Gaius said, "let us hope his habit of saving you is an indication he is loyal to you instead of his former master."

26

ASHTON

A shton woke to the smell of fresh bread. He rubbed his eyes and stretched. Taking a deep breath, he stared up at the ceiling, enjoying a moment of peace in a warm bed. He knew it was going to be the last time for a while that he'd be warm and comfortable.

He turned to see that Celeste was already awake. She was on her side watching him.

"Good morning," he said.

"Morning," she said through a yawn.

He glanced behind him at the small window in the room. Sunlight was already pouring in. They'd slept later than usual. "We better get going if we want to make any progress before it gets dark.'

Celeste pulled the blanket over her head for a minute then threw it aside. She sat up and rubbed her eyes. "We better pack up."

It took them only minutes to dress and gather their few belongings. They headed down the stairs to find the innkeeper busy in the kitchen. She looked up from a pot she was stirring as they entered. "Have a seat, breakfast is ready."

"You didn't need to do all of this for us," Ashton said.

"Just sit and eat. You two have a long journey ahead of you, breakfast is the least we could do." She smiled as she scooped warm porridge into bowls for each of them.

They set their bags against the wall and sat down to eat. The innkeeper disappeared back into the kitchen then came out a few minutes later with a bundle wrapped in cloth. She set it down between them.

"A few loaves of bread. Should help keep you fed while you're on your journey. It's about a week to cross. You'll need to move quickly. Snow will be here any day."

Ashton smiled at her. "Thank you for your hospitality and your kindness. We appreciate it more than you know."

Edward came in through the front door. His pink nose and cheeks indicated that he'd already been outdoors for a while. "Breakfast ready?" he called to his mother.

"Have a seat, Edward. These two'll need your help in a bit to ready their horses." Jocelyn scooped porridge into a bowl for him.

"That's not necessary," Celeste said. "We can take care of our horses."

Jocelyn took a seat next to her son. She brushed his long bangs away from his eyes as he ate. "We might be forgotten by the king out here but we haven't forgotten where true loyalties lie."

Ashton's heart beat picked up in his chest and he had to force his face not to react. They'd been so careful to travel as commoners. Why would she say such a thing?

Jocelyn's gaze traveled to Celeste's hand, raised halfway to her mouth holding her spoon. Celeste put the spoon down in her bowl and clasped her opposite hand over the leather bracelet she was wearing. The Ouroboros burned into it was clearly visible.

How had they overlooked that? Ashton ran his hands through his hair and glanced around the room, wondering if they needed to leave right away.

Jocelyn laughed. "Please, don't worry. I noticed it last night when you arrived. It's why I pretended to believe that ridiculous story of yours. Nobody travels across the mountains to visit a parent this time of year, dying or not."

Celeste started to pull the lacing off of her bracelet to remove it. Jocelyn reached her hand across the table and set it on top of the bracelet. "Leave it on. Nobody will turn you in to the king for wearing it. Besides, the only thing you may encounter after you leave are the king's monsters that live in that castle across the peaks."

Ashton pushed his bowl away, no longer hungry. "You know about that?"

She nodded then turned to Edward. "Son, please go see that their horses are fed and brushed."

Edward crossed his hands over his chest and scowled at his mother. "You're just sending me away so I can't hear what you talk about. I'm almost ten. I'm practically a man."

Jocelyn lifted an eyebrow and pursed her lips. Her expression was enough to send Edward away from the table. He took heavy, stomping footsteps as he left, slamming the door behind him.

Jocelyn's face darkened. "I can only protect him for so long from the truth. I know when he finds out, his childhood will be over."

"What is it?" Celeste asked.

Jocelyn wrung her hands together and looked down for a moment before composing herself. "If you traveled through the village, you'd see that there are no men here. Only women and boys. I didn't even know I was with child when Edward's father was taken from us." She moved her hands under the table and took a few breaths.

"The king came through ten years ago and demanded that all the men follow him into the mountains. Those who resisted were killed and brought along as undead soldiers. They had no choice. He sent his Reapers from home to home, tearing them apart in search of any who looked old enough to pass as a man. Some of them were mere boys of 12 or 13. The king took them all up the pass and none of them returned."

Celeste gasped and covered her mouth with her hand.

Ashton shook his head. Anywhere the king went, he brought terror and tore families apart. He was tired of seeing and hearing the stories of those left in his wake of terror. Getting rid of the Reapers might not put an end to the king, but it would weaken him and that was a start.

"You're going after it, aren't you?" Jocelyn's gray eyes stared into Ashton's. He clenched his jaw and wondered what he should say. If he told her the truth, he might get some information out of her that would help them. But he didn't know this woman and didn't know if she could be trusted.

Jocelyn took his silence for an answer. "They say it's hidden in the castle right outside the Illarian border. They say..." her voice cracked and she wiped away a tear, "that the men he stole from our village are protecting it." Her hand rose to her neck and rested there for a moment while she swallowed back the tears. "They say he turned them all into undead soldiers to guard the stone."

All this time, the women in this village had known where the stone was hidden. The king knew they wouldn't go after it. They wouldn't be able to face their husbands, brothers, and friends to take the stone. They couldn't leave their children unprotected. They might even feel like they are trapped here. The king had created a village of prisoners who guarded his deepest secret. So that was how Master Edward knew. He must have traveled through this village.

"I'm so sorry for everything you've been through," Celeste said.

"Tell me something." Jocelyn wiped her face and sniffed. "Is it true that the heir has returned? Is there hope that my son will get to grow old in a safe kingdom?"

Celeste smiled. "Yes, it's true."

"We're doing everything we can," Ashton said. "Things might get worse before they get better but you should be safe here. It's far enough away from the king's castle."

Jocelyn reached her hands across the table and rested them on top of Ashton's. "Can you do something for me?"

Ashton glanced at Celeste, unsure of how to react. Celeste covered Jocelyn's hands with her own. "What is it?"

Jocelyn looked from Ashton to Celeste, then back again. "If you come across the men from our village, kill as many of them as you can. Nobody deserves to be serving another after death."

Ashton leaned across the table so his face was a few inches away from Jocelyn's. "That," he said, "I can promise you."

HORSES READY, Ashton and Celeste waved goodbye to their hosts and rode through the quiet village. There were not many people out but those they did see were all women. Heat rose in Ashton's stomach as he recalled the night his own mother was ripped from him. The Reapers had to be stopped. Tightening his legs around the horse, he picked up the pace. They rode out of the village and onto the rocky pass toward the summit of the mountain. It would be several days to the top.

The pass was steep and only allowed for one horse at a time and could only be traveled on by daylight. This time of year, darkness set in early so they would have to go as quickly as possible during the time they had.

The first two days they made excellent progress. The terrain was difficult, but the horses handled it well. They found streams to keep the horses in fresh water and grass for them to eat. They slept on a bed of dry pine needles and listened to the sound of the nighttime insects and animals as they settled down for the evening.

On the third day, the trail grew steeper and the horses struggled to find solid footing. Their progress slowed. By the time they stopped to make camp that night, they found that the vegetation they had relied on had changed. Instead of trees, they were now surrounded by low shrubs and rocks. Their breath came out in clouds as the temperature dropped.

Ashton broke out some oats they had packed for the horses and shared the remaining bread with Celeste while a rabbit cooked over the fire. They didn't talk much when they stopped. Ashton felt his chest growing heavier with each passing day. They were getting closer to the castle and facing whatever protections the king had in place. The sword Thomas gave him was sitting next to him on the ground. He picked it up and looked at the reflection of the bade in the firelight. How was he going to defeat the king's undead guards?

"Think we'll be at the top tomorrow?" Celeste asked.

Ashton set down the sword. "Might be. We won't be able to stop at the top. It'll be too cold up there to camp. We'll have to summit and descend a bit before nightfall."

Celeste was quiet for a few minutes. She turned the rabbit over the fire. Fat dripped from it making the fire crackle and sizzle. The smell of cooking meat should have made Ashton feel hungry, but his appetite was gone. He didn't know if it was from the altitude or the impending battle.

"I'm scared, Ashton."

"Me too," he said. "We don't know what to expect. That's what makes it so challenging. But we can do this. We have to." His fingers found the ring on the chain around his neck.

"She's going to be so happy to see you when we get back," Celeste said.

He dropped the ring and reached for a stick to poke around in the fire. He wasn't so sure about that, he'd said some terrible things. Would she understand what he had been trying to do? "You think so?"

Celeste smiled. "Yes. You two are perfect together."

"She'll have to forgive me, first." Ashton poked at the rabbit. "I think it's done."

Celeste pulled the rabbit down and set it on a flat rock so it could cool a little.

"You know," Celeste said as she handed Ashton a steaming piece of rabbit. "She won't be able to forgive you if you don't forgive yourself."

Ashton ignored her as he ate his food. The guilt of listening to Sir Henry and breaking Etta's heart was eating away at him. He should have refused, he should have fought for her. How had he been so quick to let her go? It was going to take a lot of work to be able to forgive himself for making that mistake. He wasn't sure he'd be able to do it until he'd won Etta back. After a few bites, he looked at Celeste. "I'll take first watch, why don't you get some rest."

They kept the fire burring through the night. The chances of somebody finding them in the mountains was slim so the fire was worth the risk. While Celeste slept, Ashton pulled the ring out from its place behind his tunic and held it in his fingers. He could just barely make out the engraving on the sides. One half of the ring had flames and the other half had tiny snowflakes. He knew they hadn't know each other long, but he couldn't imagine life without her. When he had seen the work of a jeweler in a town near the Raven camp, he knew he had to have a ring made for Etta. It wasn't gold, it didn't have any precious gems, but it was so much more than that. It represented the two of them. His fire and her ice. It was a testament to how they came together, how their powers combined when the kissed. Tucking the ring back under his tunic he thought about Celeste's words. Could he forgive himself?

Sitting alone in the dark gave him too much time alone with his thoughts. Finally, it was time to wake Celeste. He pulled a blanket up over him and fell into a dreamless sleep.

27

ETTA

" A nd this is the ballroom," Mari threw open the double doors, revealing a huge room with a polished wood floor. "This is where we have parties. All of the chandeliers are lit and it's just beautiful."

"I'm sure it is," I said. After breakfast, I'd agreed to let Mari show me around her home. The castle was full of elaborate and beautiful rooms. I had a hard time grasping why one would need so much space. "Is it just your family that lives here?"

We walked down the marble hallway, Mari leading me to our next stop. "There's us, some high-ranking members of the court, and our servants. There's even a wing for the sorcerers and our highest-ranking guards. Though, they sometimes stay with family members when they aren't needed here."

She stopped walking. "You know, none of them have gone home since we found out about you. I'm not allowed to be part of the high council meetings until I turn eighteen. But I can tell they're planning something."

"Maybe they're worried the king will try to come here?" I suggested. As soon as the words were out of my mouth, I knew it was the truth. Why else secure an alliance with Sardinia? Why else use me to make the Darkness stronger? The king had to be planning to do what he did to Illaria in other kingdoms. Why hadn't I seen it sooner?

Mari took a deep breath. "I think you're right." She looked down, then back up at me. "You know, a lot of people around here don't take me seriously. They speak to me like I'm fragile, like I don't understand what is in store for me when I become queen. With the exception of fighting, I was educated like any prince would be."

She took my hand in hers. "You and I are coming into power in dark times. I'm glad we'll have each other."

I smiled at her. I knew too well what it was like to be treated as if I wasn't capable of the job we had been born into. "You're going to make an amazing queen."

"Your highness?"

We both turned to see a guard standing behind us.

"Yes?" Mari said.

The guard bowed. "Pardon the intrusion, but the king has asked for a word with our guest in his study."

"Thank you." Mari turned from the guard to me. "I'll show you where it is."

I SAT in a high backed wooden chair in front of a fireplace. Gaius' study was large but felt cozy. The walls were lined with panels of dark wood and plush carpets covered the entire floor. A huge desk positioned in front of three windows took up a quarter of the room.

"I've asked to meet you in private so we can discuss the conditions of our treaty and the details of your request for aid." Gaius leaned back in his chair and rested his hands on the arm rests.

"Thank you," I said.

"We'll have to meet with my council to draw up the formal documents, but I know this process is new to you. I didn't want to overwhelm you and thought you might want to know what to expect."

I felt like I was in over my head. "I appreciate that. Anything you can teach me will be invaluable."

He smiled. "I want you to know that I fully support you. I want to see you back on the throne. As a king, it benefits my country to have you in charge over that monster who currently sits on the throne. As an uncle, I want my sister's legacy to be secured."

I smiled and took another sip of tea. I wasn't sure how to respond.

He moved his hands to his knees and leaned toward me. "This is what I have in mind. I'd like to see us draw up a treaty that establishes trade benefits for both of our countries and begins the process of forming a true alliance. Our army would be at your service, and once you establish yours, you'd be expected to return the favor if we are in need. This will only help us as we prepare for the Darkness. Combining our efforts may help us destroy it sooner."

"That sounds fair," I said.

He leaned in. "There's more. I'd like to propose that once we recover from the Darkness, we declare war on Sardinia."

I SPENT the afternoon alone in my rooms. Walking from one room to the next, I tried to clear my head. You have to focus. In the wake of Gaius' request to form an alliance against Sardinia, I'd felt the Darkness creeping into me. It seemed to enjoy the idea of starting a war against a country that had been, for the most part, peaceful.

I could see where Gaius was coming from. The king of Sardinia had broken the engagement between his son and myself and aligned themselves with the king of Illaira. In doing that, he'd taken sides, denying my rightful claim to the throne. Part of me wanted to see him suffer for the betrayal and I could feel the Darkness encouraging those thoughts. Pushing them aside was getting more challenging.

They didn't betray you, they betrayed Max. I had to remind myself that when Sardinia turned against us, they thought Max would take the throne. Had the king told them the truth about Max's mother? Or did they just think we didn't stand a chance at succeeding?

Light danced across the ceiling and I turned to look out the window. The sun was low in the horizon, creating a sparkling blanket over the ocean. Pressing my face against the glass, I took a few deep breaths. If I wanted to reclaim my throne, I needed the Gallic army. That was what my advisors had said. Though one of my advisors is a traitor.

I rubbed my temples. I wasn't even officially queen yet, and the pressure was wearing on me. There were so many things to consider. I stretched my legs out on the window seat and leaned against the wall. The waves were peaceful and moved like a melody. My whole body relaxed as I watched the rise and fall of the water. I wanted to bottle them and bring them back home with me. Could I even call that little tent I slept in my home? It was home for now. Home. Where I'd have to find out who had betrayed me within my own council. Home. Where Ashton won't be waiting for me.

I hugged my knees to my chest and rested my head on them. I'd been so busy trying to be strong for everybody else lately that I hadn't let myself think about how I was feeling. Planning a war against the man who killed my parents was overwhelming. So many people around me seemed to forget that it wasn't just about the throne. It wasn't just about the kingdom. For me, it was personal. The king had to pay for what he did to my family. I'm going to make him pay. A wave of anger flowed through me. I dropped my knees and jumped to standing. If declaring war on Sardinia was the cost of revenge, I was willing to pay that price.

GAIUS WAS SEATED behind the massive desk in his study, bent over a pile of papers. I knocked on the open door to announce my presence. He looked up and set down the paper he'd had in his hands. "Come in." He gestured to the chair across from him.

I walked in, fists clenched, feeling determined. Sitting down on the edge of the chair, I straightened my shoulders and lifted my chin. I needed to look as confident as I felt. "What do we do with Sardinia after we defeat them?" I asked.

A wide smile spread across his face and he folded his hands in front of him. "We determine how we want to divide the territory between us and instate our own governors to oversee it in our stead."

"Fine," I nodded. "Let's draw up the paperwork,"

"Do you have a preference on division of territory?" he asked.

"Without my own council present, it will be difficult for me to make that decision. What about having two governors over the territory but an equal division of resources from both that we divide? That way both Illaria and Gallia will benefit from the entirety of Sardinia."

"Wise decision, your highness," Gaius said. "I'll have my council draw up the document this evening and we can finalize it tomorrow afternoon."

I stood. "Thank you."

"Etta?" Gaius called.

I turned around and waited.

"Tomorrow morning I'd like you to meet with the captain of

my guard. He's selected a few men that he thinks would be perfect for your personal guard."

"I look forward to it." I dropped in a simple curtsey, then left the room.

What had I done? I agreed to declaring war on another country in exchange for an army. My head spun as I walked down the long hallway. I dragged my fingers over the smooth, stone wall, only partially noticing the paintings along the way.

This is the right thing to do. I told myself over and over again that it was worth it to get back my throne. Perhaps Sardinia would surrender and we could minimize the loss of life. *You could be queen in two kingdoms.* Joy crept into my body with the thought and for a moment, I relished the idea. *Those that underestimated you would see how powerful you really are.* I smiled. What would the people who didn't believe in me think after I claimed Illaria and half of Sardinia? I shook my head, this was the Darkness talking. I wasn't even sure how I was going to rule one kingdom, let alone a foreign land that I agreed to help conquer by force? What had I done?

Leaning against the wall, I took a few deep breaths. The sound of footsteps echoed around me. Somebody was coming down the hallway. I wasn't sure I was ready to talk to anyone at the moment. I worried they'd be able to tell what I had done. There was only one person I wanted to see and that was impossible. Instead of waiting to see who the footsteps belonged to, I headed in the opposite direction, toward my rooms.

The peace and quiet of my rooms didn't last long. A knock on the door sounded only moments after I closed the door behind me. I hesitated, wondering if I should ignore the knock.

Before I could make up my mind, the door swung open and Master Flanders filled the doorframe, a frown etched on his face.

He looked disappointed in me. He must have already heard

about the treaty. I tried to hide the anxiety in my face and straightened my posture, then stood silently, waiting for him to criticize me.

Closing the door behind him, he walked into the room. His dark blue robes trailed behind him over the floor as he walked. Finding a seat, he nodded toward an empty chair.

I obeyed the silent command. This felt too familiar. Like my grandmother had just discovered that I ate sweets before dinner and tried to hide it from her.

His hands rested on the arms of the chair and he looked me up and down. It was as if he was trying to decide what to say.

My mouth felt dry. I licked my lips and braced myself for a lecture.

"You met with King Gaius," he said.

"I did."

"You've decided you're ready to become a queen and a conqueror?" His tone was even, making it difficult to read.

"My advisors agreed that I need the Gallic army to win against the king. I did what was necessary." My voice wavered as I spoke the words, showing my lack of confidence.

He let out a long sigh. "I will stand by your decisions. However, you need to be able to stand by them, too."

My brow furrowed in confusion.

"Once you make a choice, you have to be prepared to defend it. Don't ever let anyone see you question your decisions. You have decided to do this so you have to own it."

This wasn't the conversation I expected to be having. Scolding, perhaps, but not for what I'd done.

"Having the support of the Gallic army will help our cause." He clasped his hands and rested them on his stomach. "However, King Gaius wants more power."

I bit down on my lip. Had I given him too much power?

"Sardinia did wrong you so I don't disagree with your

actions. I will support you." He leaned toward me. "But you have to hold firm. This is your first big, public decision. All eyes will be watching to see what you do. Do not let anyone tell you the choice you made was wrong. Do not let them talk you out of it. You need to show them that you are the queen and what you say goes."

I swallowed and nodded. Declaring war on another kingdom was something I never thought I'd do, yet I understood the importance of it. What I hadn't considered was the fact that people would be looking to see how I reacted to such a decision. It was big. I would be signing a treaty as the queen of Illaria. They were counting on me winning back my throne and helping them fight Sardinia. Flutters filled my stomach. Hadn't everybody been saying that with an army, we could win? I wanted this. I wanted to defeat the king and reclaim my birthright. But it had never felt truly real until that moment.

28

ASHTON

C eleste woke Ashton at first light. His nose felt frozen and he rubbed it with his fingers to bring back the feeling. They ate the remaining rabbit and some dried fruit they had brought with them before heading out.

"I hope we reach the summit today," Celeste called to Ashton as they slowly made their way up the rocky trail.

"We have to be close," Ashton said. The shrubs kept getting smaller and less frequent. He knew that there would be little to no vegetation at the top of the peak so he welcomed the sight.

As the sun reached its midpoint, Ashton could see the rocky summit. He smiled and urged his horse forward. They were so close.

His horse slowed as they reached the top, tired from the climb. He dismounted and Celeste followed. They struggled to walk against the wind. It whipped at his cloak, burned his cheeks and nose and made his eyes water. "We should walk with the horses until we find them some water on the way down," Ashton said.

Celeste nodded and pulled her hood up tighter on her face. They made their way over the rocky, barren summit of the peak and found the trail that led them down. Ashton stood next to his horse, reins in hand as he carefully led her down the steep decline. The trail was almost too narrow for him to walk next to his horse. A few times, he felt her slip and worried she'd fall off the trail, but she managed to keep her balance.

After an hour of walking, the shrubs thickened around them and they could see trees in the distance. "Keep an eye out for signs of water," Ashton called.

They were nearly to the tree line when a deafening roar filled the air. The horses reared up onto their back legs and whinnied in distress. Looking around, Ashton couldn't see anything that could have made such a noise. Then, out of nowhere, the hair on the back of his neck stood on end and a shiver ran down his spine. His eyes darted from side to side, seeking the source of the terror that was coursing through his body. He hadn't felt anything like this since they saw the dragon smoke.

The roar came again, this time accompanied by a flapping noise. A shadow crossed over the sun and he looked up to see a beast with wings that would span a village. Its body was large and muscular, ending in a tail covered in long spikes. Horns rose from the monster's head and it opened its mouth letting out a cry that sent a chill right to his bones. Ashton was staring up at a massive red dragon. His hands trembled. This had to be the dragon that had destroyed most of Canton. He should run, but he found himself frozen in place, unable to take his eyes off of the beast.

It passed over them again, sending their horses into a frenzy. Ashton tried to hold on to the reins and calm his horse, but she pulled away from him and ran for the trees, Celeste's mare following behind his own. He wanted to run after the horses but knew there wasn't much they could do if the dragon was here for them.

The dragon swooped down and Ashton noticed that there was a person on top of the dragon. Not possible. Dragon riders were a myth. He squinted at the dragon. There was a person riding it. Somebody was telling the dragon what to do. Finally starting to regain his senses, he reached behind him and unsheathed the sword on his back. He held it in front of him with both hands.

The dragon landed near the trees. Close enough that they could see its large snout and spiked neck, but far enough that they couldn't make out the details of the person on the dragon.

Celeste put her hand on his shoulder. "Somebody's on that dragon."

Ashton gripped the sword tighter. "I know."

Dressed in black from head to toe, the figure dismounted and began to walk toward them. As the rider grew closer Ashton recognized the posture and the movement of his walk. Max. How was this possible? How did Max end up on a dragon?

Ashton lowered the sword. He knew he wouldn't strike him without trying to find out what he was doing with a dragon. Max lowered the hood of his cloak and smiled at them.

Celeste gasped. "It can't be. How is this possible?"

"Well, well, well," Max said. "Imagine my surprise seeing the two of you here."

"There's no way this was a surprise," Ashton said. "How did you know we'd be here? And where did you get a dragon?"

Max stopped in front of them and pulled black gloves off of his hands, tucking them into a pocket of his cloak. "The dragon is a friend of mine. She's going to help me defeat the king. We're on the same side, you and me. With her, the king won't stand a chance."

"So you're going to betray him just like you betrayed us?" Celeste said. She took a few steps closer to him, her hands were clenched into fists. She looked like she wanted to hit him. Part of

Ashton hoped she did, but he knew that would be a mistake. He stepped in front of her, putting himself between her and Max.

"I never betrayed you. I was the one who was betrayed. The plan was always for me to take the throne. I'm continuing on my plan." He turned to Ashton. "It's not too late for you to be on the winning side of this. After all those dragon stories around the campfire, you of all people, know the power of these beasts. The Ravens have no hope of beating the king, we never really did. But now, I've got the power we need to win."

Ashton glared at Max. "You know I'd never betray Etta."

"Still in love with her?" Max laughed. "I'm sure she's agreed to marry some Gallic noble by now. She's been in Gallia for a week already. Probably attending parties and meeting all of the eligible bachelors her uncle throws at her. You think she'll turn that down for you? A penniless sorcerer? It was one thing to believe she'd stay with you when she didn't know any better, but now that she's had a taste of the good life, how could she go back to living in a tent and associating with commoners?"

Ashton's breathing grew rapid and he clenched his jaw. He didn't know how to respond to Max's taunts. He would never help Max after everything he did to Etta, but he couldn't help but wonder how much truth there was to his words. "I've ended things with her but that doesn't mean I can't help the rightful ruler take back the throne."

"She'll never keep it. Even if you were to succeed, she can't hold that throne. But I can. Especially with a dragon by my side."

Ashton shook his head feeling disgusted. Max had been his mentor and his friend. He'd trusted him with his life and then he'd almost taken it from him. "How can you even ask me to join you after what you did to me?

"Still upset about that?" Max sighed. "You need to get over it. You're fine. I wouldn't have let you die."

"If you're going to kill us, you might as well get it over with," Celeste said.

"Ah yes, the sidekick," he said to Celeste. "You've been keeping busy the last few weeks. Secret late-night meetings with a certain new addition to the Raven camp. You'd think he would have waited the appropriate mourning period before moving on to a new girl."

Celeste's cheeks burned crimson and she lunged at Max.

Ashton pulled Celeste back.

Max laughed. "You should be nice to me, I'm here to help you get the stone."

"How do you know about that? Or about what goes on at Camp?" Ashton asked.

"You think I don't have people at the camp who are loyal to me? It was my camp long before it was Etta's."

"We're not going to let you have the stone," Celeste said.

"You are missing the point, here," Max said. "I don't want the stone. I want to help you get it. I want the king to lose his power. He'll be easier for me to defeat if he doesn't have his Reapers. And I don't want them. Those undead monsters can go back to where they came from for all I care. You can keep the stone, do whatever you want with it."

Ashton tightened his grip on the sword in his hand, trying to determine the hidden meaning in Max's words. What was his endgame? Why would he want to see the Reapers out of the king's hands so badly that he would be willing to help the Ravens? "I'm not going to join you so you can either kill me or you can leave."

Max smiled. "I'll bring a little firepower to the castle on my way out. It'll take care of some of the undead guards before you get there. Do what you want with the stone." He turned and took a few steps away then stopped. Looking over his shoulder he called out, "You're on the list as a guest for my wedding. Hope you can make it."

Ashton's insides burned with anger as he watched Max climb back onto the dragon. He didn't move until the huge beast was out of sight. "We have to get that stone and get back," Ashton said.

"We'll have to go the rest of the way on foot," Celeste said. "Good thing we can teleport back. She held up a red coin in her fingers. "Kept it in a pocket just in case."

Ashton set down his sword and grabbed her in a hug, picking her up and spinning her in a circle. "You clever girl. I knew there was a reason I kept you around." He set her down and slid the sword into its sheath on his back. "Let's get this over with."

The two of them hiked along the trail, arms out for balance. Going down seemed like it should be easier, but with all of the loose rocks, it was more of a challenge. They stopped after a few hours to catch their breath. Ashton pulled his boots off and shook some pebbles out of them. "I don't understand how these even got in my boots."

Celeste laughed. "You have a special talent, I guess. I don't have any rocks in my boots." She took a few steps away from him, into the trees. "I think I hear water. Come on."

Ashton followed her into the trees, trying to hear what she heard. He could hear the wind moving through the pine trees and birds singing. A few small animals scampered through the fallen needles. Their boots crunched over pinecones as they walked deeper into the woods. He was just about to tell her to turn back when he heard the sound of rushing water. In front of them, a fast moving stream cut through the trees.

Celeste jumped in excitement. "See those foamy areas?" She pointed to the bubbly patches of water over the rocks.

"Yes," Ashton said, "I see them."

"I might be able to catch us some fish." She looked up to the sky. The sun was low in the horizon already and the evening chill was starting to set in. "Can you build us a fire? Probably wouldn't hurt to stop here for the night."

"I miss summer," Ashton said, "we'd still have hours of light."

"Though, without the horses, we might be able to get in a few extra hours if we are careful where we step."

Ashton shook his head. "It's not worth risking injury to get there a day earlier. We wouldn't be able to make up enough time to make that much of a difference. I'll take care of the fire."

He walked away from the stream and found a flat space where he could build them a fire. He pushed the pine needles that covered the ground out of the way and set to work finding rocks to form a perimeter.

A strong fire crackled in the circle of stones when Celeste arrived back with four large, silver fish. Each fish would easily feed two hungry people. "Are we expecting company?" Ashton asked.

She shrugged. "Wasn't sure how hungry we'd be. It might be a while before we eat again."

Ashton's shoulders fell as he realized how true that was. Without their horses, they didn't have the supplies they had carefully packed to help them make this journey safer. They'd have no blankets tonight and no spare water or food. They'd have to rely on finding it along the way. He counted the days as best he could in his head, trying to figure out how long it had taken them to reach the summit. Was it five days? Six? Less? Everything seemed to blend together. And that had been on horseback. Walking would be slower. He frowned.

"What is it?" Celeste said, looking up from the fish she was gutting with a pointed stick.

"I was trying to figure out how long it might take us to reach the castle from here," Ashton sat down on a pile of pine needles.

"Without the horses, it will take us longer. We might need that extra few hours of time."

Celeste shoved a stick inside the fish, set it over the fire to roast then started to work on the next one. "We'll move faster tomorrow," she said. "We might even be as fast as if had horses. These downhills would have been tricky for them."

Ashton leaned back against a tree and listened to the fire. The smell of roasting fish filled the air. All he could think about was Etta surrounded by admirers, dressed like a queen. How could she be happy back in her tent after staying in the luxury of a castle? He needed to see her again. He covered his face with his hands. Would she want to see me? Either way, they had to find this stone quickly and get it back to the camp.

29

ASHTON

C eleste awoke Ashton right as the sky began its shift from black to gray. He rubbed his hands over his arms, trying to bring warmth into his body. "That's another benefit of getting down this mountain," he said. "The lower we get, the warmer it'll get."

"Until it starts snowing," Celeste said.

Ashton picked up the sword from the ground and sheathed it behind him. "Don't remind me."

Celeste kicked some dirt over the fire's meager remains. "Ready?"

They ate leftover fish as they walked back toward the pass. In the faint light of early morning, they had to tread carefully to avoid holes or large rocks.

"You think Max really stopped by the castle with his dragon?" Celeste asked.

"No idea," Ashton said. "I still can't figure out why he does most of the things he does."

"He wants you on his side, that's pretty clear," Celeste said.

"I don't understand it, though. He's the leader of the Order of the Dragon. He has several other fire sorcerers who will help him. I'm not that special."

Celeste sighed. "You're missing the big picture. He needs to remove Etta as a threat to the throne. Controlling you is a good way to control her."

Ashton stopped walking. It did seem like the only possibility that would explain why Max kept returning to Ashton. "If that's why he keeps coming after me, that means whoever is informing him either doesn't know about what happened between us, or they are close enough to Etta that they think she's still in love with me."

"True," Celeste said. "It wasn't public knowledge that you two broke up. Could be anybody in the camp, really. She probably hid it from everybody."

Ashton starting walking again. "I can't stand this feeling of being so powerless. We can't get news to the camp, we can't do anything to stop Max. Maybe we should just go back, skip this stupid stone."

Celeste stopped walking this time.

Ashton knew he didn't really mean it. He knew how important the stone was to remove the king from power. "Look, I -"

Celeste was pointing. His eyes moved from her outstretched finger and his breath caught in his chest. Relief washed over him as he stared at the castle in the distance. They were almost there. The relief turned to fear. They'd have to battle whatever the king had hidden in that castle very soon.

"I'd say we're still a half day's walk, at least," Celeste said.

Ashton glanced at her. "I don't want to enter that castle in the dark."

"Me neither. Let's cut through the woods and get as close as we can then make camp. We'll try to find food and get some rest so we are prepared for it in the morning."

Ashton nodded. They left the pass for the woods. Now that

they knew the location of the castle, they didn't have to stay to the main road. They just needed to continue south toward their destination. Tomorrow was the day they'd be testing their skills. Were they good enough to defeat whatever waited for them?

NIGHT FELL TOO QUICKLY. Ashton and Celeste settled in between the trees.

"What do you think we'll find tomorrow?" Celeste asked after what seemed like hours of silence.

Ashton had been staring at the orange and yellow tongues of flame eating away at the wood in their fire. He took a deep breath. "I'm not sure. But I'll probably need that sword."

Celeste poked a stick into the fire, causing the wood to shift and crumble. She jumped as the sparks flew. "Maybe we need a plan."

Ashton wondered how you make a plan for something that you have no knowledge of. They didn't know the layout of the castle, they didn't know if they would encounter threats outside of it or only on the inside. They didn't even know where the stone was being kept.

Maybe having some idea of what they were going to do would help. "We can make a plan, but we have to be willing to change it if it doesn't work."

Celeste dropped the stick into the fire. "Agreed."

"Any ideas?" Ashton asked.

"I was hoping you'd have some."

Ashton laughed. "How did we end up on this trip in the first place? What were we thinking?"

Celeste joined in, covering her mouth to stifle her giggles. She caught her breath and wiped a tear from her eye. "I've been wondering that since we lost our horses. I kept telling myself that if the others thought we could do it, we must be the right people for the job. But when Max showed up, I don't know, I just started to question everything."

"Everything?" Ashton asked.

She nodded. "Yes, everything. Like how we are going to get this stone. And how we're going to defeat the king and Max. Especially now that Max has a dragon." She hugged her knees to her chest. "Ashton, what are we doing?"

Ashton had been asking himself some of those same questions. But when he stopped to consider the alternative, living in a world where the king stayed in power, or Max took the throne, he didn't see much of a choice. "Have you thought about what it would be like if we failed?"

Celeste was quiet for a moment. "I suppose the king will stay in power. Or Max would take over."

"You can go back, Celeste," Ashton said, "but this is my home. If we don't succeed, my home will not be safe for anybody. People are scared. People are dying." He shook his head. "What kind of person would I be if I gave up without trying?"

Celeste dropped her legs to the ground. "You're right, you know, I could go home. But you and Etta are my family. I won't turn my back on either of you."

Ashton smiled. "So we're going through with this, plan or no plan?"

Celeste raised her hands over the fire to warm them then crossed them over her chest. Her face grew serious. "We're not just going through with this. We are going to succeed, no matter the cost." She reached into her pocket and pulled out the coin. "Just in case, I want you to know where I'm keeping it. No matter what happens, we get that stone back to Etta. Agreed?" She put the coin back in her pocket.

Ashton clenched his jaw as he took in the seriousness of her comment. "I'm with you."

ASHTON WOKE to a strange pulling sensation behind his head. His heart thumped loudly in his chest and he looked around for any sign of movement. It was quiet. He shivered. Celeste had fallen asleep and the fire was down to the last few smoking embers.

Maybe I'm imagining things. He rubbed his eyes and pulled his hands into his sleeves to keep his fingers warm. He should be upset with Celeste for falling asleep during her watch, but he couldn't really blame her. Neither of them had been sleeping well on the mountain. Pulling his knees to his chest, he figured he'd stay awake until sunrise and let her get some rest.

A breeze went past his ear. He tensed. It had only gone past his ear. That's not how wind works. He put his hand around the hilt of the sword and held it close. Something was out there.

"Celeste." Ashton shook her gently.

She woke with a start. "I fell asleep?" She covered her face with her hands, "I'm so sorry, Ashton." She noticed the sword in his hand. "What is it?"

"Not sure yet," he said. "But I don't think we're alone."

Celeste sat on her knees, hands on her thighs. She looked around them. "I don't see anything."

"I felt something," Ashton said. He looked to the sky, trying to find the moon. "How much time do you think we have until sunrise?"

Celeste looked up. "Two hours, maybe."

Ashton stood and offered his hand to Celeste, pulling her up. "We should get moving. We can get closer to the castle and go in right at dawn."

"You want to walk through the woods in the dark?" Celeste asked. "Is that safe?"

Ashton kicked dirt over their fire to put out the lingering embers. "Probably just as safe as staying here. Whatever is in the woods knows we're here already. It's better if we can just get this over with."

The sun was finally beginning its climb and the early dawn light filtered through the canopy of trees. Ashton headed through the woods toward the castle with Celeste right behind. Pinecones crunched under their feet and they had to push branches out of their way as they walked. If anybody was waiting for them, they would have no trouble hearing them approach.

They were getting closer to the castle but still couldn't see it yet. The lingering tingle of magic spread through Ashton's fingers. He stopped walking and put his arm out to stop Celeste. "Do you feel that?"

"Yes, do you think whatever you felt before followed us?"

"This is different," Ashton said. He took a few tentative steps forward and sniffed the air. Something had changed. The clean scent of the woods mingled with a touch of something else. Sulfur. He moved forward and came to the edge of a deep gorge. Across the gorge, they could see the castle. Red and gold shimmered inside the clouds of smoke rising from it. A dragon had attacked the castle.

Ashton ran his hand though his hair while he stared at the destruction in front of him. For a moment, he wasn't sure what to think. It didn't seem real. Why help them? "Max did it."

"Do you think he took the stone?" Celeste asked.

Ashton shook his head. "He said he didn't want it. I believe him. I didn't think he'd actually attack the castle, though."

"He wants you to know he really is openly opposing the king," Celeste said.

"I guess so."

They both stared at the smoking building for several minutes, transfixed. "What should we do now?" Celeste asked.

"We move forward. Find a way across and get the stone. Hope we can get out of there before Max comes back."

"This is turning out more complicated than I thought it would be," Celeste said. "What ever happened to just battling the undead?"

"Etta happened." He thought about how different things were from what he imagined. "I thought I'd see Max on the throne by now."

"When you put it that way," Celeste pushed her sleeves up, "bring on the dragon. I'll take Etta on the throne over Max any day."

30

ETTA

T he next morning, true to his word, Gaius took me to meet the captain of his guard.

"Antoine," Gaius said, "I'd like to introduce you to her highness, Elisabetta, Queen of Illaria."

Antoine was an imposing figure. I could see why Gaius had him as captain. He was so tall that he probably had to duck when he went through doorways. His uniform clung to the muscles on his arms and chest, showing his sheer bulk. I wondered how much he ate at meals. He was easily the largest man I had ever seen.

"Nice to meet you, Antoine." I inclined my head toward the man and he bowed to me.

"It's an honor, your highness," he said in a thick, Gallic accent. "The king tells me you are in need of a personal guard of your own."

"That's correct," I nodded once.

"I have a few men that I would like to introduce you to. I think they would be an excellent fit for service at your court." He turned to walk and I followed behind him.

We entered an open-air courtyard lined with colonnades on

all four sides. Water rushed from a fountain in the center of the courtyard making the space feel cooler and more peaceful than the rest of the castle. A breeze blew through the courtyard, filling the air with the scent of lavender. How I wished I could just sit on the edge of the fountain and lose myself in the sound of the water.

Antoine took us past the fountain to the opposite end of the courtyard where six men stood in line. They had their chins up, chests out, and arms at their sides in identical precision. Each of them had their eyes fixed on a point directly in front of them. Antoine led us to them and stopped. He saluted them and they returned his salute with sharp, direct movements.

Antoine spoke, "Men, this is Queen Elisabetta. She is here to evaluate you to see if any of you meet her expectations to become a member of her personal guard."

Antoine stepped behind me, leaving me right in front of the men. Gaius leaned over to me. "You can speak to them. Ask questions, get to know them. Whatever you'd like."

I pushed the curls out of my face and walked up and down the line looking at the men who stood alert and unmoving. They were all young. Most of them my age or close to it. They all stood at least a head taller than me and had broad, muscled shoulders. Despite their posture and uniforms, they were different looking enough that I would easily be able to tell them apart. That was a relief. In their matching uniforms, I was worried I would struggle knowing who was who. I stopped walking and stood in front of the man on one end of the line. I should probably ask some questions or something. What does one ask potential guards?

"You can relax," I began. They didn't move. Did they speak Illarian? I tried Gallic. They seemed to ease up a little when I made the switch. "Do you speak Illarian?" I asked.

One of the men took a step forward. "We all speak Illarian

though some of us have not been speaking it for very long." He had no trace of an accent and spoke clearly and without any hesitation.

"You're very well spoken," I said.

"Thank you, your highness," he said. "I received lessons in Illarian very young. Some of us do, some of us don't learn until we join the guard."

"What is your name?"

"Charles, your highness."

"Thank you, Charles." I turned so I could see all of the men in the line. "My uncle and his captain have assured me that you are highly qualified, so I do not doubt your abilities. My question for you all is simple. Do you wish to serve me?" I put my hand out to stop them from speaking.

"Before you answer," I lowered my hand, "consider that if you serve me, you'll be leaving your home. You'll be in my household and I will consider all of you to be loyal Illarians. We have a long road ahead of us and I cannot be sure of when or if you will be able to return to your home. You have to be willing to leave it behind."

The men were silent.

"If you would like to stay here, I understand," I said.

Charles stepped forward. "Your highness, I'm an orphan." He turned to Gaius and bowed. "I mean no disrespect to my home country, but there's nothing for me here. I would be honored to accept a position in your personal guard."

I smiled. I liked this guard. Something about him made me feel comfortable. "Thank you, Charles, I'm happy to have you."

The other five men stepped forward. One after another, they pledged allegiance to me and my kingdom. I was overwhelmed. Six men who didn't know me were voluntarily agreeing to leave everything behind to protect me. "Thank you," I said. "You are all the highest-ranking members of my service and will be welcomed into our country with open arms."

I turned to my uncle. "Thank you for looking out for me."

"I'm glad you are pleased," Gaius said. "And I know I'll rest better knowing you're protected."

I turned back to the men. "Charles, you'll serve as captain."

Charles lowered his head in a simple bow. "Thank you, your highness."

The men followed behind me as we walked back into the castle. It felt strange to have them following me, knowing that they'd be doing that every day unless I specifically sent them away.

WE SAT around a long oval table. Gaius sat in the middle of the table and I was sitting next to him with a document between the two of us. We went through the pages, one at a time. Each page was written in both Illarian and Gallic. The treaty outlined our alliance to each other, the promise of troops to secure my ascendency and transition to the throne, and our promise to support each other in a war on Sardinia once my throne was secured. Master Flanders was on my right and I'd occasionally whisper to him to ask about a word or phrase.

My hands were shaky as they handed me the quill to sign the treaty. I took a deep breath. You can do this. Channeling all of my willpower, I focused on stilling my hand. I dipped the quill in the ink and signed my name. Elisabetta Aqualine. It was the first time I'd signed that name on anything. It made everything seem so real. I handed the quill to my uncle. He dipped it in the ink and signed his name next to mine.

His council members who were present clapped and several of them reached hands across the table to shake my hand. Their smiles were kind and I couldn't help but smile back at them. Inside I was full of doubt. I hope I did the right thing. *Of course, you did.* Flinching at the voice of the Darkness, I tried to push it away. This wasn't the time for me to act out or let it take the better of me. *Stop fighting it. You deserve everything that's coming your way.* I took a deep breath. For the first time, I agreed with the voice.

After the treaty was signed, Master Flanders and I walked back to my rooms. It was time to pack up and head home.

"You did well, today," he said.

"Thank you." I let out a sigh. It had been a long journey and I was ready to return to the Raven camp. This time, we wouldn't have to wait for a ship. Since Master Flanders was able to create teleportation coins to the Raven camp, crossing the sea wouldn't be a danger. I was already imagining what it would be like to sleep in my own quarters. The bedroll might not be as comfortable as the plush beds in the Gallic palace, but it was mine.

31

ASHTON

T he grounds around the castle were nothing but black ashes. Crumbling trees lined the overgrown stone path that led to the front gates. Ashton gripped the sword tighter and took careful steps. His feet sunk into the ashes as he walked, muting the sound. It was eerily quiet. No birdsong, no wind. All he could hear was his heart beat and his shallow breathing.

Celeste walked next to him. Her eyes forward, jaw set in focused concentration. Her hands were extended as they walked, prepared to call on her magic if needed. Ashton wondered if he should be focusing on his magic instead of the heavy sword, but figured it would be easier to drop the sword to call on magic than try to pull the sword from its sheath on his back if he needed it.

The castle was on the smaller side. More of a large house than a proper castle. Though Ashton could see why people called it a castle. It was entirely made of large, gray stones. It was only two stories high but had a tall turret on one side. The front door was the large enough for a rider on horseback to cross through and was constructed of wood and iron.

Despite the damage surrounding the castle, the door and the

building itself were untouched. Ashton wondered if that was because Max had left it be or if it was somehow protected by magic. That's when he realized he was getting no sense of magic in the area.

"Celeste," he whispered, even though they were alone. "Do you feel any magic?"

She stopped walking and knitted her brow, frozen for a moment. "No, none at all."

A chill ran down Ashton's spine. Why weren't they feeling any magic? This whole building should be teeming with it. Were they in the wrong place?

"I don't understand," Celeste said. "This feels very wrong. It's like time has stopped."

Ashton knew what she meant. The lack of wind made him feel like they were the only living things for miles. "Stay on guard. We don't know what kind of magic we're up against."

She nodded.

Ashton approached the door and touched the doorknob quickly then pulled his hand away. Nothing. It appeared to be safe. He reached out again, this time turning it. He didn't expect it to open and jumped back when it did.

He glanced at Celeste. She shrugged.

Here goes nothing. He used his foot to push the door all the way open and stared into the entryway. The inside was dark and empty. Looking back at the castle, he realized he couldn't see any windows except for one on the top of the turret. It was going to be dark and cold inside.

"Here," Ashton handed the sword to Celeste. "You take this, I'll make us some fire."

"I don't know how to use a sword," Celeste said, but took it anyway.

"Me neither," Ashton said. "We're making this up as we go."

She gripped the sword with both hands and poked it through the door. Nothing happened.

"We've got to go in," Ashton said. He called to his fire, producing a glowing orb in his hands. "Let's go." Holding his breath, he stepped inside and walked to the center of the foyer. He held up the fireball to look around the room. It was an empty, dark space. The floor and walls were made of the same gray stone as the exterior of the building. On either side of the room was an archway that led away from the room. There were no carpets, tapestries, paintings, no decorations of any kind. It was the most uncomfortable room he had ever stood in. It had the feeling of a dungeon.

"Guess nobody lives here," Celeste whispered.

"Looks that way," Ashton agreed. "Right or left?" He held the fire to each archway.

"Left, maybe? The turret was that direction. Seems as good a place to start as any," Celeste said.

Ashton released the fire ball so it hung suspended in the middle of the room, then made a new one in his hands. He extended his arms, fire in front of him, and walked toward the archway. "Stay focused," he said. "We don't know what he has hiding here."

They walked through the archway and entered another empty stone room. This room had a long, rectangular fireplace that took up a good portion of one wall. There was no wood or ashes or even black marks showing any sign of a fire ever being built in it. "I don't think anybody has ever lived here," Ashton said. His words echoed through the large room and he winced. If something was waiting for them, it knew they were here now.

Ashton released the fireball in his hands to the middle of the room so they could look around. "We should check every room. Just in case it's hidden somewhere."

"Um," Celeste began, "do we even know what the stone looks like?"

"All I know is that they think it's the size of a man's fist and it's yellow. But that could be wrong so be on the look out for anything that looks like it could be magical."

Celeste nodded and walked around the room. After several minutes, they decided the room was just as empty as the entry way and headed through another archway. This took them to a long hallway, just as empty as the other rooms.

"We need to find some stairs," Celeste said. "I think we need to check out that turret."

"Keep your eyes open for anything strange on the way," Ashton said. The lack of magic was making him nervous. He thought he'd have to battle the undead or worse. So far, they'd been completely alone in the empty castle.

After looking through several more empty rooms, they found a door. Ashton's heartbeat quickened and he felt sweat beading on his forehead, despite the cool rooms. So far, all of the rooms had been connected through archways. They stared at the door for a moment, an unspoken tension between them. Ashton let out a long breath then reached for the handle. He pulled it open and stepped back. It was just as quiet as the other rooms had been. Where was the protection from the king? Not that he wanted to be battling the undead or something worse, but the lack of defensive magic on the building was causing his stomach to twist into knots. Every step they took, the fear inside him built up.

He floated his fireball inside the doorway to reveal a narrow, twisting staircase. "You wanted to go to the turret?"

Celeste nodded slowly. "Why am I so afraid of those stairs?"

"Probably because the longer we go without meeting a monster, the worse the monsters get inside our heads," Ashton said.

"You first," Celeste gave him a little push.

"You've got the sword," he smirked.

She lifted the sword toward him, hilt first. "You can have it back if it means you'll go first."

He placed his hand on the hilt to lower it. "Have it ready, just in case." Then he turned and headed up the stairs. As he walked, he pulled a new fireball into his hands, leaving the other one floating at the doorway. As soon as Celeste was on the steps, the door swung shut behind them with a slam.

Ashton turned and looked at Celeste, eyes wide. "Did you do that?"

She shook her head.

Ashton looked up the stairs to see a faint glow from above. His breath caught in his chest and he had swallowed. "Be ready."

He took a cautious step up the staircase and had to stop to grip the railing. The tingle of magic filled his whole body at once, overwhelming him. Whatever was up there was powerful. He looked up the stairs to see that the light was growing stronger. He extinguished his flame. It was so bright, he no longer needed the extra light. He reached behind him and Celeste set the sword in his hand. He took a deep breath and continued up the stairs.

The temperature dropped with each step up the winding staircase. Ashton's senses were on overdrive. He could hear his heart pounding in his chest and Celeste's breathing behind him. Every few steps, he paused to listen and stood on his toes to see if he could see the top of the stairs. So far, he had no idea what he was walking toward.

The light got brighter as they climbed and a low buzzing sound filled his ears. He wasn't sure if it was in his head or if it was everywhere. He stopped. "Do you hear that?" he whispered.

"Yes," Celeste's response was barely audible.

Ashton's chest felt tight and his stomach knotted. Something was up there, waiting for them. Whatever it was, it didn't feel the need to attack. It was letting them come to it. He searched his thoughts, trying to figure out what it might be. How should he prepare for what they would find at the top of the stairs? Was it undead soldiers? Was it a monster or some other creature? Maybe it was the Reapers, themselves. A shiver ran through him. What could they do against any of those possibilities?

The end of the stairway was in sight but all they could see was a large door. Ashton looked around, trying to find the source of the light. He couldn't figure out where it was coming from. He clutched the sword tighter and took a deep breath before pushing the door in. The room was dark and at first glance, appeared empty. But as his eyes adjusted he saw the figure standing in the corner. He called on a fireball and lifted it to the center of the room, illuminating the small circular space. A woman stood in the corner, staring at him. She was alone. In front of her was a pedestal with a glowing, yellow rock the size of his fist. The stone of Morare.

Ashton took a step into the room and glanced around as best he could without taking his eyes off of the lone woman. She looked familiar, but he couldn't place her. She smiled at him and he stumbled back, the memories washing over him. He dropped the sword. The woman in front of him was his mother.

32

ASHTON

" A shton," Celeste's voice seemed so far away. Time seemed to have stopped. He stood open-mouthed staring at the woman who used to be his mother. He'd been so young when she was taken from him, her lifeless body being dragged away by Reapers. Her face was burned into his memory. He'd never forget that face. Though he'd never admit it, he often wondered if she was still alive somewhere or if the king had turned her into one of his undead monsters. Ashton could feel the color drain from his face. Despite his musings, he never thought he'd actually see her again.

Ashton's dead mother smiled. "I've missed you."

Shaking his head, he worked to regain his thoughts. She's dead. This isn't real.

"Ashton, what's happening?" Celeste asked.

Ashton bent down and picked up the sword. He held the point out toward his undead mother. "You're dead."

"Do I look dead to you?" she asked.

Ashton narrowed his eyes. He imagined that the undead wouldn't look as alive as she did. "It's impossible. I watched them kill you and take you away."

She took a step toward him. "Are you sure I was dead when they carried me away?" She looked down at her hands then back up at him. "I don't feel dead."

"Ashton," Celeste rested her hand on his shoulder. "It's a trick. You told me yourself, your mother is dead."

"Who's this?" the undead woman asked. "Your girlfriend? They don't tell me much up in this tower."

"How long have you been here?" Ashton asked.

The woman pursed her lips in concentration. "A few years, I think."

LOCKED in a tower for years and you don't think you're dead?" Ashton asked. "Have you even eaten anything while you've been here?"

"You should know better than anybody that there is magic that we can't explain in this world. I'm assuming you continued your studies? You showed so much promise as a child."

Ashton narrowed his eyes at the woman. Ashton had been ten years old when he accidentally channeled fire. Before that, he'd never even known if he had the ability to channel magic. In the chaos of the years leading up to the Battle of the Dead, Ashton had never been tested. "I don't know what you are, but you're not my mother."

She took a few more steps toward Ashton.

He backed up and gripped the outstretched sword tighter. "Don't make me use this."

She raised her hands up. "There's no need for that. I'd rather you just get me out of here. We can be a family again." She smiled at him.

"I'm just here for the stone." Ashton nodded toward the pedestal in the center of the room. He took a step toward it.

The woman's eyes flashed red. "I'm afraid I can't let you do that." She moved too fast to be human. Before Ashton could react, she had crossed the room and knocked the sword from his hand. Ashton staggered before regaining his balance.

His nostrils flared and he bared his teeth. He'd hesitated, it was a mistake he shouldn't be making. Calling on his fire, he pulled the heat that was rising inside him to his hands. Flames ignited in his palms.

The body that used to be his mother backed up. "So, you can use magic," her lip curled. "When you came in here with a mere sword, I was worried." She rose her hands, green flames shot out of her palms. Ashton pushed Celeste out of the way, then ducked and rolled across the floor to avoid being hit by the fire.

"That's not possible. The undead can't use magic." Ashton stared at the creature for a moment. "You're not undead. You're something else. Some kind of monster."

"I told you, I'm not dead." The creature lifted her hands, palms facing Ashton and launched another round of green fire toward him.

He rolled away, then pushed himself up to standing. This time, he didn't hesitate, and launched a fireball in the direction the monster had last been. The fire hit the wall, leaving a black scorch mark against the gray stone. He glanced around, trying to find where she'd gone. A burst of green caught his eye a moment too late. He moved, but the strange flames caught his upper arm. He cried out in pain and used his opposite hand to beat out the flames. He could smell the singed fabric and burning flesh. Wincing, he lifted his arm to look at the injury. In just a few seconds, the green fire had done enough damage for his arm to respond in angry blisters.

"Ashton!" Celeste cried.

Ashton spun, heart pounding, toward Celeste's voice. She was in a corner and the creature had trapped her. Celeste kicked the sword between the woman's legs and it slid across the floor.

Ashton's mother turned and hesitated. It was as if she was trying to decide which person to attack. She turned her back on Ashton and ignited her green flames.

Ashton picked up the sword and charged, fighting through the burning pain in his arm. He pushed the sword through his mother's chest. It took more pressure than he thought it would. He screamed in pain as he used all of his strength to push the sword through bone and flesh.

His mother let out an unearthly howl. She stumbled backward and turned, arms outstretched, toward Ashton. The sword was stuck in her back, the point protruding through her chest. Her fingers clawed at the point of the sword and her eyes locked on Ashton. Her gaze was murderous. The creature shuddered, and started to expand. The sword fell from its body as the form shifted from a small woman to a towering figure with flowing black robes. The face was covered with a hood.

Ashton's blood ran cold. He was staring face to face with the biggest Reaper he'd ever seen.

The Reaper lowered its hood, revealing a face that was more skull than flesh. Two empty holes replaced the eyes. Maggots crawled across his skin, going in and out of the holes where his eyes should be.

Was this how all the Reapers looked under their hoods or was this something different? "What are you?"

"You need to learn your history, boy. I'm the keeper of the stone. I am the one they call Morare and I am neither living nor dead."

Ashton thought back to what Master Flanders had told him about the power stones. He'd heard that if they didn't create the stone successfully, the sorcerer casting the spell could be pulled into the stone. "You made the stone?"

Morare moved toward him. "I did. And my Reapers will help

the king to bring the Darkness back to Illaria. When it returns, I will be whole again."

The king was already powerful enough with the Reapers and his undead army. How much harder would it be to defeat him with Morare, strength returned, at his side? That couldn't happen. Ashton backed up, feeling with his feet for the fallen sword. Trying to kill the monster had failed, but that was because the monster wasn't alive. His foot felt something other than floor and he risked a glance down. He found it.

Morare faced him, green flames already lit in his hands. He launched them at Ashton.

Ashton ducked and slid the sword across the room. "Celeste, the stone!"

The flames above him subsided and Morale turned away from Ashton in the direction the sword had gone. Without waiting, he launched flames at Celeste. She screamed and moved away from them just in time. A gust of wind twisted its way around the room in a cyclone.

Struggling against the whipping wind, Ashton fought against Celeste's magic, crawling across the ground. Morare had his arms up in front of his face, leaning his body forward as he moved closer to Celeste. The sword was still on the ground, just past the pedestal where the stone sat.

Ashton reached his arm out, just able to grab the hilt, and pulled the sword closer. "Celeste, fire."

Suddenly, the wind stopped and Celeste threw a fireball at Morare. In that exact moment, Ashton jumped up and raised the sword above his head, bringing it down on the stone. The orange rock shattered when the sword made contact and Ashton was launched backward, hitting the stone wall behind him.

"No!" Morare screamed, an agonizing wail coming from him. His body twisted and slithered as the last remaining bits of flesh fell from his skull. Then the bones on his face began to crumble as his body seemed to melt to the ground. A moment later, all that was left of the ancient sorcerer was a pile of black robes.

Ashton's fingers were still gripping the hilt of the sword as he stared at the pile of fabric. His breathing rapid, he waited, half expecting it to come back to life.

"Ashton?" Celeste was next to him now, kneeling down in front of him. "Are you okay?"

Ashton looked down at his arm, still red and blistered, and felt the back of his head. No blood this time. "I think so."

Celeste stood and offered her hand to him, pulling him up.

Sword still in hand, Ashton slowly approached the place where Morale had fallen. He kicked the fabric, checking to see if there were any signs of the sorcerer. It seemed to be just fabric.

"Look at this."

Ashton looked over to where Celeste was standing in front of the pedestal. She had two pieces of what had been the stone of Morale in her hands. No longer orange, the gray pieces resembled any regular rock you'd find.

"What should we do with it?" she asked.

"Let's bring it back with us, just in case." As Ashton said the words, he breathed a sigh of relief. They were done. Not only had they found the stone, but they'd destroyed it. The king would no longer be able to call to the Reapers. "We can go home."

"I can't wait." Celeste took his hand and held the red coin in the other. They waited. Nothing was happening.

"I don't understand," Celeste said. "It's not working."

Ashton took the coin and tried to teleport them out. Nothing. "Maybe the room has too much magic. We might need to leave the castle."

Celeste took the coin back and slid it in her pocket. "Let's hurry."

They climbed back down the stairs in silence and retraced

their steps out of the castle. There were no more monsters. Max must have destroyed the others when he came by with his dragon. It still didn't make any sense why Max would help them. He'd have to think about that later. Right now, he just wanted to get back to the Raven camp.

The front door was in sight and the two of them picked up to a run, wanting nothing more than to put this castle behind them.

The bright sunlight blinded Ashton. He lifted a hand to shield his eyes from the light. As his eyes adjusted, his heart dropped into his stomach. They weren't alone. Max was standing outside the castle. His black sorcerer robes blowing gently in the wind. His arms were behind his back and he wore a smug expression.

"You're welcome," Max said.

Ashton tightened his grip around the stone in his hand. "What do you want? Why did you help us?"

"I told you, we're on the same side. We both want the same thing. The end of the king."

"You are not the rightful heir," Celeste said.

Max looked at her and shook his head. "You still don't see it, do you? Etta can never rule Illaria like I can. She's not willing to do what it takes to keep us safe. Especially with the coming Darkness."

"She's more powerful than you know," Celeste said.

Ashton's jaw tightened and he glared at Max. Why wouldn't he give up? Ashton would never side with Max. "That's enough. I haven't figured out what this game of yours is, but I'm done playing."

"I know you won't turn your back on Etta," Max said. "You've made that clear. I'm here to tell you I won't hurt her if she steps down. The king has the Skystone. How long do you think he'll let her live now that he can build an army of thousands of undead by himself? His power far exceeds that of a hundred necromancers."

"Even if she were to step down, I can't trust you. Not after what you did to me." Ashton stared at Max, not blinking. How could Max think he'd ever consider supporting him?

"I know what I put you through. That's why I helped you, and that's why I came here to tell you that the king knows where the Raven camp is. He's probably already there and he's going to kill Master Flanders." Max turned away from Ashton and took a few steps before stopping to glance over his shoulder. "If you change your mind, you're on the guest list for my wedding. There was talk of an attack so it's been moved up to tomorrow." Grey smoke enveloped Max and he vanished from site.

Ashton hardly registered the words about the wedding. At the moment, an invitation to a wedding was the last thing on his mind. All of his attention was focused on the news that the king was after Master Flanders. His heart raced in his chest. *The king knew.* This changed everything. Suddenly, nothing else mattered. Not the stone, not the upcoming war, none of it. If the king was going after Master Flanders, he was going to break the protection spell that had been cast on Etta. And the only reason he'd do that was if he wanted to attack Etta himself.

"Is he telling the truth?" Celeste asked.

Ashton grabbed hold of Celeste's hand and turned to her, eyes wild. "Master Flanders is the one who put the protection spell on Etta. We have to go now."

33

ETTA

The air was cold and the scent of burning wood filled the air. Small white flakes dropped from the gray sky. Winter was finally making its appearance. I rubbed my hands together and looked around at my new entourage. I'd have to find quarters for all of them.

"Charles?" I spun around to find him behind me. He bowed his head in response.

"I don't have any quarters set up for you yet but I'm sure we can find places for you all until we can build something to suit you," I said.

"As long as it's near your highness' quarters, we are fine with anything," he said.

"Etta! Master Flanders!" A familiar voice called out. Saffron.

She caught me in a hug before I was able to respond. "I'm so glad you're back." She held me at arm's length and looked me up and down. It reminded me of something my grandmother would do after she caught me out in the woods "You seem to be unharmed."

"What did you expect?" I asked.

Her eyes darted from side to side and she pursed her lips as she looked at the newcomers.

"Don't worry," I said. "They're with me. Gift from my uncle. Personal guard. How is everything here?"

Her face darkened. "I wish I had good news for you. A few messages came in while you were away." She looked to the guards again and lowered her voice. "They say there was sighting of a dragon."

I started walking toward camp. "We heard the same thing. We should gather the council. We have so much to talk about."

Saffron placed her hand on my elbow and I stopped walking. "What is it?"

"We received word the wedding date was changed."

"To when?" We'd planned everything around the wedding. Had they changed the date because they knew our plans? I felt like I'd never be able to get a step ahead of the king. Was this more proof that we had a traitor in my council?

Her face fell. "It's going to be tomorrow."

I took a deep breath and glanced in the direction of the portal I had just left. The blue coin was still in my palm. "I should go back and let them know. Maybe they'd be ready to fight tomorrow."

"Our army is always ready, your highness," Charles said.

I looked at Master Flanders. "What should we do?"

Before he could answer, he looked up and my eyes followed his gaze. Above us, flashes of light filled the sky and a tingle of magic filled my fingertips. My heart raced. I recognized the flashes of light I was seeing. It was the same magic the king's sorcerers had used to break down the wards at the Trials. "We're under attack."

We would need more sorcerers to win this battle. I turned to Saffron. "Are Ashton and Celeste back yet?"

She shook her head. "No word yet."

"Find Sir Henry, I need the two of you to get everyone who can't fight to the exit point." She took off at a run, leaving me with my guards and Master Flanders.

"I'll find Madame Lyndsey and see if we can round up a few more sorcerers," Master Flanders said.

"Thank you," I said. "I'm going to find Calder. We need to arm our fighters."

Charles and my guards followed me as I ran through camp. The flashing lights were increasing in frequency and intensity making my stomach knot in anticipation. I didn't know how long the wards would hold and I was terrified that we weren't ready to fight the intruders.

The Ravens were noticing the flashing lights, stopping to stare up at the invisible ward. I shouted to the people I passed by, "Fighters, get to the arsenal, non-fighters, get to the exit point."

The further into the camp we went, the more movement there was of people as they scrambled to find their place. We'd come up with a plan for attack, and the Ravens knew what to do, but I never thought we'd actually need to implement it.

Breathless, I stopped at the training grounds on the opposite end of camp from the archery range. Charles and the other guards stopped with me. Like the archery range, it was a bit secluded from the rest of the camp.

As I hoped, Calder was there giving lessons to a group of kids that looked too young to be fighting. He lowered the wooden sword he'd been using when he saw me. "What's wrong? And who are they?"

Pointing up, I took a few more breaths before I could speak. "New guards, I'll explain later. We're being attacked. I need all fighters at the ready."

Calder's jaw tightened and he nodded. "You all, go to the exit point."

"We can help," a boy who looked to be around ten said.

"Yes, you can. I need you all to go with the younger children. Who will protect them while we fight the guards? Take your weapons. This is what we have been practicing for. Get those kids out of here."

I noticed that the group of kids were all holding metal weapons. My heart sunk knowing that it was a possibility that one of them may have to fight.

"Go," Calder said.

The group of kids took off at a run, away from the training fields.

I turned to my guards. "You all, go with Calder, help prepare for the fight. I'll meet you there."

"I'm staying with you," Charles said.

I wasn't used to having someone following me around, but we'd be joining the rest of the fighters soon enough. "Alright, Charles, you're with me. The rest of you, follow Calder."

Calder glanced at the men surrounding me. "This way, hurry." He took off at a run away from the training grounds.

He'd only been with the Ravens a short time, but he had demonstrated he was a leader. The others looked up to him. I felt confident he could organize the fighters and prepare them for battle.

With Charles at my heels, I ran right for my tent. I knew magic was my best defense, but there was only so much I could do before I'd lose the energy to cast spells. I'd need another weapon. I ducked into my tent, only stopping to grab my bow and a quiver of arrows. Charles had followed me into the tent. As I clipped my quiver onto my belt, I narrowed my eyes at him. "You should know I am not as fragile as you think."

"I don't doubt that," he said.

"I won't sit back and let others fight for me."

"So I've heard." He looked down at the bow in my hands.

"I don't know what we are going to be facing when those wards fall. If you think I'm a lost cause, do not risk your life for me. Save my people. As many as you can. Promise?"

"I can't do that." He shook his head. "I'm here to protect you, I'll give my life for you if I have to."

We were wasting time. I didn't think I'd be able to convince him quickly. "Fine. You stay with me, but I want you to tell the others to focus on protecting everyone else."

He nodded. "Agreed. I'm not leaving your side."

I couldn't see the lights as the magic attacked the ward from inside my tent, but I could feel the tingle of magic coursing through me. It was almost as strong as my encounters with the Reapers. "We better run. We don't have much time."

We cut through the common area on our way to the arsenal. Nobody sat at the tables, but the remains of uneaten lunches were still sitting on the tables, reminding me of how many people called this place home. How could I protect all of them? I never thought the war would come to us. The plan had always been to bring the war to the king.

The Raven I saw before I went to Gallia had to have been sent by the king. But how had he found us? Fire rose up inside me. Whoever had betrayed us would pay. Somebody had to have given away our location. A woman carrying her child bumped into me as she ran by, bringing me back to the crisis at hand. I had to save these people.

Calder was helping pass out swords, bows, and any other weapons when we reached the small wooden building that served as our arsenal. It wasn't much, but over the last few weeks, we'd managed to acquire enough to arm all the fighters in camp.

"Just remember," Calder said, "they're still only human. They can still be killed. You just have to find the weak areas in their armor or get them while they are distracted. Work together."

"What about the sorcerers?" a man asked.

"We have sorcerers of our own, and more on the way. Don't worry about them. They will focus their attention on me." A hundred pairs of eyes turned to look at me.

"What about the Reapers?" somebody asked.

"WE SENT Ashton and Celeste to get the stone. They should have it by now," I said. "Hopefully, the king no longer has control of the Reapers." Murmurs rose up though the small crowd. I figured telling them about the hunt for the stone might be good for morale in this situation.

Heads turned in my direction as I reached the building.

This was when I needed to say something. I had to make them feel better. I knew what we were up against. I knew our odds. But I couldn't let them know how much I was trembling inside.

"This isn't what we planned, but we've been preparing for this." My voice came out stronger and clearer than I thought it could. "You've all been training and all of you can defend your-selves. They won't expect that. They think we're weak. But we're not. We know that what we fight for is the right thing. We have the will of the people and the blessing of the gods on our side. We know that good triumphs over evil. We can do this."

34

ETTA

The lights above us were coming more frequently as we ran toward the edge of the ward. How many sorcerers were there? I didn't remember seeing this much light at the trials. My grip tightened around the bow and my heart pounded in my ears.

The faces of the men and women around were fearful, but determined. I hoped I wasn't leading all of these people to their death, but my optimism was waning.

"Etta," Saffron ran toward me. Silver glinted in her belt. She'd stopped to get her daggers and sword on her way back. "Everybody's safe. Sir Henry will stay with them. They're going to flee as soon as the wards fall if it's safe."

I nodded. Everything was following the plan we had set up when we first chose this place for our camp. Though we knew having emergency plans was necessary, I never thought we'd need them.

"You all know what to do," I said to the small group around me. "Focus on the soldiers." I glanced around and my stomach felt like it dropped to my feet. I was the only sorcerer here. Our plan had always counted on having at least three sorcerers.

"Who is the best with a bow?" I asked.

"Yancey," Charles said. "He's one of the best archers I've ever seen."

Yancey, one of my new personal guardsmen bowed at me. He was probably only a year older than me and had thick, dark curls. When he looked up at me, his bright blue eyes practically glowed against his dark skin. I wanted to stare at them for a while. My own blue eyes had made me stand out more than I liked. They were rare and it wasn't often I came across someone else with this trait. Yancey returned my stare with a steady gaze, eyes unblinking. He came across as well disciplined, and fierce. I had a feeling he would be a good addition to the fighters we had in the Ravens. Forcing myself to look away from him for a moment, I broke eye contact, then looked back at him. "Are you as good as he says?"

"YOUR HIGHNESS, I have trained with a bow since I was a child. I can handle any bow."

I took a deep breath and handed him my bow. It was my most prized possession after my necklace. "I made this bow myself. Please don't break it."

He took the bow from me. "It's beautiful. Your highness. I'll treat it with the highest respect."

I handed him the quiver of arrows. "These are enchanted. They'll explode on impact. Make them count. If you can hit somebody while they are close enough to other people, you can take down several soldiers with one shot."

He nodded at me and clipped the quiver to his belt. Removing an arrow, he balanced it against the bow with one hand. He looked comfortable with it in his grip. I relaxed a little. He'd probably be as good a shot as me. Maybe even better.

Tingles shot through my fingers. Magic. We didn't have

much time before the wards fell. I turned my attention back to the group. "I'm the only sorcerer we have right now, but we stick to the plan. I'll focus on the sorcerers and as soon as Master Flanders and Madame Lyndsey are back with reinforcements, they'll help me. We can do this. They underestimate us."

The tingle spread to my arms, and began to creep into my chest. The ward was cracking. "Positions, now! The ward is about to fall."

Everybody ran to the barriers and walls we had constructed as hiding places in case of an attack. We knew with our smaller numbers we couldn't meet an army in a face to face fight. We had to be tricky. Hide and attack. Outlast.

Pointing to one of the false walls we had constructed, I turned to Charles who hadn't left my side. "You need to wait over there. You won't want to be next to me while I'm calling magic."

"I'm supposed to stay with you," he said.

"You can't for this," I said. "I'll call for you if I need you."

He hesitated, then nodded. I waited until he I saw him tucked behind a wall, then walked out to the open space between our barriers. Facing the ward that was about to fall, I focused on clearing my head. I needed to be able to channel my magic and keep the Darkness away. With the ward gone, it would be easier for the Darkness to find me. This wasn't practice with Master Flanders anymore, this was real.

I took a deep breath and hoped that the order still stood for the king's guards and sorcerers to not kill me. I was the only one who would be visible since we had no other sorcerers and I needed to see my targets so I knew where to aim my magic.

Bending my knees, I settled into my sorcerer stance and called to the energy inside me. Falling snowflakes stung my cheeks, giving me an idea. If I could make more snow, it might make it harder to see. Closing my eyes, I reached inside, feeling the icy cold of water rising in my veins. I pictured heavy, gray snow clouds filling the sky, then opening up and dumping huge, wet flakes. I called to the wind to move the flakes of snow in circles as it reached the ground.

Opening my eyes, I looked up and saw that the snow was falling harder. I reached my hands up toward the sky and pulled at the water I could feel above me. Snow. More snow. The flakes started falling harder, faster. The wind kicked up. Snow.

In a rush of energy coursing through me, I felt the ward break. I gasped as if I had been doused in cold water. That hadn't happened last time. Was I getting more sensitive to magic?

My heart stopped. At the border of our fallen wards, stood several hundred men in matching armor. The flaming Phoenix bright against the falling snow. Behind them, I could make out figures in dark robes. Sorcerers. The snow swirled around them, making it so I couldn't tell how many there were or if the king was with them. I pushed my fear aside.

Focus on the snow. In one last burst, I reached out for the clouds and pictured them tearing open and pouring snow on us. I stumbled as a gust of wind nearly knocked me over. In the blizzard I had created, I could no longer see the sorcerers behind the guards. My breathing was heavy and the approaching army seemed unstable. I'd overdone it. Scrambling away from the oncoming guards, I ran behind a wooden wall where two men with bows and arrows were waiting to ambush the guards.

Collapsing onto the ground, I leaned my head against the wall.

"Your highness," one of them knelt down next to me. "Are you all right?"

My hair was soaking wet and clung to my face. I pushed it back then wiped the snow out of my eyes. "I'm fine. Just need to catch my breath."

"You sure?" he asked, brow creased.

I nodded. "Making snow was harder than I thought."

"You started this storm?" he asked.

"Yes." I closed my eyes and focused on slowing my breathing.

"Remind me never to make you mad, highness," the man said.

I smiled. I wasn't feeling very powerful at the moment, crumbled on the ground, breathing heavily. But I had made a blizzard and that was no small feat.

In the swirling snow, I saw a man approaching us, as he drew nearer, I recognized the face of my new guard. Charles sat down next to me. "You okay?"

I nodded. "Fine."

Distant shouts filled the air as the battle began and I knew the guards were charging the camp. The men next to me stood and waited for the king's guards to reach our hiding place.

Still weak, I pushed myself to standing. I wasn't sure what I had left in me. I'd never tried anything as big as a blizzard and then continued to fight before. My mind flashed back to my first encounters with the Reapers. Those first few times resulted in me passing out. I couldn't afford to do that here. Why did I give away my bow?

"I need a weapon," I said to Charles. I didn't wait to see if he responded before taking off as fast as I could. It wasn't quite a run, but it was faster than walking. I charged on toward the arsenal, then paused. Were there any weapons left in the arsenal? Probably not. Changing direction, I headed toward my quarters. I should have at least a dagger in there and that would be better than nothing while I waited for my strength to return.

Running was proving more difficult than I thought it would be. The fancy dress I had worn to Gallia was weighing me down. Especially as it got wetter and wetter in the snow. My feet slid over the grass and I nearly went crashing into the ground. How am I supposed to fight like this?

I darted into my tent and pulled off the top layers of the dress.

Charles stepped into my quarters, and I spun around to face him, piles of fabric in my hand.

His face reddened and he turned away. "I'm sorry, your highness. I didn't realize."

"I can't fight in this stuff. You can turn around. There's still five layers of fabric covering me." I threw the overdress to the ground and looked around the tent, trying to remember where I had stored the daggers I'd been given.

"I never thought about how hard it would be to fight in a dress," Charles said.

"Remind me not to wear them again until we defeat the king." I shivered. Since I stopped moving, the cold had set in. Rummaging through a chest in the corner of my tent, I found a pair of daggers that Saffron had given me. I hadn't used them since we traveled to Greenville. Weapons in hand, I looked over to Charles. "You ready?"

35

ETTA

As we neared the edge of camp, the sounds of battle grew. The smell of burning and death assaulted my senses. My whole body tensed as I tried to prepare myself for what I would see.

Ahead of us, I could see that our men had abandoned the false walls we'd built and joined the fray beyond the original wards of the camp. I walked around a few bodies of guards and crimson stained snow. My throat tightened as I turned away from the body of one of our own. It looked like at least some of the king's guard had made it past our perimeter and into the camp.

Behind me, I noticed a trail of footprints that had erased the snow, forming a pathway through the heart of the Raven camp. It was wide enough to have been made by a large group. My heart fell as my fears were confirmed, the guards had made it through the camp. I hoped that the non-fighters had found a way to escape the onslaught. We'd been working on finding evacuation locations for the last few weeks and had settled on an abandoned castle not far from here. It hadn't been fully protected yet, but it would do if we had found enough sorcerers to teleport people there. I hoped Madame Lyndsey had found her friends who promised to help us. For a moment, my vision blurred as the crushing weight of all the things I couldn't control came crashing down on me.

"Are you alright, your highness?" Charles' voice brought me back to the present. I couldn't do it all. As Ashton had reminded me, I had to be willing to let people help me. Madame Lyndsey had her job and she would take care of them. I had to do mine.

"I'm fine, let's keep going."

"Are you sure?" Charles grabbed my shoulder. "You said yourself that you don't have any magic left."

"They don't know that." I hoped the king's orders to keep me alive still stood. "Besides, if I have to use it, you can carry me to safety." Before he could argue with me, I took off at a run toward the fire and the cries of battle.

As we approached, I slowed down. We stopped behind a freestanding wall, and looked around the edge.

Hundreds of people were engaged in the fight as it came into view. Fires burned on the wooden walls around us, the snow not enough to quench them. Smoke rose from the battlefield, which was no longer white, but rather a muddy span of land outside the fallen wards of the camp. Ravens and guards grappled with swords up close, their mud-covered bodies making it difficult to see which was which from a distance.

Knowing the greatest threat would come from any sorcerers who were going unchallenged, I searched in the chaos for the familiar black robes, pausing to assess each one when I came across it.

The first one I found was fighting someone with a sword. It took me a moment to realize the mud-covered figure was Saffron. She swung at the sorcerer who seemed to dissolve and then rematerialized inches away after every attack. She ducked when he threw a fireball at her. They were surprisingly evenly matched.

Then, I found two more black-robed figures. They were both attacking a single person. The hair rose on the back of my neck. Two sorcerers fighting the same opponent? I narrowed my eyes to see who the target was. Navy blue robes and long, loose gray hair told me this was Master Flanders. He was back. Where were the other sorcerers on our side? Were they fighting somewhere else or had they not come?

After a quick assessment of the rest of the scene, I don't find any other sorcerers. It was time to help.

I ducked back behind the wall. "Here's the plan. See if you can sneak up behind the sorcerer that Saffron is fighting. Take him out. I'm going to help Master Flanders."

"Are you sure?" he asked.

"Quit asking me that. I'm fine." I gripped the handle of a dagger and headed out at a run, not looking back.

Master Flanders was launching spell after spell at his two attackers. Most of them seemed to be invisible and caused the other sorcerers to stop in their tracks or cry out in pain. How long has he been at this?

He looked up at me. "Stay there," he shouted. "Help me. Use your power to support mine."

I stopped and grounded myself in my stance. I knew I was weak and that there wasn't much power left inside me. Hoping that the few minutes had been enough to give me something to work with I pulled on my magic and directed it out through my outstretched fingers, toward Master Flanders.

A sudden gust of wind swept past me, picking up dirt and snow, forming a funnel in the air. It swallowed the two sorcerers. They screamed and their feet lifted off of the ground. Master Flanders took a few steps away, his robes and hair whipping around him. He made a sweeping gesture with his arms and the funnel traveled away, through the snow until I lost sight of it. The sorcerers were gone.

I dropped to my knees, breathing hard. Spots danced across my vision. I knew that was all I had left. There would be no more magic from me today unless I was willing to lose consciousness.

My body swayed and my eyes went in and out of focus as I searched for the other fight. Where were Saffron and Charles? The only other person I could see was Master Flanders.

Looking behind me, I realize the other fight had moved right behind me and I had a front row seat to its conclusion. The sorcerer they were fighting let out a grunt as Charles shoved his dagger into his ribs. The black robed man let out a gurgling cry and clutched at the dagger. Saffron aimed the point of her sword at his chest and thrust it inside of him. Blood spilled out of the man's mouth and his eyes rolled into the back of his head. Saffron pulled the blade out and pushed the man over with the heel of her boot. He fell backward into the snow, blood oozing out around him.

My shoulders dropped in relief. My friends were safe, the king's sorcerers were dead or gone. Saffron dropped to her knees next to me and wrapped her arm around me. "Thank the gods you're safe."

"You've used too much magic, haven't you?" Master Flanders said.

"I'm sure I'll be fine," I said. "Where is everybody else?"

"Other side of camp." Master Flanders' mouth pressed into a tight line.

Other side? The moment of relief was over and my whole body tensed. We staged our attack to keep the battle away from those who couldn't fight. "They went after the children?"

Saffron stood and pulled me up. "You know how the king works. He seemed to know exactly where we hid them."

My jaw clenched. "Someone told him, you mean."

"Probably," Saffron agreed.

"We have to help them." I took a few steps and nearly fell to the ground.

"You're done. You need to rest," Master Flanders said. "Charles, Saffron, go help the others." He wrapped an arm around my waist. "I've got a tonic in my tent. It'll help."

"I need to help," I repeated.

Saffron lifted my chin in her hand. "Look at me. You are no good to any of us if you're dead. Go take your medicine and then come back and fight."

Letting out a sigh, I nodded.

Master Flanders' guided me to his tent, then had me sit on the bedroll while he dug through a wooden chest. After a while, he retrieved something, then closed the chest. Holding a small vial, about the size of my pinky finger, he walked over to me.

"Here." Master Flanders passed me the vial.

I took the bottle and squinted at it, trying to determine what made up the swirling, silver liquid. The contents seemed to pulse and move of their own freewill. Last time I had drunk from a vial, I had sent myself to the underworld. While I didn't think Master Flanders was trying to harm me, I still found myself facing a tangle of nerves in the pit of my stomach. "What is it?"

"Essence of the Jubilee flower and dragon scale," he said. "It's potent stuff. Only used for emergencies."

I'd never heard of a Jubilee flower and had no idea that somebody still had the means to get a hold of dragon scales. "It'll help me recover faster?"

"It will. Go ahead and drink," Master Flanders said.

I pulled the cork stopper out of the bottle and took a sip. My face puckered and I gagged. It was like eating the most sour lemon in the world.

"All of it at once." Master Flanders lifted his hand in a drinking motion.

I swallowed back the overwhelming flavor. It lingered in my mouth as I stared at the shimming liquid remaining in the vial. Just drink it. Lifting the vial to my lips, I tipped the entire contents into my mouth. It took all of my willpower not to spit it back out. Forcing myself to swallow, eyes watering from the intensity of the flavor. I coughed and handed the empty vial back to Master Flanders.

"Feel better?" he asked.

I pushed my hair away from my face and looked around the room. Nothing was spinning. My vision was clear. My head wasn't hurting. Standing, I reached inside, calling to the ice that flowed deep within. In seconds, my body hummed with power as the cold flooded my veins. I pushed the ice out of my palms, making blue sparks of cold rise to my hands. Closing my hands, I let the power recede. "How is that possible?"

"I told you, it's potent stuff." Master Flanders dropped the empty vial back into his trunk and closed the lid. "Ready to get back to it?"

The battle wasn't hard to find if you just followed the sound of angry people and fear. The edge of camp was dotted with bodies that had a fine layer of snow covering them. It wasn't possible to tell which side they belonged to but based on how few Ravens I saw, I guessed too many of them were ours.

Master Flanders stopped, eyes on the scene in front of us. "We're losing," he said.

A lump rose in my throat. Our people were dying. We weren't ready for this kind of a fight. "We don't have a choice," I said. "We have to keep fighting. We'll never get everybody out in time."

"We can get you out," Master Flanders said.

"No," I gripped the dagger in my hand. "I fight with them."

I charged into the fray, searching for somebody to help. Movement from behind me had me spinning around just in time to see a guard launching at me with a sword. I ducked, avoiding the blow, then righted myself. My upper lip curled in disgust as I faced off against my attacker, a stocky member of the king's guard with blood-streaked blonde hair. He lunged toward me and without stopping to think about what I was doing, I called on my magic and sent a rush of wind toward him. He stumbled backward. Pulling the dagger from my belt, I approached, blade held in front of me.

His eyes narrowed on me as he ran toward me. With a flick of my hand, I knocked his sword from his grip. He turned to chase after it and I shoved my blade into his stomach, removing it quickly. Backing up a few paces I watched him stumble. He let out a groan and pressed his hands on the gushing wound.

An arrow flew past me and landed in the man's throat. He coughed, spitting blood, then fell face first to the snow. I turned to see who had shot the arrow and Yancey rushed to my side.

"Are you hurt, your highness?" He grabbed my arm and pulled me away from the battle.

I shook my head. "You used up all the enchanted arrows?"

He turned to show me the quiver I'd given him. It had three arrows left. "I've been saving them. Picking up the arrows the king's guards sent our way during the initial attack."

Smart.

"Let's get you somewhere safe, your highness, you shouldn't be out here," Yancey tugged at my arm.

I pulled away from him. "No, we don't quit."

He nodded and lifted my bow toward me. I waved it away. "You really as good a shot as you say?" I asked.

Gripping the bow with both hands he smiled. "Better. What do you have in mind?"

"I'm going to move our people away, leaving just the guards.

You hit them with one of the enchanted arrows. We should be able to take out several at once." I swallowed, not sure how I was going to make it happen.

"This way." I ran for a small hill that would give us a better view of the battle. Yancey followed behind me. He nocked an arrow in the bow and turned his gaze at the battle in front of us.

Taking a deep breath, I focused on the people in front of me. A tangle of bodies collided with one another. People slid across the wet grass and the sound of steel against steel rang through the air. I locked my gaze on a group of six guards who had surrounded three Ravens. They were fighting bravely, but it was clear they wouldn't be able to hold out much longer. Clearing my mind, I imagined my energy filling each of the three Ravens, pulling them away. Inside, I focused on the sensation I felt when I teleported. Like the pin of a lock fitting into place, I felt my power grasp them. I pulled, moving my arms in a wide sweeping motion.

The three Ravens vanished from the fight and landed in a heap next to me. Gasping for air, I fell to my knees and rubbed my forehead. I looked up just in time to see Yancey's arrow strike one of the confused Guards. It struck him in the arm and ignited on impact. Six bodies flew through the air and landed, in pieces. The aftermath took me by surprise and I heaved, unable to keep it down.

I wiped my mouth off with the back of my hand and stood on shaky feet. The Ravens next to me stood and stared at me, wide-eyed. Two of them had mouths open in shock. The third, bowed. "Thank you, your highness."

I nodded, then turned to Yancey. "Again."

We repeated the process twice more, using up the enchanted arrows and removing eight more king's guard. Now that I knew what to expect, I turned away when he loosed his arrow so I didn't have to see the flying arms and legs. With each explosion, several of the king's guards ran from the battle. We were still smaller in numbers, but there was hope.

Master Flanders' tonic must have strengthened my magic. Surprised that I felt like I had more magic in me, I began to search for places where I could inflict damage. I started removing weapons from the king's guard, launching them across the battle field and rendering them helpless. The bodies dropping to the ground all seemed to be wearing the king's crest. Good. If only we could take out the king.

On the edge of the battle a figure in a long, flowing black cloak began to approach. It floated the same way the Reapers did and panic shot through me. Gathering my wits, I realized I didn't feel the Reapers. It couldn't be.

As the figure drew nearer it lifted its arms and fire shot through the field, parting the battle as people cried out in pain or ran to avoid being burned. My breath caught in my chest and my whole body tensed. The newcomer was a powerful fire sorcerer.

The fire sorcerer threw up his arms, a wall of flames rose from nothing and rolled across the ground and like a wave in the ocean. Cries filled the air as bodies were consumed by the fire. Nobody was spared, king's guards and Ravens alike were swallowed by the rising flames.

For a moment, I was frozen in wide-eyed fear, watching the newcomer's destruction. I'd never seen anything like it before. How could you stop someone that powerful? *You know what you need to do.* Dark tendrils of fear rose inside me, calling out to me. The pull from the Darkness was almost soothing. *You need more magic.* It would be so easy to let it in.

I took a step toward the battle and Yancey put his arm out, blocking me.

"Let me go." I turned on him and glared. *Don't let him stop you.*

"My job is to keep you alive," he said. "Not let you go out there to meet your death. You're too important to risk. How would it look if I let you die on my first day?"

Too important to risk. I hated when I was treated like I was made of glass, but the words brought back all the warnings from

Ashton and Celeste. If something happened to me, who would protect the people? Would someone else be brave enough to face the king? Or Max?

You make the rules. I squeezed my eyes shut and took a deep breath. I'd resisted so far. I needed a plan. How could I keep the Ravens from any more loss?

The battlefield in front of me was covered with a cloud of dark smoke. The air was thick with haze that made my eyes sting. The fire sorcerer was standing in the middle of the ruined field, arms at his side, waiting. A circle of bodies surrounded him. Charred figures, blackened from sorcerer fire. Bile rose in my throat at the sight. I'd never seen so many dead at one time before. Swallowing back the fear, I turned to Yancey. "We have to call for retreat, but we can't have this sorcerer following us. I have to do something."

Yancey pointed. "Let him handle it."

I turned to see Master Flanders walking across the open field. No. I started to run, but an arm stretched in front of my chest blocked me. Yancey put his other arm around me and pulled me toward his chest. I twisted, trying to break his grip.

He lifted an eyebrow. "I can hold you like this all day, highness."

"You have to let me go, you have to do what I say!" I yelled.

"Not if it results in your death. Don't make me take you back to camp." He wasn't budging.

I closed my eyes for a moment and fought against the fear and anger in my head. This was too much. What was he doing out there? Master Flanders was going to get himself killed.

"Please," I said. "He needs help."

A cloud of gray smoke rose up a few feet away from Master Flanders. No. It was probably more sorcerers to help him. I twisted again, trying to break free, and again, Yancey held me tight.

The smoke rose, and as it began to fade, two people emerged. My knees wobbled and I let out a long breath. Ashton and Celeste are back. The moment of relief was short lived as the realization struck me that they had arrived right in the middle of a battle. My heart pounded in my ears and I fought against Yancey's grip. "Run!"

My words didn't seem to reach them. Instead of turning toward me, the cloaked figure and Master Flanders both turned their heads toward Ashton and Celeste. They were frozen in place.

The stranger approached them and Celeste took a few backwards steps. He lowered his hood. The hair on my arms rose and my whole body tensed. Yancey tightened his grip on me but I was frozen in place. The fire sorcerer facing down my friends was the king.

Even if I could get out there, what could I do against the king? My body went limp for a moment in Yancey's arms and he kept me standing. I shook my head, not believing what I was seeing in front of me. Clenching my fists, I stood tall, maybe with all of our help, we could destroy him. "You have to let me go out there. The king can't touch me. I can help."

Yancey's face reflected sympathy but he didn't release his grasp on me. "Your Master met with us before we left Gallia. He made me promise not to let you fight the king."

"What?" Why would he say something like that? How would he have known? Master Flanders musings about the end of his life seemed to strike me all at once. Was he trying to get himself killed?

"Why would he do that?" Tears stung the back of my eyes.

Yancey swallowed and pressed his mouth tight. It looked like he was forcing himself to hold something back.

"Tell me what you know!" My face felt hot despite the fact that I was soaked through from the snow.

He sighed. "I'm not supposed to tell you."

"Yancey, do you work for me or Master Flanders?"

He loosened his grip on me a bit but didn't release me. "Some sorcerers know things. They can see the future. He gets premonitions. He saw two versions of this battle. In one of them, you die."

My vision blurred for a moment and I swayed, before the full weight of the words hit me. *Two versions.* I turned so I was facing Yancey. "And in the other version?"

He frowned. "He does."

"No! That can't be." I slammed my fists against Yancey's chest and heat rose inside me.

Yancey pulled me in tighter, rendering my hands useless. "I'm sorry, your highness, but my job is to keep you alive."

Suddenly, Master Flanders' cryptic messages over the last few months started to make sense. Like his daughter, he must have some of the sight. How long had he known about this? Tears blurred my vision and streamed down my face. They left a trail of warmth against my frozen skin. "I'm just supposed to stand here and watch?" How could I do that? Why would they make me do that?

"Just wait," Yancey said.

Master Flanders positioned himself between the king and the others. I wanted to turn my eyes away but I couldn't.

The king lifted his arms and opened them wide. An arc of fire formed between his hands and he continued his progress toward Master Flanders.

Master Flanders dipped down, then stood, lifting his hands in one fluid motion. The earth between him and the king rose, forming a wall between them. The king dropped his hands, fire extinguished. He turned to walk around the wall.

Master Flanders rushed to Ashton and Celeste and spoke to them. They nodded and readied themselves in their sorcerer stance. My stomach tightened and my breathing grew rapid. Watching this take place without being able to do anything was like torture. I felt like part of me was out there with them. If anything happened to any of those people, I don't know what I would do.

The king came around the wall and spread his arms again. Bringing the arch of fire back to him. It was intimidating, but he wasn't doing anything with it. What was he waiting for? I furrowed my brow and tried to make sense of his show of power. He wasn't causing any damage or attacking.

A loud popping noise sounded and four figures in black robes appeared behind the king, trails of smoke blowing away at their feet. I moved forward, wanting to rush in to help my friends, but Yancey's arms held me tight. "Please, I won't go to the king."

"I'm sorry," he said. "We can't afford to lose you. Do you want your brother to rule Illaria?"

I wanted to argue, to tell him that I could defend myself down there but I knew I was putting myself into grave danger if I left this spot. Ashton and Celeste would never forgive me if I died trying to save them. Feeling defeated, I watched my friends take on the newcomers.

Without hesitation, Ashton threw a fireball at one of the sorcerers standing behind the king. Caught off guard, the man screamed and dropped to the ground, rolling around to eliminate the flames. While he was down, Celeste sent a gust of wind toward him, blowing his robe around him. Ashton sent another round of fire on the current and the man was engulfed in flames. He swung his arms around for a moment, then stopped moving.

The three remaining sorcerers pushed past the king and launched spells at Ashton and Celeste. She must have put up a shield because everything bounced off of them. While they were engaged in fighting the sorcerers, the king began to attack Master Flanders.

Master Flanders blocked the king's fire and sent a rain of small stones down on him. The king spread his arms wide and the stones blew away from him as if made of feathers. Master Flanders shook the ground, causing it to split as the king walked across it. The king lifted himself off the ground and floated toward Master Flanders.

I grabbed on to Yancey's arm, squeezing as the heavy weight of dread fell over me. How was I supposed to stand here while my teacher died for me?

Yancey turned me away from the battle. "You don't have to watch."

For a moment, I buried my head in his chest and took a few deep breaths. Regaining composure, I looked up at Yancey. "Is it possible that Master Flanders is wrong?"

Yancey shook his head. "He's descended from Oracles. Predictions can change, but visions usually do not."

"What about my friends?" I asked, glancing behind me.

"He didn't say."

"Isn't there anything we can do?" I asked.

"Just wait."

"Why do you keep saying that?" I pushed away from him.

"You have to trust me." He dropped his arms, freeing me from his grasp. "And you have to trust Master Flanders. If you go down there, you undo everything he has done for you and your kingdom."

My arms fell to my side and I looked out at the battle again. I was being asked to trust a stranger. But this stranger had saved my life and given me no reason to doubt him so far. As much as I didn't want to believe it, making a guard promise to keep me away from a battle seemed like something Master Flanders would do.

I covered my ears with my hands and watched at the king and Master Flanders continued to throw magic at each other. Turning away from them, I saw Ashton and Celeste taking on two black robed figures. While I was looking away, they'd managed to take one of them down.

Celeste lifted her hands. They were shaking so hard I could see the trembling from where I stood. Though I couldn't see the magic she was using, it looked like she had created some sort of funnel like Master Flanders had done, but on a smaller scale. The two remaining sorcerers were both suspended, just a few feet from the ground, spinning in a circle. Ashton approached and pulled a sword from his back. Where had that come from?

He thrust the sword into the first sorcerer, pulled it out and then sliced across the neck of the second. Celeste dropped her hands and collapsed to the ground. The two sorcerers fell to the ground in a heap of black robes. Ashton produced a fireball and threw it at them, setting them ablaze, then ran to Celeste's side.

He helped her up and wrapped her arm around his shoulders. They started walking toward the camp, ignoring Master Flanders' battle with the king. I sunk to the ground, I didn't even feel the wetness of the ground through my soaked clothes. If Ashton and Celeste were not going to help Master Flanders, he'd said something to convince them to leave.

Yancey extended a hand to me. "Get up. It's time."

Feeling numb from both cold and the scene in front of me, I reached up and let him pull me to my feet.

"Watch," Yancey said. He raised his hands, palms pressed together, then spread them apart making a wide "V" above his head. He closed his eyes, then slowly moved his arms further apart until they were resting on either side of him against his body.

"What are you doing?" I stared at him, forgetting about the battle going on.

He pressed his hands out in front of him and an arc of blue light appeared, then traveled toward the battle like a ripple in a pond, expanding as it moved away.

Master Flanders stopped fighting. He turned his head in my direction, then lifted his hands to his chest. The king's outstretched hands sent a burst of red and gold flames. They swallowed Master Flanders in an instant, leaving nothing behind.

"No!" I knew it was coming, but I couldn't believe it actually happened. "No!" Before I could realize what I was doing, I ran toward him. The king turned toward my cries and cradled a fireball in his hands.

Then, the blue arc of light went through the king, and he vanished.

I slid to a stop, chest rising and falling rapidly as I struggled to catch my breath. Where'd he go?

Yancey rested a hand on my shoulder and I pulled away. "What did you do? What was that?" I took several steps back. "What are you?"

"It's okay, you're safe, for now. I'm a sorcerer, just like you," he said.

I shook my head. "No, not like me. I can't make people disappear."

He lifted an eyebrow. "No? I saw you do it today. You teleported people out of danger's way. What I did wasn't much different. I sent him away. He's not gone for good, though. So right now, I have to get you, and the rest of your people to safety."

"Wait." I shoved him with both hands. "Why did you wait so long? If you could send him away, why wait?"

He grabbed my wrists to stop me from pushing him again. "I had to wait. Master Flanders made me promise. Where I come from, we take promises very seriously. I'm so sorry."

Tears rolled down my cheeks. I looked behind me to where Master Flanders had been. Was he really gone? How was it possible? My teeth chattered as the cold started to sink it. In the midst of the battle, I hadn't noticed how cold I was. Shivering, I wrapped my arms around my chest.

"Come on," Yancey draped his arm around my shoulder and guided me forward. "I have to get you warm."

37

ETTA

"Thank the gods, Etta." Saffron ran to me as soon as we reached the edge of camp. She put her hand on my face. "You're freezing. We need to get you warm."

It was getting difficult to get words out through the shivering. "We have to get out of here." It was all I could manage. Would the king send in more guards? Or would he return for wherever Yancey had sent him?

Saffron replaced Yancey next to me and put her arms around me. "We will. As soon as you are in dry clothes."

She led me to my quarters. It wasn't much warmer in my tent, but at least there wasn't any new snow falling on me. Saffron peeled off my wet clothes and pulled off my slippers while I continued to shiver. She wrapped a blanket around me. "Can you move your fingers and toes?"

My fingers were throbbing. Slowly, I bent them in a fist, then straightened them, repeating the process until the pain dulled. My toes tingled, which I hoped was a good sign. I wiggled them. They seemed to be responding.

"Good," Saffron said, looking between my hands and feet. She led me to a chair and sat me down. Then she began to walk around the mess that was my quarters, searching for something for me to wear. She returned with a pair of trousers and a heavy dress. "Wear both. It'll be warmer."

I nodded and stood so she could help me step into the clothes. As I began to warm up, my thoughts drifted back to the battle and what needed to be done next. If I focused on what we had to do, maybe I could keep myself from thinking about what had happened and who we had lost. There had to be something good to come from all of this. Perhaps it wasn't as bad as it seemed in the midst of the fighting. "Saffron, how many survived?"

She was bent down, lacing up a dry boot. She frowned. "I don't know the numbers yet, but it doesn't look good."

I rubbed my forehead. "Has everybody been evacuated?"

She nodded. "Most people have been. Madame Lyndsey's friends came through and were able to teleport the non-fighters out. A few people stayed behind to wait for you."

"My guards?"

She paused before she answered, as if she was deciding how to word her response. "And a few others. If you feel up for their company."

My stomach flipped. "Ashton?"

"I can send him away, if that's what you want," she said without looking up.

Did I want to see him? I'd spent the last two weeks missing him, but was still so angry at him. Now he was back and he was safe. I was relieved that he was safe but I didn't know how I was supposed to act around him anymore. If we weren't together, what were we? Were we even friends?

"There." Saffron stood. "You should be warmer now." She handed me the blanket. "Wrap this around you so you can keep your clothes dry."

I stood and threw the blanket over my shoulders. "Thank you."

"Ready to go?" she asked. "Madame Lyndsey can take us to everybody else. Is there anything you need to bring?"

I looked around the tent. Another abandoned home. Would I ever get to stay in one place? I reached for my pendant and squeezed it in my hand. At least this stays with me wherever I go.

"I just need my bow," I said.

Saffron lifted her hand, she already had it. Yancey must have given it to her.

"Thank you." I took the bow from her. Holding it made it easier to walk away from the place I'd called home for the last few months. My fingers brushed against the carved wood of the bow. It helped me to focus on the things that mattered. My friends, my people, my throne. "After you," I said, sweeping my arm toward the front of the tent.

Saffron nodded once and opened the flap, walking out into the blowing snow. I followed her. While I had been inside, my entire guard has assembled in front of the tent. Doing a quick count, I noticed that all of them had survived the battle. That's a good sign.

Charles stepped up to me and dropped into a low bow. "Your highness, forgive me for letting you down. I should have been able to stay with you. I understand if you'd like to name a new captain."

"Please rise, Charles," I said. "You stay as my captain, but you might have to get used to losing me. I'm hard to keep up with."

He smiled. "I'll be ready next time."

"I know you will," I said.

My guard shifted, making a hole for me to walk through. Behind them, Ashton and Celeste stood with Madame Lyndsey. The two of them looked terrible. Their clothes were torn and burned in places. Their faces were smeared with blood and soot. Celeste's long hair was knotted and blew wildly in the wind.

At the sight of them, tears welled up and my knees buckled. Charles steadied me and Ashton reached for me, but then pulled his hand back. Words escaped my mind. I didn't know what to say or how to react. They were here, they were alive.

Celeste smiled, tears in her eyes. She ran between my guards and caught me in an embrace. I squeezed her back and we both started laughing.

"Am I happy to see you," Celeste said.

"I'm so glad you're safe," I said.

Celeste pulled back and clasped my hand. We stood there, hand in hand, for several long seconds before she dropped my hand and gave me a little push toward Ashton.

He stepped forward and for a moment, we just stared at each other. I had missed him the whole time he was gone but the things he said seemed to echo through my mind. Part of me wanted to move closer to him, to feel his arms around me, but part of me was afraid of being hurt again. I'd let him in, trusted him. More than I'd ever trusted anyone in my whole life. *And he broke you. He broke that trust.*

I could feel the Darkness wrapping itself around my heart, tugging at it, protecting it. *You can't let anyone in. You'll just get hurt again.*

"Etta." Ashton's brow was furrowed, eyes pleading. "I'm so sorry. I never should have said those things."

The Darkness squeezed, and my breath caught. *Don't believe him. How can you trust him?* I knew I shouldn't be letting it in, I shouldn't be listening, but what was so wrong about protecting my heart?

"Can you ever forgive me?" Ashton's eyes were still locked on me. He didn't move closer. It was as if he could sense my internal struggle.

This was Ashton. My closest friend. The one person in the world who knew everything about me. *Not everything.* I furrowed my brow at the thought. He didn't know that the Darkness was speaking to me, trying to pull me in, doing its best to control me. *Maybe he's not the monster here, you are.*

Every time the Darkness called to me, I felt like I was losing part of myself. *It's his fault, you know.* If I hadn't gone to the Underworld to save Ashton, I wouldn't have opened the bridge to allow the Darkness in. I wouldn't be channeling it the way I am now. He never asked me to do that. I took a deep breath and imagined the dark tendrils that had closed around my heart, releasing. Today wasn't the day I was going to let the Darkness win. "We have all done things we regret."

His face brightened. "Could you ever give me another chance?"

The group around us shuffled and I could feel the tension raise around me. Everyone was watching. I kept my gaze on Ashton, not wanting to know what those around me were thinking. Something between us had shifted. Things had changed. Until I could control the Darkness, I was a risk. It was too much. For now, I needed to figure out who I was and focus on saving my kingdom. "I can't think about that right now."

Ashton stepped back away from me and I had to tighten my jaw to keep it from trembling. He looked like I kicked him in the gut. *Now he knows how you felt.* Ignoring the dark thought, I steeled myself. This was the right thing to do. "The important thing right now is to move up the attack on the king and finish what we started."

My heart raced in my chest, as if begging me to change my mind, but I knew this needed to be done. Unable to look at him anymore, I turned to Celeste. "What happened with the stone? I'll need to know what to tell my uncle."

Celeste held out two pieces of gray rock in her hands. "This is all that's left of it."

My heart leapt at the sight of the broken stone and I reached to touch the pieces. "You destroyed it." I looked at Celeste and Ashton, finally feeling a rise of hope. "Does that mean the Reapers are gone?"

"I think so," Celeste said. "The sorcerer who made the stone was guarding it. Ashton destroyed him and the stone."

Hands reached out to touch the remains of the Stone of Morare. I could feel the energy shifting in the group. My guards, Madame Lyndsey, Saffron, Celeste, and Ashton closed in around me. All of them had risked so much already and we hadn't even gone after the king yet. Master Flanders missing from the group left a hole inside me. There was no way I was going to lose anyone else. These people were my whole life. They deserved to be free of the fear of the king. They deserved to be happy. It was time to act. "I have to go to Gallia and see if we can move up the battle. We can't let this attack stop us. It's time to rid Illaria of evil once and for all."

"He might have the Skystone, but he's lost his Reapers. There's no way he'll expect us to attack so soon. We'll catch him by surprise," Saffron said. "I say, we do it."

"Etta, there's something you should know." Ashton took a step toward me. "The king attacked because he was after Master Flanders. He found out that he was the sorcerer who cast the protection spell on you. There is nothing stopping the king from harming you."

I swallowed back the lump that rose in my throat at the thought of Master Flanders. There would be time to mourn the dead later. "Then it's even more important now that we don't fail."

"You need to go now," Saffron said. "We can take care of the

Ravens. We can be there, hiding in the woods before sunrise after the wedding. Go. Get us an army."

"I'm coming with you," Celeste said. She leaned down to pick up something set on the ground. I recognized the orb that we had wrapped in fabric. She must have retrieved it from my room before I arrived.

I glanced at Ashton, half expecting him to say something. He remained quiet. I wanted to say something to him. He'd left without a goodbye and this was the last time we'd see each other before we would be fighting the king. Looking at him made me feel broken. There was still a part of me that felt a pull to him, but I knew it wasn't the time. I couldn't be trusted with my own emotions until I took control of the Darkness inside me.

Turning to Celeste, I nodded. "Alright, you come with me."

I gave Saffron a quick hug. "See you on the battlefield."

A hand caught hold of my upper arm and I turned to see Ashton, pulling me closer to him. We moved a few steps away from the group, who turned their backs on us at Saffron's urging.

"Be careful," Ashton said.

I couldn't tear my eyes away from his. "You too."

"I'm sorry," he said.

All I could do was nod.

He broke his gaze away from mine. "You better get going."

Without another word, I gripped my bow and walked away. Celeste and my guards followed me back to the portal. It was time to end the king.

38

ETTA

I marched through the marble portal room in my uncle's castle. Without waiting for a formal greeting, my guards, Celeste and I made our way through the doors into the window lined hallway.

As soon as we opened the doors, we found ourselves face to face with a row of guards. At the sight of us, they hesitated. Charles stepped forward. "Make way for her highness, Queen Elisabetta of Illaria."

The guards stepped back, lowering their weapons and bowed their heads. I was sure I didn't look the part of a queen today, but did my best to keep my chin high as we walked through the guards.

"This way to the study?" I pointed down the hall.

Charles was next to me, matching my pace step for step. "Yes."

About halfway down the hall, I saw a group of people walking toward us. My uncle Gaius was at the center of the group.

He stopped in front of our group. "What happened?"

"The king attacked us at our camp." I paused, torn between

giving him all the details or just telling him the news. Master Flanders had died to see me on the throne. He wouldn't want me to dwell on the past. When this was over, we'd mourn the dead. "The king has moved the wedding and he won't except us to come to him after what he did. We have to move up the attack."

"When is it?" he asked.

"Tomorrow."

He turned to one of his sorcerers, "Master Acel, let the others know we need to get the portal ready."

Master Acel nodded and headed away from the group.

"Come." He offered his arm to me and we started walking again. "Let's go meet with my generals."

"I'm sorry we weren't able to give you more warning," I said.

"The fact that this was moved up and the attack on the Raven camp tells me that the king is nervous. He probably thinks you're going to do something and figures you won't be ready. This might give us an edge."

My stomach was in knots and I tried to find something positive about this situation.

Gaius glanced over at me. He seemed to know how I was feeling. He put an arm around my shoulders. "Don't worry. You could be back on your throne by tomorrow night if all goes to plan."

My breath caught in my chest. Was I ready for that? Since deciding to fight for my throne, it had seemed so far away. Now that it was within my reach, it seemed so foreign. How was I going to fix this kingdom?

Gaius led me down the twists and turns of the hallways until we reached an area of the castle I hadn't been in before. A series of doors lined the hallway.

"This is where my guards and generals stay," he explained. We continued down the hallway to a large room. The walls were lined with maps and in the center of the room stood a large table. No chairs surrounded the table but a semicircle of chairs surrounded a small fireplace in one corner. Three men were standing around the table. They stood at attention and bowed as we entered the room.

Gaius put his hand up to stop them. "No time for formality now. The plans have to be moved up."

"How much?" a tall man with dark hair and a thick beard asked.

Gaius took a breath. "The wedding is happening tomorrow."

The man nodded. "We're ready." He looked at me. "Your highness, we are ready to fight for you."

"Thank you." I had to swallow back the lump that rose in my throat. Everything was coming together. These men were going to stand up to defend my throne on my behalf.

"We heard about what happened in Greenville. Nobody should be attacking unarmed civilians, ever." His face darkened and his hands drew up into fists. I knew his anger well, and I'm glad he shared it with me.

Gaius turned to me. "Any word on the search for the stone?"

"Yes." I gestured to Celeste. "This is my friend, Celeste, she was on the journey with Ashton. They were able to destroy the stone."

Gaius stretched his hand out to Celeste. "Many thanks, to you. You are a hero and your bravery will help make this attack more successful."

Celeste shook his hand. "Thank you, your highness. There is one thing you all should know." She looked over at me. "We had a run-in with Max. He has a dragon and seems to be planning to betray the king."

The good feelings that had come with recalling the destruction of the Stone of Morare went out like a candle being snuffed.

I had worried about Max or the king being the ones with ties to the dragon. What did that mean for our plan?

The men around me grew quiet. Gaius broke the silence. "That could work to our advantage. If Max is fighting against the king, it will be easier to take the king down."

"We don't know if he'll be openly opposing him yet," Celeste said.

"We'll find out when we get there. If he keeps playing the king's pet, I'd guess the dragon won't be there. That's all he has to compete against the king. He wouldn't want him to know about it," I said.

The general nodded. "We'll have to figure that out when we get there. Either way, it can play to our advantage. If Max isn't fighting against the king, we go about everything as planned. If a dragon is helping to attack the king, we'll let it. Once the king is gone, we'll turn our attention to Max."

I nodded. It was as good of a plan as any. "Do you think we can really take down the king?"

"We've got 10,000 men and 45 sorcerers who hate the impostor on the throne as much as you do," the general said. "He won't stand a chance."

"I hope so," I said. "I don't know how much help we'll have from the Ravens, but they will be waiting in the king's woods before sunrise."

The general narrowed his eyes at me. "You sure you should be fighting in this battle? I've never heard of a queen who does her own fighting."

"Except for her mother," Gaius cut in.

The general straightened, eyes wide. Then, he lowered his head. "I'm sorry, your grace, I didn't mean any insult."

"I know," Gaius said. "Etta is her mother's daughter, and I'm sure the sorcerers will benefit from having her in their ranks."

"Your highness." Charles turned to me. He hadn't left my side since leaving the Raven camp. "You should know that being in a battle of this scale will be unlike anything you have experienced before. There will be loss of life on both sides. You won't be able to stop when you see somebody fall. There are going to be people you can't save. You have to stay focused on keeping yourself alive."

My stomach knotted and I dug my fingernails into my palms. I wasn't a stranger to death or losing those I loved. As much as I hated to recall the terrible things I'd done, I'd killed. These things weren't new to me, but this was still going to be different from anything we had experienced so far.

We'd been in battles, but it was with less than a hundred men. We didn't have an army so we could rely on moving quickly, hiding, and having the advantage of the land. That wasn't going to work here. It didn't even matter if I was ready for this. It was happening. It had to happen. We had to win. If we didn't we were all dead.

The Darkness seemed to vibrate inside me, it welcomed the battle, it wanted it. I wasn't in the mood to hear the dark thoughts that found their way inside my head and closed my eyes for a moment, preparing to send it away at the first sign of betrayal into my mind.

"Your highness?"

Opening my eyes, I looked at Charles and the rest of my guard. "Don't worry. We'll be ready."

Gaius turned to me. "You will be. But tonight, you need to recover. Tomorrow, I'll introduce you to all of my sorcerers and you can prepare for the attack on the king."

As we walked back through the hallways, I tried to fight off the nauseous feeling rising inside me. I knew we had real chance at beating the king, but something didn't feel right. Perhaps it was pre-battle nerves or maybe it was the fact that all

I wanted to do was ask Master Flanders for advice, and for the first time since I started training as a sorcerer, I couldn't.

"You can stay in the same rooms you were in during your visit, Etta. Celeste can stay in one of our guest rooms." He paused in front of the door.

"That's not necessary," I said. "There is more than enough room for us to share this room."

"Of course," he said. "I'll send some ladies to help you get cleaned up and some food. I'm sure you'll want to rest before tomorrow."

"Thank you." The last thing on my mind right now was getting cleaned up but I was a guest here and didn't want to be rude.

Gaius opened the door for us, pausing with his hand on the handle. "What you are about to do is a great risk."

"I know," I said.

"I want you to know, that if the worst should happen, you're always welcome here."

I nodded, hoping that I wouldn't end up spending the rest of my life as a refugee living in my uncle's castle. While there were worse things that could happen, spending my life knowing I'd failed my people while I returned to a life of privilege didn't seem like a viable option. No, I wouldn't be coming back here unless I was victorious.

39

ETTA

Somehow, despite the questions in my head, I slept. When I woke, Celeste was still asleep in the bed next to me. She'd thrown off all the covers and managed to turn almost sideways while she slept. If the bed weren't so large, she'd have knocked me off. I couldn't help but smile.

Walking over to the windows, I threw open the curtains, flooding the room with sunlight. Celeste grunted and turned over, covering her head with a pillow. I wished I was as sound a sleeper as she was.

A gentle knock sounded on the door and I padded across the floor in my bare feet to answer. When I opened the door, my guards stepped aside and I found my cousin, Mari, smiling at me. "Father caught me up on everything." Her face fell. "Are you alright?"

I stepped back and moved away from the doorway so she could enter. "I'm fine. Just ready to have this over with." My stomach was a tangle of nerves as I considered what I was saying. I was ready to be done fighting, done hiding, done feeling afraid all the time. What I wasn't sure about was if I could do it.

Mari entered and I closed the door behind her. "Good morning." She waved in the direction of the bed and I tuned to see that Celeste was awake, sitting on the bed. Her dark curls surrounding her face like a cloud of hair.

"Good morning." Celeste got off the bed and walked over to us.

"Mari, this is my friend, Celeste," I said, "Celeste, this is my cousin, Mari."

Turning to Mari, lowered her head, and greeted Mari in Gallic. "It's so nice to meet you, your highness."

Mari smiled, and spoke to her in rapid-fire Gallic. I caught some of the words exchanged between them, but my study of the language had typically been done with practice conversations and reading books. True conversation was challenging to keep up with.

After a few minutes, Mari switched back to Illarian. "I'd love to stay and talk, but father sent me to invite you to breakfast. He says you'll be meeting the sorcerers after."

"Of course," I said, glancing down at the nightgown I'd been given. "Let me change, then we can go."

As Celeste and I changed into the fresh dresses that had been left for us last night, Mari asked us questions about the battle and what had happened in the few hours I'd been away from Gallia. She seemed horrified by everything I told her.

"You're still going to go fight after all of that?" she asked. "I mean, you have the Gallic army, you could stay here where it's safe and let them fight for you."

I laced up the ribbon on the sleeves of the far too-fancy dress I was now wearing. "I have to fight. What sort of message will it send to my people if I'm not willing to fight for my own throne?"

Mari's forehead creased. "You must hate me."

"Why would you say that?" I asked.

"Because I grew up here." She opened her arms and gestured

around the opulent room. "I never had to struggle or fight for anything. I just get to be queen and you have to go out there and fight for it."

"Oh, Mari." I walked over to her and rested my hand on her shoulder. "I don't hate you. It's not your fault I'm in this situation. And I know you're going to make an amazing queen."

"So will you." She pulled me in for a hug.

I was going to have to get used to all the affection from her. If everything went according to plan, I'd be Queen of Illaria and one day, she'll be the Queen of Gallia. She was family, something I'd spent my whole life dreaming of. She tightened her grip on me, adding a sense of urgency to the embrace. I could feel her fear coming though. Like she had said, she'd grown up protected. Even though she wasn't going out to fight, the upcoming battle had to be causing her fear. I squeezed back. "It's going to be fine. We're going to win."

She let go of the hug, and took a deep breath. "We have the best army in the word, of course we will."

Despite her confident words, I could still sense the tension in her. What did it mean that someone who wasn't even going to be anywhere near the battle was afraid? I swallowed back the flicker of fear that had cut through my nerves. This wasn't the time to worry. We still had another day before we'd challenge the king. Glancing behind me, I saw Celeste standing in silence. She seemed lost for words. I wondered if she was feeling the same thing I was.

"Shall we go?" I asked Mari.

The three of us walked away from the room, my guards following silently behind me.

CELESTE and I followed Gaius down a long corridor lined with paintings of serious looking men in armor. They appeared to follow me with their eyes. I shivered. When we exited the corridor, the marble floors I had grown accustomed to in the castle changed to gray stone. The walls were made of the same gray stone and the lack of windows made the space darker. I crossed my arms over my chest against the sudden temperature drop.

"We're in the sorcerer wing," Gaius said. "This part of the castle is actually the original castle built by my family 600 years ago. The sorcerers asked to have this part of the castle after they joined our household when my great-grandfather was king."

I looked up at the high, gray ceilings. There was nothing in this space to personalize it or make it look in the least bit cheerful. It reminded me of a dungeon. We passed several closed wooden doors then the hallway opened into a large common room with two massive fireplaces. The room had no windows and was lit by candles in sconces along the walls.

Several chairs and thread-bare couches were scattered about the room. On a few small tables, books were piled up so high they stood taller than me. I worried some of the piles may fall if a breeze were to pass through the room.

Two men occupied a semicircle of chairs in a corner near one of the fireplaces. My heart leapt at the sight of man with long gray hair. For a moment, I thought he was Master Flanders, then I remembered I'd never see him again.

Gaius cleared his throat. Both men turned, then stood and bowed at the king.

"Masters," Gaius said. "I'd like to formally introduce Elisabetta Aqualine, rightful Queen of Illaira."

The man who I had first taken as Master Flanders smiled. He had warm brown eyes and a kind face. "I'm happy to see you return to Gallia, Master Moreau." The man turned to me and bowed his head. "It's a pleasure to meet you, your highness, I am Master Colin."

I inclined my head. "Nice to meet you, master."

The second man, a squat, bald man with watery gray eyes approached. He was wearing the long green robes that the sorcerers who were at my arrival had worn, though I didn't recall seeing him that day. He stopped in front of me and dropped into a low bow.

When he stood, I realized he was a little shorter than me, which was unusual for a man. "It's a pleasure to meet you, your highness. I am Master Marcus, head sorcerer of Gallia."

I curtseyed. "Nice to meet you, Master."

Gaius turned to Celeste. "And this is -"

"Celeste Moreau." Master Colin said. "It's nice to see you again, Master Moreau."

I looked over at Celeste. To me, she'd been my friend Celeste for so long now, I had forgotten that she was a full sorcerer after the trials. I'd never once referred to her proper title.

Gaius raised an eyebrow and looked from Celeste to Master Colin.

"She was one of our star pupils at the Academy, your grace," Master Colin said. "She never returned after completing her trials."

"She stayed to help me," I said.

"Well, isn't that extraordinary," Gaius said. "I knew a few of our sorcerers had offered to help. I didn't realize we had such a recent member in the inner circle of the queen of Illaria." He smiled.

"I wouldn't be here without her," I said.

"I can't wait to hear all of the stories when this is finished," Gaius said.

"If you'll excuse me, Masters." Gaius looked around at everyone gathered. "I have a few things to see to. Master Marcus, can you see to it that Etta finds her way to my study when you are finished?"

He bowed to the king. "Of course, your majesty."

"Can we sit?" he gestured to the chairs they had just come from. I inclined my head and followed him.

Arranging my dress, I sat into a chair covered with a faded, pink fabric. It had probably been red at one point but time had taken the vibrancy from it.

Master Marcus and Master Flanders took seats across from me. Master Marcus didn't waste any time with formality. "I hear you can produce arctic fire."

I glanced at Celeste. Was this how people started conversations in Gallia? She nodded.

"That's correct." I smoothed the skirt of my dress and folded my hands in my lap.

Master Marcus made a whistling sound and leaned back in his chair. "I'm impressed. I've never met any sorcerer who can do that." He leaned closer to me. "Though, there are so few water sorcerers in existence as it is."

His comment made me squeeze my hands together. Was he downplaying my abilities? I'd grown so used to people being in awe of my powers, I couldn't tell if he was trying to dismiss it due to the lack of people who aligned with water in the first place.

Master Marcus rested his chin on his hand. "I suppose that you are still learning to control it?"

"I practiced with Master Flanders every day for the last few weeks. I'm getting better at control." My stomach flipped as I recalled our training sessions. There wasn't anyone to train me anymore.

"I was hoping you'd bring your Master Flanders with you again, he's a very talented sorcerer and we could use his expertise," Master Colin said.

My shoulders sunk and I looked down at my hands. "He was killed by the king when we were attacked yesterday."

The room was silent for a moment. "I'm sorry to hear that," Master Colin said.

"He will be missed," Master Marcus said. "There will be many losses tomorrow, but if all of us sorcerers work together, we should be able to change the tide."

I looked up at him. "What do you need me to do?"

"First," he said. "I need you to not get killed. That arctic fire of yours might be the key to helping bring down the king. He's not undead, but his life has been magically prolonged. We're not sure what will truly kill him, but based on my research, your fire might be our best bet."

I nodded. All this time, we'd been working toward killing the king. We needed to remove him from power. There was nothing I liked about the king and while I wanted to see him dead, I never thought I would be the one who would deal him the killing blow he deserved. Something dark rose inside me at the thought. I had kept the Darkness contained for the last few days, but the thought of taking down the king, of ending this war and claiming my throne sent my emotions into overdrive. I took a deep breath, working to clear my mind. If I did kill the king, I was going to do it on my own. I wouldn't let the Darkness in. "I'll be ready."

40

MAX

Max paused in front of the double doors that led to the royal chapel. The guests had already arrived and every eye would be fixed on him as he walked to his place at the front. He looked down at the black velvet tunic he wore. The gold embroidery was stitched on in a subtle pattern that incorporated the phoenix and flames of the house he was marrying into. It should have been the other way around, his family crest being the focus, but given his illegitimate birth, the king had insisted on retaining his own crest.

Taking a deep breath, Max nodded to the guards in front of the doors. This wedding was the last thing he would have to do as the king's supporter. Once he and Nora were married, there was nothing stopping them from taking over the kingdom.

As the heavy doors swung open, Max held his chin high and kept his eyes forward. He didn't want to look at the faces of the people who were gathered for this. They weren't loyal to him or Nora, they were the king's supporters. His own Dragons were absent today, making sure that the king felt no threats.

Out of the corner of his eye, Max could see the important people of Illaria watching him. He smiled as they rose when he walked by. These people who had shunned him because of his lesser birth now had to at least pretend to respect him. All of the people here had been asked to denounce the king and rise up with the Ravens. None of them had been willing to sacrifice their comforts and their titles to do what was right. Max was going to enjoy making them all pay for their choice.

At the end of the aisle, Max greeted the priest, then turned to face the heavy doors. They'd been closed again in anticipation of the arrival of the princess. A bead of sweat trickled down Max's forehead and he ignored it, trying to maintain an expression of indifference. As if he'd always known he'd marry the heir to the throne.

Horns sounded from outside the doors and they swung open to reveal Nora, bathed in sunlight from the windows in the hall-way. The music grew louder as the musicians moved through the door and stood on either side of it, moving into a festive processional tune.

The people in the chapel stood and lowered themselves into bows as the king walked up the aisle with his daughter. Nora had shed her usual black in favor of a gold and ivory gown heavy with pearls and lace. The train of her dress trailed behind her leaving a golden river in her wake. The pattern woven on the dress matched the pattern on Max's tunic. Every detail had been planned to demonstrate the importance of this wedding. The king had made it clear to his inner circle that the unfortunate death of Nora's first husband would not leave his daughter as a widow before she even turned twenty.

They walked slowly up the aisle, pausing when they reached the altar. As was tradition, King Osbert took hold of his daugh-ter's hand, and Max's hand, bringing the two together. He faced the gathered crowd. "Blessings on this day, the day that two become one."

King Osbert clasped Max and Nora's hands together and

held them up to for all to see, then he lowered them, and let go, leaving the couple joined hand in hand. Max bowed to the king, eyes lowered, trying to look as humble as possible.

Nora curtseyed to her father, then took hold of Max's other hand, signaling the beginning of the ceremony. Max glanced at the front row, which had been left vacant. King Osbert sat alone, watching the ceremony.

The priest raised his hands above his head, indicating the start of the ceremony. Max's stomach twisted in anticipation. This was what they had been waiting for. If the king was going to stop them, he would have done it already. Once the words were spoken, Max and Nora would be married. Only death could undo a royal wedding bond.

The priest began the wedding rite, telling the story of the gods blessing the first people and teaching them to care for each other. The next several minutes were a blur to Max as he repeated the words the priest asked him to say. He hardly registered what was being said. This had been the plan, but now that he was in the midst of the wedding, now that he was actually going through with it, it didn't seem real.

Even during his time with the Ravens, Max had known he'd need to marry to secure his legacy once he gained the throne, but it had seemed so far away and so out of reach. He hadn't ever paused to think about who that partner would be. Now, he was staring into the face of the woman who was about to be his wife. Soon, he'd be the heir to the Illarian throne in his own right. He'd always wanted to be king, but he never thought this was how he would gain the crown.

Nora squeezed Max's hands, bringing him back to the present. He looked over to see that the priest had produced two wreathes for the couple. The bride's had been made of flowers woven by children to promote fertility. The groom's was a circle of carved oak to represent strength and wisdom.

Max smiled at Nora, trying to reassure her. She had taken just as much of a risk as he had by going through with this plan. While she made it clear she held affection for Max, he knew she could have been with any man she wanted. If it weren't for her desire to be queen and to put an end to her father's reign, they wouldn't be about to exchange wedding wreathes.

Max took the flower wreath from the priest and placed it on the princess' lowered head. Her bow was symbolic of her submission to her husband. The priest himself put the wreath on Max's head. With the exchange complete, the couple faced the priest for the end of the ceremony.

Max hadn't seen a formal wedding ceremony performed since before the Battle of the Dead. He wasn't quite sure what happened next. In front of them, the priest held a bound, leather book. He began to read from it, something in ancient Illarian, that Max could barely make out. He'd neglected his studies after joining the Ravens and until this point, hadn't needed to know language of his ancestors. Cheers erupted around them as the priest closed the book. Max turned to Nora in surprise. The priest leaned down to them. "You can kiss her now."

Max leaned in, kissing Nora and completing the wedding rite. A swell of pride surged through him. They'd done it. Max and Nora were officially the heirs to the throne. Now all they needed to do was take what was theirs.

The room was dark and quiet. Shadows played across the ceiling from the flickering firelight. I knew I should be in bed but sleep wasn't coming easy tonight. I sat on the couch in front of the fire, tracing the etchings on my pendant with my finger. The metal glowed in the light of the fire, making the Ouroboros of my family's crest even more dramatic. The fire cracked and a few sparks flew out, landing on the already singed rug in front of the fireplace.

Leaning back against the couch, I tucked the pendant back under my clothes. Tomorrow, we would be making our run for my throne. If we won, would I start feeling like the queen I said I was?

Closing my eyes, I tried to imagine what the battle might look like. What would it feel like to be surrounded by that many armed men and sorcerers? Would I even be able to get to the king? What if our plan failed? What if it didn't? When faced with the chance, would I be able to kill the king? Would I be strong enough? What if Max showed up? Could I really kill my own brother? The questions kept filling my mind, churning over and over. Occasionally, the slither of the Darkness found its way into my thoughts. So far, I'd been able to send it away easily, but this was a safe room away from the dangers of a war. Taking a deep breath, I worked to clear all my thoughts away. I needed to be focused for tomorrow. I didn't even want to consider what would happen if we didn't win.

Fear washed over me as I realized what a loss would mean. I hadn't let myself think about it before, but I knew that if we didn't win, there probably wouldn't be a day after tomorrow for me. If we lost, it would be the end.

MAX

Max and Nora led the way outside the castle into an outdoor courtyard that had been transformed for the celebration of their wedding. Above them, hundreds of glowing fireballs floated, filling the night sky like giant fireflies. They let off heat, keeping the space warm despite the cold weather. Bare trees free of their leaves were wrapped in gold silk and the fountain near the castle at the back of the courtyard was pouring purple water. Tables covered in purple and gold fabric dotted the space and tables laden with food were set up on the edges.

King Osbert held back near the entrance, giving Max and Nora a moment of pretend privacy. Taking her by the hand, Max guided Nora to the opposite end of the courtyard, as far from the door as they could get. He looked into her eyes and brushed the flowing red hair away from her face. The whole wedding had been part of the plan to gain the kingdom, but Max couldn't help but feel a little proud of the woman he now called his wife. "We did it."

She smiled. "Almost."

He knew what she meant. The night wasn't over yet. "True. Almost."

The guests from the ceremony began to flood into the space and servants walked around with bottles of wine, filling the glasses that were left on the tables. Max mingled with the crowd, accepting begrudging congratulations and well-wishes from people who wished it had been their child standing in his place right now. His face hurt from the fake smile he wore and he counted down to when he would no longer have to pretend to be something he wasn't.

As people began to fill their seats at the tables, servants served the guests. The courtyard was filled with quiet conversation as everyone ate. With each course, and each round of wine, the conversation grew louder, dotted with boisterous laughter.

Max and Nora sat at a long table at the far end of the courtyard right next to the king. Nora was keeping her father distracted and entertained, filling his wine glass frequently from the bottle that had been left on their table. Max hardly touched his food. Nobody seemed to notice how distracted the new prince was.

All eyes turned toward the castle as the servants arrived with dessert. Huge platters of pastries and sweets were carried around to each table. Despite the amount of food that had already been consumed, the guests continued to fill their plates with the rare treats.

Max leaned over to Nora. "It's time."

She nodded, then turned to her father. "Excuse me, I'm feeling a bit ill."

King Osbert whispered to her, concern showing on his face. It wasn't an unusual symptom of pregnancy and Nora had made sure she'd excused herself from most meals the last few weeks. Rumors had started to spread about the princess' condition, but it wasn't unheard of for a wedding to come after a baby. Being the daughter of the Necromancer king, nobody would dare openly question her.

When Nora stood, it took a few moments for the guests to take notice, but once they did, everyone rose. She lifted a hand. "Please, sit."

Hesitantly, people returned to their seats as Nora walked back to the castle. Max now sat alone with the king. An empty chair between them. Flutters of anticipation filled his stomach as he waited. The seconds ticked by, time seemed to have stopped. Then, the chatter of conversation was masked by the thunderous flapping of wings.

Glasses dropped to the ground, shattering. Max smiled. They couldn't see the dragon yet, but he knew they could feel her. Everyone gathered would feel the creeping fear the creature brought with her before an attack.

King Osbert turned to Max, a scowl on his face. Max smiled. He was going to enjoy watching his dragon kill everyone.

The dragon was larger than the entire courtyard and she circled above, sending gusts of wind from her massive wings. A rush of wind extinguished all the fireballs and screams filled the air as people began to realize the cause of the events taking place. Max left his chair and headed toward the castle. Standing next to the fountain, he called to his dragon. "Kill them all."

In a rush of heat, dragon fire poured out of the beast's mouth, Max lifted his arm to shield his face from the blaze. The sound of people crying out in pain was deafening. Then, all at once, the cries stopped. The heat lessened. Max dropped his arm and looked in front of him. Everything in front of him was black and smoking. Piles of ash stood where the tables and people had been. He couldn't tell the difference between them.

"Max?" Nora stepped out from the castle and walked over to him. She stared out at the destruction.

Max still had his arms raised toward the sky. He lowered them then turned to face his wife. "It's done." A wicked grin stretched across his face. "You're looking at your new king."

"I wouldn't be so sure about that." A strong, clear voice rang out above them.

Max looked up, seeing a figure still standing in the smoke. Somehow, the king had survived. Flames ignited in Max's hands, a momentary loss of control, as the heat of rage flooded through his body. He squeezed his hands into fists, extinguishing the flames. How could this be? How could he have survived dragon fire? After all that planning, what had Max missed?

The king's upper lip was curled in disgust. "My own daughter." He shook his head and locked his gaze on Max. "You may have won the battle, son. But you'll never win the war."

Max scowled at the king. "This isn't over." He grabbed his wife and in a cloud, he vanished.

43

ETTA

It was still dark when we gathered in the portal room. Since the sorcerers had determined that I needed to stay hidden until we could find the king, I would be entering with only my guards. Even Celeste would be in going through the portal with the other sorcerers. I was to stay at the rear of the army and wait until we found the king. I'd insisted on wearing trousers and a tunic today. My bow was slung across my back with a full quiver of arrows clipped to my belt. I gripped the bow, feeling a sense of security at having my trusted weapon with me. My magic was what we were counting on and I needed to conserve it so the bow was my go-to weapon until we found the king.

Master Marcus waited with us in the room. "Remember, we need you to go after the king, so don't die."

The words were blunt and exactly what I needed to hear. I was beyond the point of sugar-coating. I knew what we were all risking by doing this. He passed me a coin so I could travel through the portal and I squeezed it tight in my palm.

Butterflies swam in my stomach. This was it. We were going to attack the king. Everything had been leading up to this since I was first introduced to this world. The execution had changed, but the goal remained: eliminate the king.

I stepped forward to go through the ripple. Charles dropped his arm in front of me. "Wait."

Two of my guards went through, then Charles and Yancey stood by my sides while a third guard stood behind me. "Now," Charles said.

A wave of cold washed over me as we stepped through the ripple. It momentarily took my breath from me and I let out a deep breath as we stepped on the other side. We stood in a muddy field filled with yellow grass. I could see the castle in front of me. We were far enough away that the guards looked like tiny specks. They wouldn't be able to make us out at this distance.

The sun was just beginning its ascent across the sky, illuminating everything in a warm, yellow glow. The last few purple and pink clouds of sunrise were being washed away by the increasing brightness of the sun. I glanced to the woods, wondering where the Ravens were hiding. Were Saffron and Ashton there? Did they see us when we arrived? Part of me wanted to run to the woods, see if I could say something to my friends before this started. My heart ached to see Ashton again. Had I made the right choice by telling him I couldn't be with him right now? Whatever happened today was going to change everything.

We all stood there in a group, silently clutching whatever weapons we had. All around me I could hear rapid breathing and I wondered if everybody else could hear my heart pounding inside my chest. I adjusted my bow and kept staring toward the castle.

My fingers were starting to go numb from the cold and the lack of movement. I rubbed my hands together, then stuck them under my armpits for warmth. Feet around me started to fidget. I shook my hands out, they were starting to tingle. At first, I had mistaken the magic for the cold, but as the tingle crept up my arms, there was no mistaking it. Letting out a gasp, several heads turned toward me. "They're on their way," I whispered.

Hands gripped tighter around weapons and bodies tensed around me. Eyes fixed in front of me, I watched as the first wave of soldiers appeared in front of the king's castle. Everything moved very quickly after that. A horn sounded from the castle, breaking through the early morning silence. It was time.

We broke out at a run, heading right for the growing Gallic army. Waves of soldiers were continuing to come through the portal. Banners held high, the soldiers moved in unison toward the castle.

We were close enough now to see the response from the castle. Archers lined the front, releasing arrows at the encroaching army. The Gallic soldiers held shields above them, deflecting most of the arrows. A regiment carrying siege weapons stepped through the ripple as we arrived. The other soldiers parted, making a clear path for them to head for the castle, battering rams at the ready.

A group of cavalry on horseback came through right as the ripple faded. The general was seated on one of the horses and he rode to the back, waiting for me. I met up with him, my guards behind me. He looked down at me. "You're to stay behind us until someone finds the king. Don't worry, your highness, we'll take care of his soldiers." He called out to his men, and the mass of bodies moved toward the castle.

My guards formed a horseshoe around me, following me everywhere I went. I gave them dirty looks.

"We have to keep you alive till the sorcerers arrive," Charles said. "After that, we'll ease up."

I wasn't sure if I believed him, but I let it go. We'd need every sorcerer we had against the king and his sorcerers.

Cheers rose from the soldiers at the castle wall. I looked up to see that they had already breached the castle and were streaming inside. I shook my head. "That was too easy."

"Something isn't right," Charles said.

The sound of shouting came from behind me and chills crept up my spine. I turned to see the king's army headed right for me. They weren't in the castle, they'd been waiting for us.

"Run!" Charles screamed. He grabbed me around my waist and lifted me off the ground, running away from the charging army.

"Put me down!" I yelled. "I can run on my own."

He set me down and we all took off as fast as we could. My chest ached and my legs were burning as we raced away from the oncoming army. We charged up a hill, finally managing to get out of their path. I doubled over, struggling to catch my breath. Looking up, I watched the king's army clash with the Gallic army. In a surge of bodies, steel met steel and the air was filled with the sounds of battle. I wiped the sweat from my brow. "What happened?"

Charles shook his head. "I don't know how they knew."

A shadow passed overhead, as if a cloud had blocked out the sun. Then I heard the flapping of giant wings. My blood ran cold and my heartbeat quickened.

Looking up, I saw a great, red dragon. Its wings stretched across the sky. As it flew over us, I saw a rider on its back. A man dressed in all black with dark, curly hair. Max.

"I don't think the army was waiting for us," Charles said. "I think we stepped into the middle of another battle."

The dragon flew over the soldiers and flames poured from its mouth. Tears streamed down my cheeks as I watched the dragon make another pass over the soldiers. There was so much fire, so much death. My eyes were glued to the scene. I couldn't move.

"Etta," Charles said. He never used my name and the word broke me from my trance.

"We have to do something," I said, pushing up my sleeves and raising my arms toward the sky. Charles pulled my hands down. "We have to stick to the plan. You wait for the king."

"We didn't know we'd be fighting a dragon when we made that plan," I said.

"Fine. We need to find the other sorcerers. You won't be strong enough to bring down a dragon alone," Charles said.

He was right. The sorcerers should be here by now. Our original plan was for them to focus on the king and his sorcerers since he usually kept them close by. I would take down the king when we had weakened him enough or eliminated his bodyguards. Now it seemed we'd have to turn our powers to Max and his dragon. I'd read about how destructive dragons could be, but I never imagined that a single dragon could destroy two armies.

Our plans had been thrown off by the appearance of the king's army behind us, and with the dragon in the air, nobody was where they were supposed to be. "Where do you think they'd be?" I asked.

A fireball out of the corner of my eye caused me to turn my head. It wasn't dragon fire, it was sorcerer fire, and it was being launched at the dragon. "There!" I pointed to small group of figures in colorful robes.

The field between us and the sorcerers was filled with people engaged in battle. To make things more complicated, Max and his dragon continued to rain fire down on all of the soldiers. "I'll have to teleport there."

Charles surveyed the scene, then nodded. "It's the only way. You're bringing me with you." He turned to the others. "Yancey, can you teleport yourself there?" He pointed to the other sorcerers.

"I think so," Yancey said.

"Do it," Charles said. "The rest of you, do what you can to bring down that dragon."

I grabbed Charles' hand and squeezed it tight. The smoke rose around us and before I had time to think, my feet appeared on the other side of the battle field.

Celeste was standing with the other sorcerers. She was wearing a satchel across her body, the bag shifted to one side of her. I could see a faint purple glow shining through the bag. She'd brought her orb. We were going to need it.

Madame Lyndsey stood in the center of all of the sorcerers. I ran over to her. "What can I do to help?"

She never took her eyes off the dragon. "Whatever you can throw at the dragon, do it."

I bent my knees to find my sorcerer stance, and lifted my arms to the sky. I wondered how arctic fire would react on a dragon. Calling on the power inside me, I reached down for the ice. My fingers tingled as the cold filled my veins. My eyes followed the dragon, preparing to fight its fire with my own.

Just then, Charles threw me to the ground and landed on top of me. My breath was knocked from my lungs and I sucked in a huge breath of air as I sat up. What was he thinking? I turned to yell at Charles, then shut my mouth quickly. He had an arrow in his back.

"Are you okay?" I asked.

"Don't worry about me." He pulled me up to standing then dragged me back, away from the encroaching battle. All of the sorcerers fell back. For some reason, there seemed to be more people fighting. It didn't make sense. The dragon fire should have killed so many. I watched so many bodies fall. My eyes found a group of people who had fallen, skin blackened from the dragon fire. To my horror, they stood, reached for their weapons and headed toward us. "That's not possible. They should be dead."

"Necromancers," Madame Lyndsey said. "Max is killing them and the king and his sorcerers are bringing them back."

"No." Max and his dragon were aiding the king. He was giving him more soldiers. Soldiers that didn't feel pain or stop after they'd been hurt. How could we fight against them all? The day had started with so much hope. Now I was beginning to feel trapped. How had things gotten to this point?

The dragon swept down in front of us, breathing fire on the soldiers that had just been poised to attack. Had Max done that on purpose? I stepped away from Charles, who still had an arm around me.

Flapping wings sounded above me and the dragon hovered directly above us. I looked up, fear seizing me, making me unable to move. My heartbeat quickened and my breathing was rapid.

Somebody tugged on my arm, pulling me back. I stumbled and found my feet, stepping away from the giant red beast.

The dragon reared, shaking its head and howled. I covered my ears against its sharp cry but it was too late, a ringing sound muted the sounds of the battle. I couldn't even hear the wing flaps.

It fell to the ground, knocking Max from its back. Somebody had managed to wound the creature. It tried to stand, failed, and collapsed to its side. Part of me felt sorry for it and I had to remind myself of all of the destruction it had caused.

Max seemed unscathed and walked toward us, leaving the dragon behind without a backward glance. "It's me and you, little sister," he called out. "We finish this right here, just the two of us."

I gripped my bow, wondering if I should try to shoot him, but I hesitated. How could I kill my own brother? "Why are you doing this, Max? I never wanted this."

"All you have to do is step down from the throne. Give up."

My nostrils flared, jaw clenched. "Never."

Puffs of gray smoke began to rise around him and as it cleared, I was staring at 12 other sorcerers. All wearing black robes like Max's. These were the other members of the Order of the Dragon. We were surrounded by fire sorcerers.

Madame Lyndsey moved in front of me. "You're not going to hurt her."

"Look at you, traitor," Max said. "I never seem to know whose side you're really on."

"At least I chose a side," she said.

Another gray cloud of smoke appeared and as it faded, a young woman with red hair stared back at us. She was wearing the black robes of the Order. I stared at her, eyes narrowed. She looked familiar but I couldn't place it.

"I think you've all met my wife." Max nodded to the newcomer.

We stood there, facing each other down for a moment. My sorcerers behind me, Max's Dragons surrounding him. As I looked at the smirk on Max's face, I had an overwhelming desire to lash out at him. I wanted to make him suffer. I wanted him to feel the pain that I'd been through.

Before I could decide on the best course of action, a fireball was launched from one of Max's sorcerers. Ducking and moving out of the way, the battle began. Madame Lyndsey threw fire, Celeste called to wind. The ground under me shook and I was knocked down just as a ball of fire came at me. I rolled away from it, and turned to see my opponent. Everything happening around me seemed to come to a standstill as I stared up at the face of my brother.

Max looked down at me. "Come on, little sister. Let me see that blue ice you make."

Heat rose up inside me. I wasn't going to let him kill me. As much as I didn't want to kill Max, I knew it had to be done. The

Darkness pulled at me, begging to be released. It was taking most of my energy to keep it away as I struggled to my feet. *It's time to show him how much he underestimated you.* There was truth in the words but I ignored them. Today wasn't going to be the day the Darkness won.

I glared at Max, knowing that if I didn't fight back, he was going to kill me. Reaching down inside me, I found my ice. Pure adrenaline ran through me, helping me to make faster decisions, less thinking. Time was moving too quickly for me to question what I was doing.

Blue flames rose into my palms, cold raced through my veins. Forming the flames into a ball, I threw them at Max.

He sent up a shield of bright orange fire. My ice was absorbed by his flames.

"You'll have to do better than that," he said.

I was vaguely aware of the battle raging around me. The other sorcerers were attacking Max's friends, but my focus was only on Max. The edges of my vision blurred as the Darkness tugged at me. It would be so easy to give in. So easy to let it guide me. It could help me win. It could help me defeat Max. I hesitated as a vision of Max burning alive flashed through my mind. *Just accept it. You deserve to defeat him.*

No. I won't give in. I took a deep breath and pushed back against the Darkness, sending it from my mind. Max took advantage of my internal struggle, throwing a fireball at me.

I crossed my arms in front of me, calling to the Arctic Fire in the same way Celeste had taught me to create a shield. Nearly transparent blue flames rose in front of me, blocking the fire. Spreading my arms wide, I released the arctic fire that had been protecting me out in front of me, sending it toward Max.

He dropped to the ground to avoid getting hit and was back on his feet before I could take advantage of his moment of weakness. He was faster than me, more experienced than me. My breathing was heavy and I had never trained for a battle like this. Teeth bared, I threw another round of arctic fire at him.

The ground rumbled under me, shaking. Arms extended, I tried to maintain my balance but lost. Rolling over to my front, I pushed myself back to standing but the damage had been done. Orange flames caught my eye too late for me to do more than try to dodge them. The fire caught my hip, spreading in a surge of screaming pain up and down my side.

I dropped to the ground and rolled, extinguishing the flames. Crying out in pain, I laid there on the ground, unable to move. The smell of burned flesh filled the air and I knew most of that came from me. Tears streamed down my face as I tried to push myself back up.

Max grabbed my chin and looked at me, his nose practically touching mine. "Everything would have been so much easier if you had just done what I asked." He pushed me down to the ground and cracked his knuckles, smiling at me.

Wincing, I tried to call on my powers, to do something. I raised a hand toward Max, hoping to find anything to push him away. Even just some wind. Something to buy me time to call out for help. My gaze was fixed on Max and his was on me. He lifted his hands, ready to end my life. My vision blurred as I fought to stay conscious.

Max turned away from me, and I moved my head in time to see someone with a sword run into view. Without hesitation, the newcomer thrust the sword into Max's chest. Max turned his gaze back on me, eyes wide. He dropped to his knees, then fell forward, pushing the sword further into his chest.

My head swam, and my vision darkened. I couldn't fight it anymore. Everything went black.

44

ASHTON

Ashton dropped to the ground, not even pausing to remove the sword from Max's chest. He slid his arm under Etta's head. Her trousers were burned, exposing the blistered red skin that spread from her chest to below her knee. Steam was rising off of the wound in the cold. Ashton didn't know what a burn this bad from sorcerer fire would do to a person. She needed help.

Yancey knelt down next to Ashton. "Is she breathing?" The guard's face displayed signs of panic and Ashton believed his sincerity.

Her chest rose and fell. She's alive. Heart pounding, he looked through the mass of bodies engaged in battles all around him. "She is, for now. We have to get her out of here." Ashton looked around, he had to find Celeste. Her orb was the only thing that might have enough power to heal Etta's wounds.

"I'll take her," Yancey said. "I can get her somewhere safe."

"She needs Celeste, find her." Ashton's tone made it clear that this was the only option. With a nod, Yancey stood. He pulled his sword from its sheath and ran into the fray.

Everybody seemed to be so caught up in their own fight that

they hadn't yet noticed the fallen royals. Hurry, Yancey. It wouldn't be long before Max's supporters saw him on the ground. Would they leave without their leader or would they try to avenge him? Ashton didn't know what their plan was so he had to hope for the best and prepare for the worst. Taking a deep breath, he called on a shield spell, wrapping the two of them in a bubble. It would keep out any weapons thrown at them but wouldn't stop somebody from charging at them. It was the best he could do right now.

"I'm so sorry, Etta." Ashton pushed her hair away from her forehead. He glanced over toward Max's fallen body. He would have to burn it so the king couldn't claim him. Ashton took a step back as the reality of what he'd just done sank in. He looked down at the fallen body of his teacher, his friend. His vision blurred. He'd killed Max. Heart racing, he fought to swallow but couldn't. How had it come this far? They'd talked about it but he never thought he'd be the one to do it.

"Ashton."

The sound of his name pulled him back to reality and he turned to see Yancey with a breathless and bloody Celeste.

Her eyes fell on Etta and she dropped to her knees. "No," she said. She reached out a hand and rested it on her chest, feeling the weak beat of her heart. "She doesn't have much longer. We need to get her out of here."

Ashton lifted Etta, cradling her against his chest and passed her off to Yancey. "Go, help her."

"Come with us," Celeste said.

He shook his head. "I've got to call for retreat. Take her to the bookstore in Canton. I'll come when I can."

"Don't do this, Ashton. Don't be the hero."

"I have to," he said. "Now go. Save her. You're the only one who can."

Celeste blinked away the tears that had pooled in her eyes.

She nodded then reached her hand out to grip Yancey's. The guard shifted his grip on Etta so he could better support her. A cloud of gray smoke rose up around them and they vanished.

Ashton took a deep breath and looked around. The noise from the battle rushed into his ears as if he had been inside a vacuum while worrying about Etta. Things were moving too quickly. Sorcerers were engaged in combat against each other. The dead were rising from the piles of bodies on the field. A dragon lay on the ground, unmoving.

They'd lost. There wasn't anything else they could do. He needed to call for retreat. Out of the corner of his eye, he saw the glow of a fireball. He ducked just before it could hit him, then spun around to face his assailant.

Her hair was wild, forming a tangled main of red around her pale face. Green eyes flashed with hatred. "How could you?" She screamed as she launched another fireball at Ashton. "You owe everything to him."

Ashton dodged her fireball and ignited his own flames in his palms. Her aim was poor. She hadn't been training long enough to be a threat. He could finish her in seconds, but he hesitated. If what Saffron had said was correct, the princess was pregnant. Despite everything, could he really kill Max's child?

Nora charged at Ashton, letting out a scream as she did. Ashton extinguished his flames, then caught her in his arms. She twisted, trying to pull out of his grip. "Let me go, you bastard."

She called to her flame, and Ashton jumped from the heat. It would take a lot more fire than that to harm a fire sorcerer, but the surprise was enough to cause him to loosen his grip. She broke free and ran toward Max's fallen body. With a look of pure hatred aimed at Ashton, she wrapped her arms around Max. Gray smoke circled her as the two of them disappeared.

Relief flooded through Ashton. He wouldn't have to burn the

body. Then fear gripped him. Max had just left in the arms of the king's daughter and she now had the sword. What did that mean for them? Stupid. He knew he should have just burned the body. He couldn't worry about it right now. It was time to end this battle.

Checking to make sure he wasn't under attack, he lifted his hands in the air to launch red sparks over the field. It was the signal to retreat. There was a shift on the battle field as people noticed the sparks. The momentum reversed as the soldiers and sorcerers began to flee.

A roar cut through the human sounds of battle and retreat. He froze. He knew that sound. Fingers trembling, Ashton turned to see the dragon, color drained from its once red body. The grayish beast's eyes were milky white, dead. The massive creature rose into the sky, letting out another roar that sent Ashton's heart into his stomach. The dragon opened its mouth and emitted a bright green flame across the battlefield. Cries of pain rose from those in the flame's path. Living and dead alike, crumbled to the ground, unmoving.

As the monster flew away, the king's sorcerers began to disappear in clouds of smoke. The members of the king's undead army stopped what they were doing and walked toward the castle.

It was over. They had lost.

He turned around to where the other sorcerers had been fighting against the Order of the Dragon. Two figures were still engaged in combat, despite the call for retreat. He recognized the blonde curls and ran toward Saffron. Just as he neared her, a dark cloud descended on them. Reaching his hands around his throat, he struggled for air. Blackness descended upon him and he felt his feet leave the ground.

45

ETTA

Every part of my body was screaming. Everything hurt. My eyes were closed and I was afraid to open them. Did I die? Was this what it was like? Voices in the distance only added to my state of confusion. I couldn't make them out clearly enough to tell who they were or what they were saying. My mind replayed the last thing I remembered: Max. Was he really dead?

Cautiously, I moved my fingers. They felt like they were moving. I tried my toes. They felt like they moved, too. One, two, three I opened my eyes, then squeezed them shut again. It was so bright. I tried again, squinting this time. I was in an unfamiliar room lit by a single candle. Looking down, I noticed that I was on a small cot. My heart started pounding harder in my chest. This wasn't a familiar place.

Grunting, I tried to sit up, and found that I couldn't.

Footsteps raced toward me. I turned my head, at least I could do that.

Relief washed though me as I saw Celeste come into view.

"What happened?" I managed.

"Max burned you," she said.

"But don't worry, you're healing quickly." She pointed toward the end of the bed. I looked down by my feet and saw that the purple orb was resting on my bed.

"You're going to be okay," Celeste said. "You're safe."

"What happened to Max? To everyone?" I asked. "Where am I?"

Celeste took a deep breath. "Max is dead. Ashton killed him."

TEARS STREAMED DOWN MY FACE. "He's really gone." I closed my eyes and leaned my head against the pillow, taking in a deep breath. After everything, Max was dead. I should be relieved, but I struggled to find any. He had tried to kill me, and I still struggled to celebrate his death. I looked back over at Celeste. "Where's Ashton?"

She looked down.

My heart seized. "No, no bad news, Celeste. Tell me something good, please."

"I don't know where he is." She looked at me, forehead wrinkled in concern. "I don't know where anyone is. I had to get you out of there. It's just me and Yancey. When you're healed more, we can move you to Gallia."

If she wanted to take me to Gallia, we were running away. A lump rose in my throat. We'd failed. "The king?"

"He lives."

"And he's stronger than ever." Yancey was standing in the doorway.

Celeste glared at him.

"It's true and she'd want to know the truth," he said.

"Help me sit," I said.

Yancey and Celeste exchanged glances. I glared at them.

Stationed on either side of me, the two of them helped pull me to sitting. I clenched my jaw and held back from screaming in pain as they adjusted me. I looked down at the left side of my body. It was still red and swollen. It looked bad. I couldn't imagine what it had looked like before.

"How bad is it?" I asked.

Celeste climbed up on the bed next to me. "Your burns?"

I shook my head. "The war." Neither of them looked like they wanted to tell me anything. "Tell me. Or I'll find someone who will."

Yancey frowned. "We've lost almost everything. We don't even know who survived yet."

"How long has it been?" I asked.

"You've been asleep for two days," Celeste said. She lifted the orb. "This saved your life."

I rubbed my eyes, wiping away the tears. "Two days? And we haven't heard any news?"

"Nobody knows where you are," Celeste said. "Except for Ashton."

My stomach twisted and a wave of nausea passed over me. If Ashton knew where we were, he should have come for us by now. I knew things weren't going well for us, but he was loyal and he'd want to see if I was okay. He'd want to see if Celeste was okay. I didn't want to say my fears out loud. I'd already lost too much. "How could we have gone through so much, just to lose everything?"

"We'll find a way, Etta," Celeste said.

"How?" I asked. "What's the point? All I do is get people killed. Maybe I should end this."

"Don't you do that," Celeste said. "Don't you give up on me. We've been though too much. Too many people are counting on us. There's still hope."

"Where?" I asked. "Where will we find hope?"

The room fell silent. Nobody had an answer for me. How could anything fix this? We had nothing to offer the people. It seemed like every time we went after the king, he grew more powerful.

A strange tapping noise filled the room. I turned my head toward the door, but didn't see anybody. "What is that?"

It grew louder. Celeste moved closer to the orb, bending down to stare at it. I couldn't move closer but in the silence, I could now tell that the noise was coming from the orb. Without warning, the purple glow vanished, revealing the dragon egg at the center. The tapping grew louder and the egg moved on the bed.

I stared at it, holding my breath as we waited. Suddenly, the tapping stopped. Then a thin crack began to spread down the egg. It was hatching.

<<<<>>>>

AUTHOR'S NOTE

Thank you for spending your time in Illaria! Want to know what happens next? Visit my website and join my newsletter for updates on new releases and lots of other book-related goodies!

I'd love to hear what you thought of the book! Reviews are a great help to authors and readers. I'd love it if you'd take a minute to leave your thoughts in a review.